The Cliff

Adrienne Leigh Summers

We dedicate this novel to all the people who dare to dream. It is never too late to follow your dreams or chase a new one. Perseverance, dedication, and hard work will make them a reality! Never give up and keep dreaming!

Contents

– 1 –

The Cliff

Allison

Allison Evans pulls open the French doors and steps inside the mansion's sprawling living room. The party is over on this side of the property, which is not a good thing for her. Most of the guests, including her friends, are now frolicking out back by the pool and the hot tub or are ensconced in private rooms.

Get a grip, Allison commands herself. *Stay calm.*

She spots a couple sprawled on a love seat in a darkened corner, legs entwined, and she smiles with relief.

"I'm in search of a nightcap," Allison says to the pair before realizing she knows them. "Oh, hey, Bobby, hey, Siobhan. I can't get enough of those martinis, you know?"

Bobby nods back and points to the back of the room. "Bar's still open."

Allison strides over and pours herself a seaweed martini, the evening's signature cocktail, from the pitcher the bartender left for late-night revelers. She raises her glass to the couple.

"Enjoy your night," Allison says. "I'm going to soak up some more of that sweet sea air."

9

"I might join you soon," Siobhan replies with a shiver. "It's getting chilly in here with the AC cranked up."

Allison steps out onto the empty deck and leans against the cedar railing. She sips her cocktail and takes in the view. The house sits atop a majestic clifftop that snakes and bends along the island as far as she can see, towering above the dark waters below.

She watches the whipping of the whitecaps, follows them as they crest and crash, illuminated under a full moon. July in New England is sticky, but the ocean breeze is a salve. She lets the air fill her lungs.

With the drama unfolding tonight, with all the hurt feelings, jealousy, betrayals and the fallout of a summer spent on the edge, Allison shouldn't be surprised everything seems to be building to its final act tonight, an inevitable crest that is fated to crash as hard as the waves down below.

A cloud shifts and the moon illuminates the scene in front of her as if with a spotlight. At that moment, Allison sees an object fall off the cliff in front of her. There is no mistaking what it is, because she can see arms and legs flailing.

It is a body. A *person.*

Allison hears a scream that tears through the night. It happens so fast she can barely register this is happening in real time.

The roar of the ocean covers her gasp as she watches the body fall out of her sight, and then she screams too, loud and shrill.

Allison drops her drink and races inside to call 911, her martini glass shattering on the deck behind her.

– 2 –
Anticipation

Allison
Six weeks earlier

Allison finishes her seven-mile run along Cisco beach and decides to cool off with a dip in the ocean. She stops at the base of the steps leading to the dirt road that winds back up to her house and leaves her sneakers, sweaty socks, hat, and glasses.

Barefoot and carefree, she runs to the shoreline and dives into the rolling waves. A born athlete and a competitive swimmer throughout high school and college, Allison is at ease cutting through the rocky waters with her powerful free-style stroke. Before she knows it, she's a hundred yards offshore.

Growing up spending summers on Nantucket, Allison never feared the ocean and has fond memories of jumping off the docks at night in the harbor without hesitation. But lately, local island news is all about the burgeoning seal population and the increase in great white sharks that inevitably follows. Allison can't help but feel uneasy, especially with the beach still empty so early in the morning.

In a few weeks things will be different. Once the Fourth of

July celebrations kick into high gear, Allison will be in the company of dog walkers and fellow runners also enjoying the peace and tranquility of the dawn of a new day.

She cuts her swim short and heads back to shore, finding her belongings, and speed-walks toward home. There's much to do before she has to pick up Marc at the airport this afternoon. They usually don't spend the week apart—thankfully, Marc runs his law practice from their beach home during the summer months—but he was swamped with work this week so he stayed on the mainland.

Allison knows she's lucky he gets to work on the island most weeks, but it hasn't always been this way. The early years of their relationship were full of ups and downs, barely survivable salaries, and coupon cutting. But Marc took a chance and left his grueling, thankless prosecutor position not long after he and Allison married. He decided to hang out his shingle, as they say, and start his own law firm as a solo practitioner. Within six weeks he was so busy he hired a receptionist and a full-time paralegal. Within the year he brought on a partner and the firm has been wildly successful ever since.

It's Friday morning and Allison misses him terribly after five days apart. Running and swimming are her therapy, and she needs these workouts to lift her up and help stop her anxiety from rearing its ugly head.

Allison picks up her pace. She needs to get back to the girls, who will be awake soon, and she wants to make sure the house is ship-shape for Marc's return.

Allison intends to make this summer perfect. She and Marc are closer than ever lately, spending quality time together on this beautiful island, and she will never take that for granted.

Still, however fast or far she runs during these extended workouts, she hasn't been able to shake the feeling that an underlying tension between her, Marc, and their closest friends on Nantucket could bubble over if they're not careful.

Allison plans to do everything she can to keep her bond strong with Marc this summer, no matter who might be waiting in the wings to try and fray it.

– 3 –
Grief

Brooke

Brooke Doyle takes her husband's hand and steps gingerly out of the car. He wraps a strong arm around her shoulders and guides her through the doors of their Boston condo, then upstairs and into their bedroom.

Kevin pulls back the covers on their king-sized bed and Brooke slides in. He plumps her pillows, then strokes her blonde curls.

"The doctor says you need to get some sleep," Kevin says. "I'll be in the other room if you need anything. I mean *anything*. You want hot chocolate flown in from Switzerland? A celebrity chef to make you some mac and cheese? Done. I'll even get you a bell."

Brooke attempts to smile, but fails. Her eyes are red-rimmed and puffy from what feels like weeks of crying. She has no fight left and should have no more tears to shed, but somehow one last tear slips out and runs down her cheeks.

Kevin tiptoes out of the room and closes the door behind him with a quiet *click*.

Brooke knows he's trying. He hasn't made an effort like this to be attentive and protective of her in many months, maybe years, but she's too drained to play the game. She feels empty, like the procedure scraped her out.

She hears the suction and fizz of Kevin opening a can of beer, though it's barely noon. This is hard on him, too, but it is Brooke who bears the physical trauma, so she doesn't possess the energy to worry about him right now.

Brooke closes her eyes and drifts into a fitful sleep, dreaming of hospital gowns and crying babies.

She's awakened by the sound of Kevin's phone ringing. He must be passing by her room for it to interrupt her slumber. She can't tell how much time has passed, but she needs the bathroom, needs to move, so she sits up slowly, swings her legs out of the bed, and plants her feet on the ground.

She opens the door soundlessly and pads toward the kitchen, stopping outside Kevin's office when she hears him on the phone.

"She's OK," he's saying. "I mean, as OK as can be expected. The doctor said it would do her some good to get away, but I don't feel comfortable leaving work right now. I can't leave you to deal with everything—what?—oh, no, definitely not. That wouldn't be fair to you—"

Brooke can tell he's talking to Mona, his overqualified assistant who's put up with him for too many years. She and Mona struck up a friendship due to the sheer number of times Brooke has called the office when Kevin wouldn't answer his cell. Mona thinks her husband is a "schmuck." She knows this because Mona once forgot to hang up the phone with Brooke before she whispered to someone else in the office, *I don't know why that lovely woman puts up with that schmuck.*

Far from feeling insulted, Brooke was amused, mostly because Mona wasn't entirely wrong. Her husband could be a schmuck, and worse—but he also had a side to him no one else saw like she did.

After a pause, Kevin says, "You know what? You're right. That's what remote working is for. My wife needs me. You tell Brian I'm taking some personal time and he can hold down the fort until I'm back. OK? Great. Yep—I'll tell her."

Kevin hangs up the phone without saying goodbye. Brooke, her loose, silky nightgown flowing around her like a ghost, appears next to him.

"Sweetie! Honey," he says, leaping out of his chair. "You shouldn't be up. I *told* you—I'm here to wait on you hand and foot."

"I had a little nap," she says. "I wanted to stretch my legs and get a seltzer. But now I want to know what you're up to."

Brooke wonders what Kevin is planning. This isn't the first time she has sensed that her husband is up to something he doesn't want her to know about.

‒ 4 ‒

Bon Voyage

Carla

Carla Rossi watches the vein on her husband's neck throb as he navigates the Range Rover through heavy traffic heading south on Route 495 towards Cape Cod. Carla cranks up Bob Marley, hoping to get them all in the mood for summer, but it's not working on Lawrence. He's too stressed about traffic.

Carla turns to check on the kids crammed in the back seat. The three of them have been troupers on the long drive. Their two oldest have earbuds in and are texting with friends, and their youngest daughter, Marley, is singing along with the reggae on the radio, which is fitting because the child is named after Bob Marley.

Carla brushes strands of long chestnut hair out of her face as the wind from the open windows blows it everywhere. They left town well before the typical five p.m. rush hour, but a Friday in June heading to the Cape will always be a travel nightmare. Lawrence got tied up at work, so they didn't hit the road until close to eleven-thirty a.m., and now he's worried about making the two-fifteen p.m. ferry out of Hyannis.

Carla is struggling to get in a relaxed mood herself, but she's making a grand effort to put on a happy face.

As fate would have it, as they approach the Bourne Bridge things inexplicably open up and the roadway clears. The whole family cheers as they sail over the bridge without hitting the brakes.

Lawrence, smiling with relief, turns to Carla. "That was a miracle," he says. "I think we might have time to fill our gas tank and pick up a bike helmet for Marley since we forgot to pack hers."

"We?" Carla tilts her head. "You mean *you* forgot Marley's helmet. I swear I saw it in your hands. How could you have forgotten it?"

"I did have it in my hands, but I put it down when the office called," Lawrence replies. "I had to deal with work. It distracted me."

Carla takes a breath. "That's OK, honey. Sorry I snapped. I'm sure there are other things we forgot. We can always buy her helmet on the island. But there will be a better selection in Hyannis, if we have time."

"Not to mention everything is twice the price on Nantucket." Lawrence adds.

He's acting like nothing happened, but Carla can see he's wondering why she's been quiet and irritable. She needs to do better at hiding it, she decides. She's not in the mood for questions right now.

Carla pastes on a smile. It's a big moment for their family, after all. They're heading to their dream summer home for the first time since they bought it back in April with a cash offer in a tight market. Three weeks later, Lawrence and Carla spent one hour and $6.7 million in their attorney's office in exchange for one small key on a red, white, and blue lobster keychain.

This key would unlock their new Nantucket home and a lifetime of memories. Carla was pinning hope—maybe too much—on this new chapter in their marriage.

"I can't wait to see what they've done with the place," she says now, pulling the key out of the handbag and dangling it with a grin. "I've been holding onto this since the realtor handed it to us. I even slept with it under my pillow the night after we closed. Goofy, right?"

"Not at all. You know all I want is to make you happy," Lawrence says, taking her hand and bringing it up to his lips for a kiss.

"I can't believe we'll be unlocking the front door in three hours," she says as he lets her hand drop. They're almost at the ferry terminal. "We've had this dream for so many years, babe. And here we are…on our way! Is it weird I'm not even worried about how it's all going to look?"

They made the risky decision to put their trust in the contractors, decorators, painters, and others who they hired to whip the house into the shape they wanted it in, and Carla has been working with them all remotely to make the place their own.

She is finally feeling giddy, forcing the worries away, feeling present with her family.

Their son, Will, a sixteen-year-old who thinks he knows everything about everything, starts to laugh.

"What's so funny?" Lawrence asks.

"Oh nothing, just a text from Trevor."

Will has been MIA since he got his driver's license. He was ready when the day came, having already bought himself an old clunker with money he'd earned working since the seventh grade doing odd jobs and mowing lawns around the neighborhood. Carla and Lawrence were on the same page about that. They had more than enough money to buy him a new one, but Lawrence was determined to teach their children the value of a strong work ethic.

Will, however, is the least of Carla's worries this summer. Their middle child, Gabriella, a spitting image of her mother, hit her teen years running with a wild side that would strike fear into any parent. Marley, ten, is a delight. She's precocious and curious and adores her father. Carla suspects she'll always be daddy's girl.

The children will be OK. It's their marriage Carla worries about. She's made a promise to herself that her children will no longer act as a convenient buffer between her and her husband of seventeen years. The unspoken stakes hang heavy around the couple on today's trip. This summer feels like a last chance for Lawrence and Carla to reconnect and reignite a romance that was quickly dampened long ago when Carla became pregnant with Will.

It's hard to believe it's been sixteen years since she was a law school student living in Beacon Hill. Time went so fast, and Carla wants to take this summer to hit the brakes. She knows Lawrence is planning on some serious alone time with Carla, late night beach walks, maybe a bonfire, and she feels ready to reconnect.

The Rossis arrive at the ferry terminal with plenty of time to spare, so Lawrence heads to Baxter's and puts in a few orders of fried clams and lobster rolls. After they're stuffed full of seafood, they head back to the car with ten minutes to spare.

Carla and the kids pile out and head up the stairs to the main deck. She breathes a sigh of relief as they begin the final leg of their journey to their new home.

All she wants to do is forget everything that happened over the last twenty-four hours and enjoy the summer that lies ahead. Carla only hopes that when she does finally return to her small hometown in Massachusetts, all will be forgotten.

– 5 –
Welcome

Allison

When Allison makes it back to the house after her run, she's greeted by her nine-year-old golden retriever, Reilly. She'd thought about bringing him along this morning, but he can't run the distance he once could and Allison needed a longer one.

"Sorry, buddy. I promise we'll go for a short one tomorrow," she says, giving him a little rub behind his ears.

Allison is relieved to find her girls are still in bed. She cherishes these moments to herself before they wake up and start arguing (or laughing, on a good day), turning on the TV, or cranking up their new favorite song.

She figures she has just over seven hours until Marc's arrival. She needs to stock the fridge, tidy up the house, and make some appetizers. She also promised Savannah they would hit the beach so she could get on her surfboard.

It's only been four nights, but Allison misses having Marc around, especially at night when the children are in bed. While she once enjoyed that quiet time to herself, she misses him like crazy now that she and Marc have been spending more quality time together. Allison feels butterflies in her stomach at the thought of him walking off the plane, and she can't wait to wrap her arms around him.

She pours herself some coffee, then tiptoes into the bathroom and cranks the water to hot, setting her mug on a marbled ledge in the walk-in shower.

When she's clean and dried off, she heads to the kitchen and hears her girls up and about.

"Good morning, girls," she calls as she pours herself a second cup of coffee.

"Hi, mom," Abigail, so sweet at ten years old, chirps.

"Hey," Savannah offers.

Allison is amazed at how much they've grown since last summer. Savannah's straight blonde hair has grown long. At just thirteen years old, she now stands nearly as tall as her mother.

"Come join me on the deck once you're done fixing your breakfast," Allison says, cradling her mug and holding a rolled beach towel under her arm. "It's a spectacular morning out there."

Allison, wearing her favorite green Tommy Bahama bikini she always thought makes her hazel eyes pop, grabs her kindle and steps onto the deck, admiring the unobstructed view of the ocean.

She sets down her mug, raises the white umbrella, and loses herself in an action-packed novel full of cloak and dagger and international intrigue.

In between organizing and entertaining the girls all morning, Allison finds time a bit later to get back to her sunbathing and her book. Within minutes she jumps as she's jolted out of the story by the crackling and crunching of shells.

Allison looks left and spots a silver Range Rover pulling up to the house next door.

Finally, she thinks, *the new neighbors are showing themselves.* She sees a handsome man jump out and head to the back of the SUV to unpack.

Allison feels a tingle of nerves and anticipation. Her home is an oasis meant to be in the family for generations to come, and the inhabitants of the house next door can affect their lives in ways she knows too well.

It was a horror show last summer when the neighbors rented weekly, and each new tenant was rowdier and more obnoxious than the next. There were beer cans tossed over the fence onto Allison's lawn, music blasting, and packed pool parties into the wee hours. It got so bad that Marc didn't like to leave Allison and the kids home alone.

When the home went on the market Daffodil Weekend in April, Allison and Marc had watched the open house crowd with great interest. As they cleaned and scrubbed—a ritual to breathe life back into the winter-battered home every spring since they acquired this beachfront property—they'd subtly watched potential buyers stream in and out.

Marc and Allison spent the weekend guessing and arguing about who might buy it that they decided to make a bet: whoever guessed correctly could choose their prize. Allison put her money on the beautiful brunette and her slightly shorter, well-built, dark-haired husband. Marc was convinced it was going to be the older preppy couple with the woman dripping in expensive jewelry. Allison and Marc shook on it and each put $100 into the candy jar—along with folded squares of paper with their secret prize written on them.

The girls race up to the deck to join Allison; they've noticed the new people, too.

"Who's *that*, mom?" Savannah says in a stage whisper.

"I think it's *them*," Allison whispers back.

But the girls are already gone, bounding down the steps. Allison wants them all to greet the new neighbors together, but she wants to do it right, so she'll wait to visit them.

Allison throws a beach wrap over her suit and follows the girls down to the driveway.

Savannah prances toward the beach with Abigail in tow, but Allison puts a stop to it, calling out, "No beach yet. We need to run to Bartlett's first. Just a quick stop."

Savannah glares at her mother with the fire of a thousand suns, but dutifully lopes back toward the house, and Abigail follows along.

Allison wants to grab a couple of her favorite items from Bartlett's Farm to welcome her new neighbors, but she also needs to stock up on some of Marc's favorite apps for their reunion tonight. When she pulls the car up to the bustling specialty store, she catches sight of a close friend.

Kate Gibson looks like she stepped out of a Gucci catalogue as she glides out of the store in flat sandals and a floral sheath, her smooth, highlighted hair tied at the nape of her neck. Always impeccably put together, naturally elegant. Allison always feels her attempts at beach chic will never measure up to Kate.

Allison is covered in a sheen of coconut sunscreen and is

hiding under a shapeless dress she threw over her bathing suit. Kate is with people Allison doesn't recognize, real estate clients or perhaps friends visiting the island, so she doesn't want to interrupt. She waits for Kate to drive away before ushering the girls into the store.

Back at the house, Allison stocks the fridge, then finds a picnic basket and pulls together a perfect assortment of elegant elements. As she arranges the basket, she feels like something is missing. She steps onto her first-floor deck, snips a beautiful purple and blue hydrangea, and slips it through the wicker top. *There, perfect.*

The girls are ready on cue. It doesn't hurt, Allison thinks, that Savannah caught sight of a teenage boy getting out of the Range Rover earlier. She heard her tell Abigail, "He's *hot*."

Then again, Savannah looks beach ready, so maybe it isn't boys she's after. "Can we surf now. Pleeeease?" her teen pleads.

She's practically hopping with excitement, so Allison relents. "We'll meet you at the beach after we greet the new neighbors. No surfing until we get there."

With that, Savannah is off like a shot.

As Allison and Abigail walk to the house and up the shelled driveway, they're met by a curly haired girl with dark brown eyes and an ear-to-ear smile.

"Hi!" The girl says. "I'm Marley."

"Hi, Marley," Allison greets her. "This is Abigail, and I'm Mrs. Evans. Welcome to the neighborhood!"

"Hi," Abigail smiles shyly. "How old are you?"

"I'm ten! How old are you?" Marley asks.

"Oh cool, I'm ten too," Abigail lights up.

"Do you want to see my room? It's brand-new," Marley offers, then sets off toward the house.

"Sure," Allison says, following along. "Are your parents around?"

"Yep!" Marley races into the house. "Mom-Mom-Mom, the neighbors are here!"

A woman who looks about Allison's age glides down the spiral staircase from the second level. Allison immediately covets her thick, flowing chestnut hair. She has green eyes and looks like she's already spent the first part of the season in the sun.

Allison couldn't be more excited and relieved. First because their families seem to be similar ages, and second, because this is the home buyer she put her bet on during the open house—and Marc's going to owe her big.

"Hello," the woman smiles, extending a hand to shake Allison's. "I'm Carla Rossi. Please excuse the mess, we just arrived late last night."

Carla gestures around the unpacked bags in the foyer.

"Welcome! I'm Allison Evans and this is my daughter Abigail."

"Hi, Mrs. Rossi, it's nice to meet you," Abigail says.

Marley eagerly pokes her head out from behind her mother. "Come see my room!"

Abigail looks to Allison, and Allison looks to Carla, who replies, "Oh, of course. Please, go ahead."

As the girls run off, Carla says, "It's so nice our daughters are around the same age."

"Isn't it? I brought you a little something," Allison says, handing over the basket with the beautiful hydrangea gracing its top.

"Oh my gosh, thank you," Carla beams. "You didn't have to do that…"

Allison puts up her hand. "It's my pleasure. We're thrilled to have a family next door instead of random weekend renters every week, I cannot even tell you. By the way, I noticed you've been using Rick as your contractor. He's great, right?"

"He is. We love him and cannot believe how fast his crew updated the paint," Carla agrees.

"It looks as though he's done an amazing job," Allison observes as she looks around the house, trying to be subtle about it.

"Would you like the tour?" Carla asks.

Allison follows her new neighbor through the home, and she's floored by how beautiful the interior is. Carla's house is decked out with top-of-the-line furnishings, and Allison especially loves the turquoise and tangerine accents throughout the second floor living room. It looks as though it belongs on a magazine cover. The wall of sliding glass off the living room is open, and the white linen drapes wave ever so gently within the room. The view is like Allison's, with a sweeping meadow and the sand and waves behind it.

"I love your taste, Carla. Everything is impeccable," Allison tells her as they work their way though.

Carla explains how she arranged for her decorator to coordinate with Rick to ensure that all their home furnishings, draperies, and wall hangings would be in place prior to their arrival. As Carla continues the house tour, Allison notices new surfboards and boogie boards lined up on the lower deck along with brand new sand chairs and pastel Vineyard Vines beach towels.

Back in the foyer, Allison remembers Savannah's waiting for her at the beach, no doubt fuming by now. "It's been so great to meet you," she says to Carla. "I've got to run. My other daughter, Savannah, wants to surf, and I was supposed to meet her on the beach about fifteen minutes ago."

"No worries," Carla smiles. "My husband Lawrence is down there surfing with our two oldest, Will and Gabriella. Why don't we grab the girls and take a walk down together?"

Carla and Allison talk like they've been friends for years. Allison treasures those rare connections where everything flows effortlessly.

They head to the water with their beach bags in hand and folded chairs tucked under their arms. Their ten-year-old girls run ahead like they can't get there fast enough.

＜center＞– 6 –＜/center＞

Tipsy

Kate

Kate Gibson streams her favorite summer playlist over her state-of-the-art Bose home stereo system, opens the fridge, and pulls out a bottle of Bollinger. *I deserve this*, she thinks. *It's noon somewhere.*

She tries not to think about how much she's "deserved" treats like this more and more. Depending on the hour, she finds herself downing a pot of coffee, popping painkillers for her headaches, or mixing up a cocktail (the last one seems to be happening earlier and earlier each day). It's an accomplishment to make it until noon lately.

Kate pours the chilled bubbly into a crystal flute and feels a pang thinking about what good shape she was in last summer. She was all about self-care, eating healthy food, running, swimming, and writing in her journal. That was the summer she was going to write her book, and write she did, for two hours a day, five days a week.

But this past winter was not an easy one, and Kate embarked on a destructive path starting around Christmas. Spring was cold and depressing, and she slid into summer on the same trajectory. Her definition of self care has shifted from long-term goals to doing whatever it takes to stay sane in the moment. If that means champagne at eleven a.m., so be it. She holds the glass in the air for a lonesome cheers and takes a long sip of the fizzy liquid.

Seeing Allison at Bartlett's that morning triggered her, though Kate has become adept at stuffing her insecurities down. Her friend didn't know Kate could see her—as she drove out, she watched Allison walk into the store with her two girls—and she somehow looks younger than last summer, robust, healthy, glowing.

By all accounts Allison is in a thriving marriage. Kate could see Allison's runner's endorphins lighting up her face, and all that did was remind Kate she's going in the wrong direction.

She's wondered for a while now why Jon hasn't said anything to her. There's no denying she's been looking like hell. Ironically, Kate's been getting regular compliments on her appearance because she doesn't eat much anymore and she is skinny, really skinny, which is still the gold standard in her social circle.

But Jon always loved her strong, athletic body. Now that she thinks about it, Jon probably hasn't even noticed the deterioration of her health. They rarely talk anymore, not about anything important. In fact, they're rarely even in the same part of the house.

Jon's M.O. this summer has been to head down to his "man town" in the basement with his laptop and six pack of Cisco summer ales while Kate watches him go, at which point she'll duck into the four-season sunroom with not just a glass, but a bottle of wine that she'll polish off by herself. Most nights she'll torture herself by fishing around Facebook and looking at past pictures of her family from back when things were normal.

Kate's daughter used to be her entire world. Then Kate and Jon got all caught up with their new partying lifestyle, which was glamorous and fun and exciting at first, but left her feeling out of touch with the old Kate and her life priorities. Oddly, she'd found all the excitement ultimately led to a kind of numbness.

Every now and then Kate longed to go back to the simple days. This was happening more and more when she awoke in the morning to a new day, and she would tell herself she could live it any way she wished. *Maybe I can go back*, she'd think. *I'm going to change things. Somehow.*

But after a few cups of coffee and texts from her new circle of friends, she'd fall back into the same pattern and think, *What the hell. I'm in the thick of everything now, Jon and I are the ones everyone on the island wants to know, so there's no going back.*

She has the rest of her life to sit around the house and play boring normal housewife and mom. This is what she tells herself this morning as she pours herself another generous glass of champagne.

As she sips her drink, Kate daydreams about Marc Evans and his muscular body. She knows her growing attachment to him could bring trouble down the road, but then again, Kate has never been one to follow the rules.

What the hell? She thinks, giving in to temptation. *My own best friend's avoiding me anyway.* She reaches for her phone and shoots Marc a quick text.

When are you back on the island?

Three dots pop up. She waits to see what he'll write back to her.

Sand Chairs

Carla

As Carla and Allison settle into their beach chairs, the younger girls perform cartwheels in the sand. Lawrence keeps a close eye on the three surfers, so Carla will wait for him to leave his post before launching into introductions.

"How long have you been coming to Nantucket?" Carla asks Allison.

"All my life," Allison replies. "My parents bought a house when my older sister was a baby and it's been in the family ever since. They've done some renovations to keep it in good shape, but most of the original house is just as it was when they bought it almost fifty years ago. Marc and I bought ours oh…about ten years ago now."

"Wow," Carla raises her eyebrows. "I bet you know every nook and cranny of this island."

"It wasn't a bad way to grow up, summering here," Allison admits.

"It must be great to have your parents on island," Carla observes. As soon as the words are out of her mouth, she wishes she hadn't said them. Allison's eyes cloud over.

"They're usually not on the island for the Fourth," she says. "They go back to Boston to spend time with my sister, Laura. They get a fortune renting it out for the holiday week, though." She tries to smile and says again, "We're very lucky."

Carla shakes it off and figures there's a story there, but not one Allison wants to share. She feels lucky she found this place, too, albeit later in life, thanks to Lawrence. They've made a wonderful life together, and it's taken one day of vacation to remind her of what she has. She winces at her own stupidity.

What was I thinking about with the baseball coach?

The guilt starts to creep in once again. Thankfully, her shame spiral is interrupted by Allison, who doesn't appear to notice Carla's unease.

"The house is actually just down the road from here, but you can't see it because it's one story and so many larger homes have been built around it," Allison says, pointing toward the south. "But they haven't managed to ruin my parents' views of the water. If you walk out your driveway, and go straight along the shoreline, they're four houses down on the left."

"Oh, I think I know what home you're talking about," Carla says. "Is it the one with the farmer's porch, white rocking chairs, and red, white, and blue flowers in the window boxes?"

"That's the one! You have a good handle on the island for a newcomer," Allison remarks. "What made you decide to buy a second home here?"

Carla applies more sunscreen to her face. She comes from an Italian family and has beautiful skin tones naturally, and add to that tons of sun in June, she thinks she's had enough sun this season. At thirty-nine, she doesn't want or need premature wrinkles.

"We've been vacationing on Nantucket for years, but we always stayed at Jared Coffin House," Carla explains. "We got the bug on our last trip. We took a last-minute break without the kids, and a trip out to the brewery and Cisco sealed the deal— we decided it was time to make it permanent."

Carla always smiles when she thinks of the weekend that ended up changing their lives. It was daffodil weekend, a springtime tradition on Nantucket, and she and Lawrence rented a Jeep and went out to the brewery for a quick beer. They bought some growlers of Sankaty Light and made a quick stop at Bartlett Farms. With a cooler packed full of drinks and snacks, they headed to the surf beach of Cisco. They had always wanted to check it out, but their kids were too little for the big waves Cisco beach is known for. They bundled up in jeans and sweatshirts and packed fleece blankets to sit on and snuggle under.

Cisco beach remains one of the most beautiful places Carla has ever been. She's always in awe of its raw beauty, mesmerized by the waves curling and pounding the sand with a boom so loud and soothing that it blocks out all of life's distractions, and it's easy to sit in the sand until the sun goes down and be entirely present.

Cisco is on the south-facing side of Nantucket, exposed to the open ocean, and on a sunny day the rays dance across the waves. The Rossis fell in love immediately.

"You made a great investment," Allison says. "Your kids and their families will enjoy the island for generations. How long have you and Lawrence been together?"

"Seventeen years," Carla says. "We met when I was in law school."

Allison perks up. "You're a lawyer? My husband is a lawyer too."

"Well, I never actually practiced law," Carla says. "I graduated and passed the bar that same summer. I gave birth to Will three weeks later, and I've been practicing motherhood full-time ever since."

Allison says, "You have a beautiful family." She throws a glance over to where Lawrence is keeping a hawk-eye on the teen surfers. "How did you two meet? I love a good origin story."

Carla smiles at the memory. "It was the first week of my third year in law school, and I was taking a bunch of night courses so I could work during the day and make some money," she says. "After class I'd usually stop by the Beacon Hill Pub, where I was a regular, and I remember how crowded it was that night. But still, Bill the bartender—he made the best drinks—had my usual gin and tonic waiting for me.

"Anyway, long story short, I take one sip and in walks this handsome, dark haired, brown-eyed Italian with a group of guys. Lawrence was by far the best looking. I mean, you could see how built he was through his polo and jeans. That's definitely my type, you know?"

"Oh, I know," Allison laughs.

Carla smiles. "Right? So he orders a Jack and Coke and he starts talking to me. The last thing I wanted was to meet someone. I was exhausted with school and work, and I wanted to unwind with a cocktail and go home and catch up on some sleep. But I was so attracted to this guy, it was like I was in a trance or something."

"So what made you give up sleep for him?" Allison asks,

pulling the kids' sunscreen out of her beach bag as Abigail and Marley skip through the sand toward them. "Did he have some magic line he used?"

"You know," Carla recalls, "to this day I can't remember anything we talked about. It was like I was in a daze. We had pure chemistry. I took him back to my place that night, and we've been together ever since."

Abigail skids to a stop in front of them. "Mom, can we go back to the house? I need the bathroom."

Carla is thrilled to see the girls bonding already. Marley clearly already adores Abigail.

"Me too! Mom, can I go?" Marley pleads.

Allison lifts herself out of her beach chair. "Sure, girls. I'll walk you back."

"Thanks, Allison," Carla replies. "I'll keep an eye on Savannah while you're gone."

Carla finds herself alone for the first time since they arrived on the island.

She enjoyed telling Allison about her origin story with Lawrence, but what she didn't mention was how the lust spun out of control pretty much immediately. They barely took their eyes off one another from the moment he approached her. Carla was not the type to go home with a guy in a bar, but she had never been so sexually attracted to anyone.

After several gin and tonics Carla had blurted, "I live in this building." Her apartment was upstairs.

Lawrence kept his eyes locked on hers. "May I walk you home?"

Carla opened the first door to the stairwell. As she turned to gaze at her suitor, she held her breath. His long dark lashes fluttered over his sexy dark eyes. She could not resist this man, so she grabbed his stubbly face and teased him with her mouth and tongue. He returned the kiss with even more passion. As she slung a leg up to his hip, she did not feel in control of her own body. Carla didn't know if it was love or lust. All she knew was that this feeling was like nothing she'd ever felt before.

He whispered into her ear as he stroked her hair, "We should get inside your apartment. Now."

Carla gasped as she momentarily realized what she was doing. Releasing him from her grasp, she started to back up the stairs. Still not taking her lips or hands off him, she trusted him to guide her to the apartment door. She stumbled back, and he caught her right before she hit the stairs. They were now lying on the stairs, anxiously grinding and groping.

Lawrence stopped, pulled her up, and asked, "What are you doing to me?"

"I never do this," she'd said breathlessly. "Get me inside before I change my mind."

He did.

Carla's thoughts now are interrupted by the sounds of her husband calling to her. She watches Lawrence swim to shore behind the three surfers. When they hit the beach, they take off running, boards in hand. At that moment, the youngest ones return from their bathroom break. Abigail and Marley run ahead of Allison and continue doing cartwheels in front of Carla's chair.

Lawrence greets them and grabs a towel.

Carla stands up to introduce her husband to Allison.

"You must be Lawrence." Allison offers her hand. "Carla has

already told me so much about you."

"All good, I hope," Lawrence responds with a smile, shaking her hand.

"This is Allison," Carla tells him. "She and her husband own the house next door to ours. You should see the beautiful welcome basket she brought over. That's her daughter Abigail, and you've obviously met Savannah."

Lawrence and the teens towel off, then they all lend a hand picking up chairs, towels, bags and boards to lug home.

As they trudge back along the path, Allison says to Carla, "I plan to bring my dog Reilly for a run tomorrow morning. Any interest in joining?"

Carla pauses for a moment. The move has been exhilarating but also exhausting, and she'd love to sleep in on her first full day in vacation mode.

"Sure, I love starting my day with a workout," she says, surprising herself by agreeing. "I'd love to learn some routes around here and you can give me the dirt on all our neighbors. What time are you going?"

"I head out at six," Allison replies. "I know, it's early, but it's a magical hour out here."

Carla hesitates again; she is not a morning person. "OK," she says finally. "Should I meet you at the end of my driveway?"

She figures with the dog, Allison can't be going too far or too fast, so it sounds like the perfect way to get back into running.

Allison smiles, "It's a date." Then she turns and heads towards her home. "See you in the morning, Carla."

– 8 –
Wounded

Brooke

Brooke wakes at two a.m. with a pounding headache and puffy eyes that feel glued shut. It's still dark out and her mouth is as dry as cotton balls. She feels around the top of her nightstand and touches a glass of water Kevin left for her.

She's noticed how hard he's been trying to take care of her since that dreadful doctor's appointment. Brooke rolls over to go back to sleep and notices Kevin isn't in their bed. She thinks about getting up to look for him, but can't muster the strength and dozes off. When she wakes again later, Kevin is asleep next to her.

Brooke sits up and focuses on her surroundings, becomes fully awake, and then the trauma of yesterday hits her again like an anvil dropped from a building. Couldn't it all be a bad dream? Can't she turn back time to when she was pregnant? And how is she going to make it through today? She wants to sleep again. She wants to be knocked out.

Kevin must have sensed she was awake; he opens his eyes and looks up at her.

"How are you feeling, sweetie?" He asks with such concern in his voice that Brooke can barely look at him lest she break down again.

Keeping her eyes focused down in her lap she tries to respond, "I…I don't know how to answer that." Brooke can't decide if she is mad, sad, or something else entirely.

"Hey. That's OK, honey. Fair enough," Kevin says kindly, sitting up and rubbing sleep out of his eyes. "Why don't I get up and fix you some breakfast? You could use a nice hot meal. I'll bring it to you in bed."

Brooke can't even think about eating right now but has no desire to explain this to Kevin.

"OK," is her one-word reply, simply because it takes less energy and it encourages Kevin to leave the room.

Brooke glances at the clock. It reads 7:32 a.m., which means she's been in bed for over nineteen hours. And she still feels tired. She puts her head back on the pillow and dozes off again.

This time when she wakes up, she feels better. Not much, but enough. She notices Kevin left a tray of food next to their bed. Orange juice, scrambled eggs with spinach, dry wheat toast, and some sliced strawberries.

Kevin peeks around the corner and Brooke, still groggy, says, "Thanks, honey. I know you're trying. I just need time."

"That's okay, Brooke. I know how upsetting this is for you, for us." Kevin steps inside the bedroom and lifts a piece of toast. "Do you think you can at least have a bite?"

"I can do that. And I wouldn't mind a cup of hot tea. Do you think you could…?"

"Of course."

He heads to the kitchen, and Brooke decides to eat her toast in there with him. She slowly raises herself from bed, wraps her light-weight robe around her tired body and shuffles into the kitchen, toast in hand.

"You're up! You look good." Kevin leans in for a kiss and pulls a stool out so she can sit at the island.

As he pours her tea, it occurs to Brooke he shouldn't be here.

"Aren't you going to work today? It is Friday, isn't it?"

Brooke looks up at him, watches his face.

"You caught me. I took the day off to take care of you." He hands her the steaming mug of tea.

As she tries to shake off her dark mood all she can say is, "Thanks."

She can see something is up. She knows him, knows when something's bubbling under (though she often doesn't know what the *something* is).

She scans the room, then feels a stab of nausea when she sees a lineup of luggage, golf clubs, and a cooler waiting at the back door.

"Whoa, Kevin," she says. "What's going on?"

She points to their belongings all in a row, clearly waiting to go on a journey Brooke knows nothing about.

"I'll tell you all about it after breakfast," he smiles. "Please, honey—eat something. Drink your tea. Stay hydrated."

"What's going on," she says flatly.

"OK, OK," he relents with a sigh. "I've booked us a luxurious getaway to a place we've been before and absolutely loved. I'm trying to do everything I can to make you feel better. I wanted it to be a surprise." He pouts, clearly annoyed she's dared ruin it.

Believe me, she thinks, *this IS a surprise*. Kevin is what is commonly referred to as a workaholic. He doesn't usually do vacations or "getaways" unless pressured by Brooke.

"Kevin…" She wants to cry again. "I'm not in the mood for travel. To put in effort. To see people. To be in crowds. I'm not ready."

"You won't have to be," he insists. "This is about rest, relaxation and reconnecting." He grabs his tablet off the counter and brings it to her at the kitchen island. "Check out what I booked for us while you were sleeping."

She dutifully leans in to check the photos as he clicks away on the screen.

"It's on the beach, out of the fray," he says. "No White Elephant or The Cottages this time around. Believe me, it wasn't easy finding a place on Nantucket so last minute. I'm spending a fortune, and you know what? You're so worth it."

A gorgeous house with weathered grey New England-style shingles by the ocean bursts onto the screen. "See? Think sandy beaches, amazing sunsets, great restaurants, shopping, beautiful people. And you're one of them for the next four weeks!"

Brooke's mouth falls open with shock. He's rented a place in Nantucket. She and Kevin hadn't been there for five years and even then, they only visited for weekend getaways.

"Check out how spacious it is," her husband continues, oblivious to her growing panic. "And look at that kick-ass view. It's less than a hundred yards from the beach."

He clicks through the images on the rental, and Brooke can acknowledge it is stunning, with a modern interior design and airy glass doors, but still can't imagine dragging herself out of her cocoon so soon.

"You don't have to do a thing," Kevin says. "You don't even have to think. While you were sleeping, I booked us a flight out of Logan direct to Nantucket. The cooler's packed. I even stopped by the bookstore to grab you the latest summer trash novels. None of this *How to Recover From Loss* self-help stuff. That'll only keep you depressed. You need something to lift you out of it."

"That book was highly recommended by the doctor to help us heal emotionally," is all Brooke can say. Come to think of it, she'd noticed the book was gone from her nightstand when she checked the time this morning. She assumed it fell to the floor; now she knows Kevin took it.

Brooke's head is spinning. Setting foot out of bed and padding to the kitchen was as far as she thought she'd be expected to go this morning, and now he's talking about a flight?

"We'll be grilling steaks and sipping margaritas by seven," he pleads. "And you'll forget all about the hassle of traveling. Just you, me and the beach. Won't that be perfect?"

She knows he won't calm down until she shows gratitude for this aggressive plan he made without consulting her, so she does it, because there's no other way around it right now.

"Sure," she says weakly. "But there's so much to pack…"

"That's just it!" He's almost manic now. "Throw in some sunscreen, toothpaste, books. Toss some clothes in your suitcase. I had Molly at Nordstrom's pick out some island outfits for you already, and they're hanging in the closet in a garment bag. Go check it out!"

Brooke is in a panic, which might actually be a good thing. Any feeling other than sadness is welcome right now.

As she rushes around the room, Kevin brings their bags and cooler of goodies downstairs. Brooke finishes her packing then focuses on pulling herself together. She slips on her J.Crew sundress and some espadrilles, she then brushes her curly blonde locks, applies some of her favorite lip plumper, and nearly knocks her husband over as he runs up the stairs for the seventh time.

"I'm ready when you are," she says.

Kevin, hot and sweaty from his hard work, trips up the last step, catches his balance and grabs his wife by the back of the neck, giving her a little spin as he passionately kisses her.

Brooke pulls back and blinks, speechless.

Kevin kisses her again, this time more gently. "Brooke, you know I love you, right? I really want this to be a fresh start for us. No talk of babies. Let's just chill out and relax. We both need it."

His attempt at pushing past the pain backfires. He's minimizing their loss again. Brooke's eyes fill with tears at just the word *babies*.

Kevin takes Brooke's bag in one hand and her hand in the other and heads outside to the car waiting for them in the driveway. He opens her door to let her in the spacious backseat. The air-conditioning is thankfully cranked up; it's nearly 90 degrees outside. Brooke spots a bottle of crisp, white wine sitting on ice with two glasses, and she wants to retch. Alcohol will be like acid in her already roiling stomach.

"Why don't you pour yourself a glass of wine while I lock up and set the alarm?" Kevin suggests.

He shuts the limo door, hands Brooke's bag to the driver, and locks up their home. He climbs in the backseat of the limo with Brooke and settles in next to her, then pours himself a glass of wine.

Brooke watches him. He's doing everything to keep on a happy face, but she knows he has a dark side. He's worried about something, she can tell that much, but he's not the kind of man who would spontaneously share with her what it is. Not unless she really pushed him.

She's not ready to do that yet.

$$-9-$$

Pick Up

Allison

Allison is more than ready to welcome her husband home. The house is organized, the fridge is stocked, and two bottles of their favorite Sauvignon Blanc are on ice. The girls, freshly washed in the outdoor shower after the beach, are quietly engaged in a game of cards at the kitchen table.

Allison brings her cell into the bedroom and shoots Marc a quick text before stepping into the shower herself.

Our new neighbors arrived today. Take a guess who won the bet!

She hops in the shower, and seconds later her phone chimes. Allison loves this game, and takes her time before checking her phone. Finally, after she's clean and dried off, reads Marc's response:

I bet it's the older preppy couple. I'll be ready for the massage you owe me for winning when I get there!

Allison smiles and texts back, *maybe yes, maybe no. You'll have to wait and see. The girls are coming with me to pick you up, so neither of us will be cashing in yet.*

Another chime. *Come on, Allie! You can't make me wait any longer. Tell me who it is!*

Allison doesn't give in. She knows Marc is going crazy on the other end awaiting her response, and she loves it.

She can imagine that anyone looking into their marriage from the outside would think he'd been gone for weeks with how excited she is for his return.

She digs through her closet and finds Marc's favorite white, borderline-sheer sundress and pulls a lace camisole out of her top drawer to wear underneath. She applies a few spritzes of her favorite lilac body spray and then checks her phone again, but there's nothing more from him. She assumes he's boarded his plane.

Allison heads back to the kitchen and sees the girls are comfortable and quite content. She decides to leave them by themselves so she can have a more intimate reunion with Marc.

"Savannah, I'm heading out to pick up your dad. You're in charge. There are plenty of snacks in the fridge, but I shouldn't be long."

"Really? You're leaving us here?" Savannah seems shocked, which makes sense since Allison has never left her home in charge of her sister for more than ten minutes.

"I am, and don't make me regret it." Allison responds with as much firmness she can muster considering the euphoric mood she is in.

"We won't!" Allison hears as she heads out and shuts the door behind her.

She checks her messages again after she pulls into the airport and parks in the tow zone, hazards blinking. Surely, he must have landed by now. He didn't check a bag, so he should be walking out any minute.

Allison settles in for some people watching. It's one of her favorite hobbies in Nantucket. Many emerge dressed in preppy outfits, accessorized with Louis Vuitton travel bags and Chanel sunglasses. Everyone has a story, and Allison takes a guess at each one, wishing she could really know.

Her husband will be one of the best-looking travelers, that much she knows. She'll never forget the day she first laid eyes on his six-foot-plus frame, piercing blue eyes, thick wavy hair she still loves to run her fingers through.

They met when Marc joined Allison's running group in Boston after his roommate talked him into signing up for his first road race. Back then Marc was not a runner. He always worked out and was in phenomenal shape with broad shoulders and a solid build, but in those days, he was bulky and didn't have the cardio endurance for running.

Allison, on the other hand, always had the typical runner's body, long and lean, and she had the bug. As the story goes, Marc stuck with it because of Allison. He's always been an athlete, and speaking of which, she's still not seeing his gorgeous body emerging from the airport.

The stream of vacationers pouring out of the building has turned to a trickle, and Allison suddenly realizes Marc is nowhere to be seen. Her phone sits quietly on her lap. She's growing uneasy. *Where is he?*

She leaves her car, not caring if she gets a ticket, and races to the ticket desk.

"Excuse me," she asks the attendant. "Are you already boarding the plane that just arrived from Boston?"

"Yes, ma'am, it's scheduled to take off shortly. Can I help you with something?"

"My husband was supposed to get off that plane. But I don't see him anywhere." Her voice is growing high-pitched.

"Maybe he's in the restroom, ma'am. Everyone has been off the plane for a while now."

"Is there any way to confirm he made the flight?"

"I'm sorry," the man says. "I'm not allowed to provide that kind of information."

Allison stomps away furiously. She parks herself outside the men's room hoping the ticket clerk is right. After what feels like an eternity during which not one person comes or goes, she opens the door and calls his name.

The only thing she hears is the sound of her own voice echoing back at her, joined by a rancid whiff of a well-used urinal.

She checks her phone again. Nothing from Marc. Maybe her phone's not working. She sends herself a test text, and immediately it chimes at her. She calls Marc's number and it goes straight to voicemail.

Allison walks back to her car and climbs behind the wheel. She slides the key into the ignition but doesn't turn it. Where is she supposed to go? What is she supposed to do with herself? She picks up her phone again but this time she calls the girls. Allison doesn't want to alarm them, but maybe Marc called the house.

"Don't worry, mom," Savannah, a mini adult all of the sudden, says. "We're fine. We're eating our snack. Awesome guacamole by the way."

"Glad you like it." Allison keeps her voice chipper. "I'm still waiting for your dad. Did he call the house by any chance?"

"No, you're the only one who's called." Savannah seems to

shuffle the phone around, and then Allison hears her voice again, now muffled. "I'll get it for you in a sec, Ab! I'm just hanging up with mom." Then more clearly again, "Gotta run mom, see you guys soon!"

Allison knows it's pointless, but she dials Marc's number once more.

Getaway

Brooke

Brooke is already exhausted by the time they make it to the check-in desk at Logan Airport. Kevin insisted a glass of wine in the limo would relax her, but all it did was make her nauseated.

The desk agent is shaking her head as she checks her computer screen. "I'm sorry, sir," she says. "I don't see your reservation, and I'm afraid this flight is fully booked. Can I ask—"

"What do you mean, *booked*?" Kevin interrupts, his face like thunder. "I spoke with someone this morning and confirmed two seats on this flight."

Brooke closes her eyes for a moment. She knows he wants everything to be perfect, but she's too fragile for a public scene. She notices a man looking up from his phone from his seat in the waiting area. *Great.* Kevin's raised voice is already drawing attention.

Tears begin to well up in her eyes. It's obviously too soon. She needed at least one more day to heal, physically and emotionally, before getting out into the world again.

Get a grip, Brooke.

"I told you this wasn't a good idea," she says quietly to Kevin. "Let's just forget it. I want to go home."

"No way," Kevin snaps, staring right at the ticketing agent. "This vacation is on doctor's orders. My wife has been through hell. We need to get on that plane."

The airline employee keeps cool, continues scrolling, then perks up. "Wait...I *do* have one seat on this flight. And then there's one on the 6 p.m. flight, so you can go one after the other, if you'd like."

"*No,*" Kevin barks. "We're sticking together."

Brooke squeezes his hand, relieved. She doesn't relish a flight alone on one of those tiny, bumpy planes.

"I'm afraid your next option is the Eight a.m. flight. We're terribly sorry for the mix-up, sir, but we can certainly get you seats together in the morning," the agent replies.

Brooke says to Kevin, "Please, honey. Just take me home."

She notices the curious man, the one who'd been watching them, is now approaching the desk. Kevin is enraged, but hasn't unleashed on the agent, so Brooke braces for a confrontation.

The stranger is tall and good-looking, with brown, sun-streaked hair, and looks to be about Kevin's age.

"Hello," the man says to both of them. Brooke sniffles, holding in tears best she can, refusing to break down over a travel mishap.

Kevin eyes the man suspiciously.

"I couldn't help overhear your trouble with the flight," the man says kindly. "Believe me, I've been there, done that. Listen...I have some flexibility, and I have a seat on this flight.

Please, take mine, and I'll catch the six o'clock. I insist."

"We couldn't," Brooke protests.

"It's already done," the man says, handing his ticket to the agent, who's nodding and booking him on the later flight.

"Hey, man," Kevin says, offering his hand to the stranger, "I can't thank you enough. This is really good of you. Can I pay you for this? Honestly, I'm—"

The man shakes his head. "Not at all. It's not going to cost me anything. But I do have one small favor to ask, if you wouldn't mind…"

The flight from Boston to Nantucket is under an hour, and it's an exciting flight. The plane has only eight passengers and Kevin lets Brooke sit up front with the pilot. She gets lost in the views out the window as they fly past the Boston skyline, over the little islands peppering the coast, past Cape Cod then over the open waters toward the island of Nantucket.

The further they fly from Boston, the lighter she begins to feel, losing herself in the deep blues and greens of the waters below.

She has a brief thought about jumping and leaving everything behind, but she could never do that to Kevin. And deep down in her soul she knows she'll have a child…someday. Even though she's not supposed to be thinking about babies, she can't help it; she isn't ready to give it all up for good.

She suddenly remembers what her massage therapist said as Brook was leaving the appointment: *Just be open as to how your wishes will come true.*

Letting this sink in, Brooke admits to herself there are many ways to have a family. She knows one thing for sure: her body simply can't take any more of the drugs, the shots, the hormones, or the cycles. She must have aged twenty years over the past five. It's time to reclaim her youth.

Maybe they could adopt Charlie? God, she loves that poor boy like her own. She would keep that to herself for now; she knows Kevin cannot handle any more stress.

Before Brooke knows it, the plane approaches the small runway, located a few miles outside of town. The pilot turns to Brooke. "Make sure your seatbelt is on tight, we are going to have to be creative landing this bird with these crosswinds."

The old Brooke would have panicked at this statement from the pilot. But with all she's been through, she feels like she has nothing to lose. She's ready for any adventure, whether good or bad. Nothing could be worse than this last pregnancy. At least, she *hopes* nothing could be worse.

The landing is as rough as promised, and her knuckles turn white grabbing the sides of her seat. But they land safely, and Kevin takes her hand as they deplane.

"I remember this airport like we were just here," Brooke smiles as she breathes in the fresh air while walking toward the tiny airport building fifty yards away. It's light and airy and full of happy memories. The sun is shining, and her skin soaks in its warmth.

"I rented us a jeep," Kevin tells her as they enter the building and head to the car rental counter. "I requested yellow since I know how much you love yellow Jeeps."

Kevin seems more relaxed too since they had landed. There are two people ahead of them, and when it's their turn, the desk clerk nods and smiles. "You're in luck," she says, tapping away on her keyboard. "Our most popular color is red, so you've got the yellow Jeep you requested."

"Perfect," Kevin nods, giving Brooke's shoulders a quick squeeze. "And there's an off-road beach sticker on the bumper so we can take it onto the beaches for afternoon lunches and sunset cocktails. Oh, the fun we have ahead of us, Brookie!"

She manages a genuine smile in return. As much as she was starting to relax, the word "fun" has not been in her vocabulary for years. She hopes she can remember how. But Kevin went through all this effort to plan this trip, so she's going to have to try.

– 11 –

Reunion

Allison

Allison listens to her phone ring over and over and her mind goes to all sorts of dark places. *Where are you, Marc?*

"Hey, Allie." Marc's voice interrupts her negative thoughts. His voice startles her.

"*Marc?* Where *are* you? Are you okay? I've been here waiting for you for almost an hour!"

"Didn't you get my text?"

"What text? No, obviously I didn't!" Allison's voice is frayed with residual panic.

"Hey, hey," he coos. "I must've punched in the wrong number. I was on someone else's phone so I was rushing, I'm so sorry. I'm fine, I promise. I'm still at Logan. My phone died, and I was finally able to borrow a phone charger from a couple eating dinner next to me for a few minutes. But I still barely have any power."

"That doesn't explain why you're still in Boston," Allison says, irritated now from the wait, the lack of communication, the worry, and the long delay to a reunion she was excited for in more ways than one.

"It's a long story, but I'm on the six p.m. flight. Gotta go—about to run out of juice!"

The phone goes dead, and Allison is left with a sense of relief mixed with a hint of unease.

For the second time in one day, Allison waits outside the airport behind two SUVs in the tow-zone. She made a point of *not* arriving early, as she's losing patience for sitting in the car.

She leans forward and watches vacationers pour out the double doors, trying to single out her husband. No dice.

She glances idly to her left, which gives her a view into the arrivals lounge through the building's glass wall. She can see people grabbing luggage and chatting from where she's sitting, and as the incoming flight empties out, she sees a familiar figure.

Marc.

Her heart leaps into her throat. She sees the duffel bag, the backwards baseball cap and the tailored suit, and any unease she felt dissipates. She can't wait to get him home.

Her heart full, she smiles and grabs the car door handle, ready to hop out, run in and greet him, parking ticket be damned.

Before she can open the door, she sees another familiar figure step into view inside the airport. She's in a different flowing sundress this time, but has the same perfect, sleek, low pony she had on earlier that very morning.

It's her good friend Kate.

Kissing Allison's husband.

Marc emerges two minutes later, sees Allison, and races over to give her a peck through the driver's side window.

He takes his place in the passenger seat, rushed, sighing, with an aura of travel fatigue.

Allison checks her mirrors and pulls out. Only when they're on the road does Marc seem to realize there's something very wrong.

"Whoa," he says, clearly confused, turning to her. "I can cut the tension in here with a knife. What's wrong, Allie?"

"I saw you."

"Saw me what?"

"I *saw* you in there with Kate," she says icily. "So I have to ask myself: where have you really been for the last four hours? Are you breaking the rules?"

"Wait a minute. What *is* this?" he asks, instantly on the defensive. "Kate was at the airport picking up a friend. Jon was with her. Did you happen to see him? Jesus, Allison! Kate's your best friend on this island and we always greet each other with a kiss. What's gotten into you?"

She says nothing.

"For your information," he goes on, "I was late because there was a couple who got bumped off the three o'clock and the woman was clearly not well. She was crying, he was freaking out, and I knew three hours either way wouldn't affect us much. I gave up my seat because it meant they could stay together. She clearly wasn't in any condition to travel alone."

His explanation has the expected effect, and now Allison feels awful for doubting him.

She understands why he's so shocked. This kind of tension is new for them. Neither of them has ever been the jealous type. Any problems they've ever had in a sixteen-year marriage have been the expected bumps from newborn exhaustion, stress from work seeping into their home life, maybe some winter blues over the years. But never this. They've always had trust and an attraction that kept them both happy in the bedroom *and* out of it.

Until lately. What started as a fun and exciting addition to their sex life is turning volatile. Allison is confused by her own growing feelings of jealousy. Kate isn't after her husband, and Marc isn't looking to blow up his family life. She knows this on an intellectual level.

So why does she feel so scared her marriage might be in trouble?

Allison grips the steering wheel so hard her fingernails dig into her palms. She gets a grip on herself, too.

"I'm sorry," she says, turning to him. Now he's the one staring out the window with a face like stone. "I was worried sick, and then I saw her with you and…well, can we reset, please? I've been so excited for you to come home. I've got a very special reunion planned."

He turns to her, his face softening. "I'm in for that," he says. "Consider us reset."

He takes her free hand and squeezes.

Allison stops at Pi to pick up a pizza for the girls on their way home. When they arrive, Allison carries the pizza so Marc can enjoy a chaotic reunion with the girls and a bouncing, joyful Reilly.

Marc heads straight into the shower as Allison settles the girls downstairs with pizza and a movie. Once Savannah and Abigail are absorbed in the latest teen release, Allison heads to the kitchen to open a bottle of wine. She pours herself a full glass, takes three big gulps, and sighs.

All begins to feel right in the world again.

She lets the nerves even out, the doubts fly away, and her worries recede about how suddenly attached she feels to her own husband. She never needed a man to feel whole. This is a new, and frankly unsettling, feeling. She always prided herself on her independence.

Allison tops off her glass and fills one for Marc. She picks up both glasses and wanders into their bedroom. He's toweling off as she walks in. She can see the beads of water still on his tanned skin, his hair wet and wavy. He is clean and smells of Ivory soap.

She hands him his wine and pulls his towel out of his hands. She plants a kiss on his wet shoulder, moves up his neck, then finds his mouth with hers. He tastes like home.

Eventually she pulls away, then reaches for her glass and swallows the last of her wine. Marc does the same.

Allison reaches for a bottle of aloe. They're supposed to be attending the first Upside-Down party of the season tomorrow night, but right now she wants Marc all to herself. Hopefully that will change by tomorrow.

"Let me rub some lotion on your back," she purrs. "It's starting to peel from your sunburn last weekend."

"Now we're talking," Marc, still standing, says with a devilish look in his eye. "But didn't you win the bet? I thought I owed *you*."

"You first."

Allison finishes rubbing Marc down and takes his hand, leading him to the bed.

"You're wearing my favorite sundress." Marc finally notices as she strips it to the floor.

Allison stands on her tippy toes and presses her lips to Marc's ear and whispers, "Not anymore."

The wine has gone straight to her head and she loses her balance on her toes; she wraps her arms around his neck and they both fall together in a tangled heap on the bed.

While she wants to straddle him right then and there, she still needs to cash in on their bet. Marc begins kissing her, first on the mouth, then her chest, then her tummy, and as he creeps lower, he runs a hand down one thigh.

"Woman, your legs will be the death of me."

Allison feels a rush inside her chest and is filled with desire for this man.

"Not until after my massage," she orders.

He complies. What happens after he rubs her down makes her want to argue with him more often.

One thing a truly solid marriage is short on is make-up sex, and Allison wonders if it might even be beneficial to have more of it in the future.

After all, there are still things she hasn't felt comfortable enough to confide in him yet, and when she does, she'll need to brace herself for conflict in their usually placid marriage.

– 12 –

Wake up Call

Carla

Carla is jerked out of a sound sleep by the shriek of her alarm. She's on vacation, so she instinctively turns it off and rolls over. Then her eyes pop open as she remembers she agreed to join Allison on her run this morning.

She yawns, slips out from under the sheets and forces herself to get up and dressed. She casts a look at Lawrence—he's snoring like a chainsaw. Carla's no running fanatic, but she senses this new neighbor could be a lifelong friend. She's not going to risk irritating Allison on day two.

Ten minutes later she spots Allison on the road outside her house, trailed by a gorgeous Golden Retriever.

"Aw," Carla squeals, kneeling to greet the dog and stroke his thick fur. "Who's this?"

"This is Reilly. He's slowing down a bit," Allison says with some sadness, scratching the dog's head.

"You're a very good boy," Carla says to the dog, standing again.

"He is. I have to say, if I wasn't meeting you, I would still be in bed," Allison confesses.

"Ha, so would I," Carla laughs. "But I'm glad we're doing this. I want to get in shape this summer. Lead the way—I'm in your hands."

Allison and Reilly lead Carla on a gentle three-mile run through the neighborhood. The two women chat the entire way, picking up right where they left off on the beach yesterday.

Carla decides she can trust her new friend, and shares with Allison all about her hometown, a suburb thirty minutes west of Boston. She tells her about a certain scandalous baseball coach who is rumored to have taken pictures of his wife with a cucumber, and then allegedly texted them around to his friends.

Carla and Allison agree this should be appalling but for some reason both find it hilarious. With Allison showing an openness and humor about raunchy sex-related stories, Carla blurts out a secret she's been holding in.

"There's more," she says sheepishly, trying not to pant too much as she fights to keep up with Allison.

"Ooh. Do tell," Allison demands.

"So I was dropping my son off at the coach's son's house after a game, and the baseball coach offered me a cold drink. I knew what he was really asking, but I went. I could see it in his eyes, and I went anyway. And…well. He kissed me."

"Wait, wait, *wait*. Are you telling me you *kissed* Mr. Baseball Coach?" Allison's mouth is agape.

"Ah…yeah. I am."

"When did this happen?"

"Just before we left." Carla is breathing heavier.

"Really? Does Lawrence know?" Allison seems shocked, but also utterly fascinated.

"God, no!" Carla shakes her head. "He has no idea. He'd kill me. *And* the guy, come to think of it. I mean, not literally. But he'd be *pissed.*"

Suddenly, having said it out loud, it hits Carla that this is a big deal. A huge deal. A stupid mistake that could hurt her family. "It happened so fast," she adds. "I feel awful about it. As soon as I realized what was happening I put a stop to it. And the weird thing is, things have been even better with Lawrence ever since. The guilt, I guess, makes me a bit more eager to please…"

Allison remains quiet for a moment. All Carla can hear is their deep breathing and shoes treading on pavement as they pick up the pace.

"I can't even believe I told you all that," Carla says finally. "But it's been eating me up and I have no one to talk to about it. Everyone in my town knows everything about each other. Sorry…I shouldn't have said anything."

"Don't be silly, Carla," Allison says kindly. "I don't pass judgment on anyone. Believe me, I've seen and heard a lot worse. A quick kiss from a coach in town is nothing."

And somehow, Carla believes her. She feels so much better about it now that she's aired it out. *I mean, what's the big deal, really?* She thinks. It'll never happen again, and it has only brought her closer to Lawrence.

When they finish their run, Reilly is breathing the hardest of all of them, but he's happily wagging and clearly enjoyed the company and fresh air.

"Listen, Carla," Allison says before they part ways outside her house. "Marc and I are hosting a little party next week with a few friends. Why don't you and Lawrence plan to come? It would be a great way to meet some of the other people who vacation on the island."

Carla is relieved that her admission hasn't turned Allison off.

"That sounds great!" I'll talk with Lawrence and let you know for sure, but it sounds wonderful. Thanks so much for the invite, and for the run."

"Perfect. Let me know if you would like to run again this weekend." Allison waves and jogs down her driveway, Reilly at her heels.

Carla shuts the door to their new home behind her. Their first island party invite!

Thoughts turn immediately to what she'll wear.

Carla heads upstairs and hits the shower. She's already curious about Allison's social circle. If they're half as cool as Allison, Carla will have a solid group of friends she can look forward to spending her Nantucket summers with.

She still can't quite believe she shared something so personal and explosive with her neighbor after knowing her less then twenty-four hours, but for some reason Carla feels she can trust Allison. More to the point, her life back home feels so far away that it almost doesn't matter.

Carla has no one she can talk to about this stuff in her small hometown of Westbury. Everyone knows the baseball coach and his reputation. The last thing she wants is to be associated with him in *that* kind of way and risk becoming a pariah in her social circle, where rumors spread like wildfire.

Her thoughts turn to her favorite sexy black dress for Allison's party. From a young age Carla was body confident and embraced her frame, which was both curvy—she was a D-cup by sophomore year of high school—and athletic. But, like many of her friends, she lost some of her confidence after giving birth to three children. She knows that was a factor in her recent transgression: the coach's interest in her made her feel sexy again.

Carla towels off and heads to her closet quietly because Lawrence is still sleeping, and she pulls out the fitted low-cut number. She slips it on to make sure it fits like she remembers, and searches for a statement piece of jewelry to adorn her neck. After trying on a few pieces, she is not fully satisfied.

Then she remembers her good friend back home told her about the Blue Beetle, apparently a *must* for summer's trendiest accessories.

Carla decides she'll run into town after lunch and check it out. Maybe she'll even bring her girls with her. She can look for some fun shoes too while she's in town.

– 13 –

Impulse

Allison

As Allison heads inside her house, she wonders if Carla and Lawrence will join their little soirée, and if they do, will they partake in the after-midnight action? She can't wait to tell Marc about their run.

The stakes are higher than usual, considering her potential new party guests live next door. No matter what, it's going to be an interesting summer.

Marc's waking up as she enters the bedroom. Before she heads to shower, she fills him in on her bonding session with Carla.

"Do you think that's a good idea to invite her so soon?" Marc asks, stifling a yawn. "You just met her, and if they get any inkling of what goes on at our parties after hours, it could set us up for an awkward situation later. This isn't like you to move so fast."

"I know, I know!" Allison can't argue. This impulsive behavior is *not* like her. "But it's a week away and I've been getting some good vibes from Carla, so I went for it. You only live once, as the girls love to say."

Allison tells Marc a few details about the baseball coach and swears him to secrecy.

"Apparently Lawrence will go apeshit if he finds out," she says. "But honestly, Marc…it seems to me maybe she got a little taste of someone else and I think it left her wanting Lawrence more, even if she can't admit it to herself yet. I mean, this woman spent half the day on the beach yesterday explaining how this is the summer for them to reconnect like the days before they had kids.

"Our party could be the perfect way for them to do that," Allison goes on. "And I think she has a bit of a girl crush on me. You know I'm a good judge of character."

Marc sighs and counters, "They seem like a really nice family and the girls have hit it off. I don't ever want our girls to suffer because of our lifestyle choices. It all feels a bit too close to home—literally."

Allison understands, but the deed is done. "I don't see any harm in inviting our neighbors over for a drink with our group, and I'll be responsible for keeping it that way, OK? We can easily make sure they don't stay too late. Our guests will understand and respect the rules concerning early-night versus late-night behavior."

Marc reaches for his phone and checks his weather app, clearly resigned.

"I guess it would be fun to share a cocktail with Carla and Lawrence and get to know them," he says. "Let me meet them both, too, and we'll go from there. Deal?"

Allison gets an idea. She knows how much Marc loves to make bets, so she decides to give him a chance to redeem himself after the last one.

"Want to make a bet about whether or not I can talk them into our lifestyle before the summer is over?"

It works like a charm. Marc takes the bait, grinning and looking up from his phone. "You're on." He pauses, then adds, "Of course I'm interested if you are. And it sounds like you are?" Allison knows what he's really asking: *Are you attracted to Lawrence?*

"Yes," she nods. "I am."

Allison already adores Carla, and after watching a shirtless Lawrence surfing the waves and running on the beach, she knew the couple were great candidates to join their group.

"We don't need Kate and Jon coming over and luring them away," Allison adds, slipping up and showing another hint of jealousy.

"Jon's in Boston for a big client dinner the night of our party," Marc points out. "Which means Kate probably won't come either."

Allison rolls her eyes. "Don't count on it. You know she doesn't always follow the rules."

Marc looks surprised at her continued negative references about her close friend.

"What is going *on* with you two? This is the second or third time you've made snarky comments about her. Did something happen?"

"No," Allison lies. "I want to branch out a little on our own instead of it always being with them or…just Kate."

Marc puts his phone down and sits up straighter, leaning against the tufted headboard. "I thought you were loving it with them?"

"I did, I do," she says. "It's just that I am getting a little bored with Jon is all, though I still love Kate."

Marc shrugs. "Fair enough. Let's see where all of this leads and what the others think. They all have more experience than we do."

"You're right," Allison says. "We've never courted another couple before. It was always us being courted."

Allison, satisfied with the plan, leans into Marc for a quick kiss and even with that, she gets butterflies.

She'll never *not* be attracted to this man. Allison and Marc were smitten with each other from the start, from the moment they met in their running gear, with just-got-out-of-bed hair, half asleep due to the early morning hour. Of course, Allison never let on about her feelings because she had a serious boyfriend, Billy, at the time. So she and Marc became running buddies along with thirteen other Bostonians.

They got to know each other on those runs, when their talks were long and deep and completely uninhibited. Allison loved that she could always be herself. After all, they saw each other in the early hours of the day when vanity had no place, there was no make-up or cute outfits, and she was completely in her natural state, physically as well as mentally. Their relationship has thankfully maintained that honest, vulnerable rawness over the years.

Although they tried their best to be friends, they slipped up one night when the group went out for drinks after the Boston Run to Remember half-marathon on Memorial Day weekend. They were tossing back a few beers and laughing about a silly story Marc was telling about one of his law school friends and then, out of nowhere, he leaned in and kissed her.

The electricity was undeniable. Marc grabbed her hand and led her out of the bar, and Allison followed willingly. They found an alley off the sidewalk and he pushed her up against a wall and they made out for an eternity.

Marc pulled away, and they both took a breath, and Allison felt a stab of guilt. She was officially cheating on her boyfriend now; she didn't see herself that way and she was profoundly uncomfortable but also felt more alive than she ever had.

He whispered, "Let's take a walk down to the Charles. It's a beautiful night."

Allison had wanted to say yes, but instead she said, "We shouldn't do this, Marc. We're both in a relationship, and I don't want to ruin our friendship."

Marc surprised her with his response. "You're right, Allie," he said. "I'll end things tomorrow with Sara. Will you do the same?"

Allison hesitated. She'd expected him to press her for more tonight, not to admit his feelings were so strong for her that he was willing to end a relationship. She was afraid to go down this path. Marc leaned in as she stuttered something about *I don't know if I can…*

He kissed her again, deeply. Allison lost herself in the kiss and gripped his ass, pulling him into her, and all she could think about was this man and this moment.

Until the guilt struck again. "We really should keep things the way they are," she said, and pulled away one final time. Marc had backed away, running his strong hands through his thick hair, now slick with sweat.

He inhaled sharply, adjusting himself, and then smoothed

out Allison's pin-straight hair. He kissed her nose and escorted her back to the bar. Neither one of them spoke a word about it for the rest of that night, and Allison had to fight her dread over Billy and what he might do if he found out.

Now she and Marc had come full circle: Both of them still desiring other people, but always keeping that raw honesty between them that they cherished so.

At least Allison hopes so.

Nothing Left

Brooke

Brooke tries valiantly to work up some excitement for the steak Kevin sets before her, but her appetite is still nonexistent. It's been an unbelievably long day. It's hard to believe it was only twelve hours ago she was in bed in a puddle of tears.

She forces herself to try a forkful of steak. "Mmm," she smiles at Kevin, who's watching her closely. "You cooked it perfectly."

Brooke knows Kevin expects nothing but gratitude for this surprise four-week vacation at their old stomping grounds, but she's growing weary of his sudden hovering. Kevin hasn't done anything like this for Brooke since they first started trying to have a baby three years ago. He's been grumpy as hell and stressed over work, or not around because of the nighttime entertaining his job requires. Brooke still hasn't decided which is worse for her.

"Your margarita's melting," Kevin says, pointing to her hand-blown glass. The cocktails did nothing but make her more tired. All she wants to do is go to sleep.

"Kev, I'm sorry, but I am just exhausted," she starts

tentatively, laying her fork down. "Would you mind if I went to bed? I know it's still early and our first night, but we have four weeks, right?"

"Sure, Brooke, I know you've been through a lot." He smiles tightly, but Brooke recognizes the look of disappointment and annoyance in his eyes all too well.

She crawls into bed and feels cold and vulnerable. And all she wants is to feel nothing at all.

Brooke wakes the next morning feeling almost human after nine hours of uninterrupted sleep. Kevin is snoozing next to her, smelling of scotch, and she guesses he stayed out on the deck last night having a few solitary nightcaps.

As he often does, he seems to sense she's up, feels her rustling under the covers, and his eyes fly open.

She smiles down at him, hoping he forgives her for bailing early on their romantic dinner on the deck last night.

"What time is it?" He croaks.

"I don't know," she replies. "Kev—"

"*What.*" He growls, grasping his head with two hands and groaning.

One of his headaches; she's not surprised, given all the liquor she's sure he drank last night.

She flinches, then begins to tear up. She wonders when she'll be dried out, drained, out of salt.

"I'm so sorry, Kev," she cries. "I've been trying to put on a happy face because I know how much effort you put into planning this vacation, and I love you for it."

Kevin rolls over and his face and mood changes on a dime.

He reaches out and smoothes her hair back, then sits up and leans on some pillows against the headboard. He kisses her streaming salty tears and licks one from the corner of her mouth as he softly kisses and consoles her.

"It's been a rough couple of years. But that's all it is, Brookie. Life is tough, and when it puts you down you have to stand up and try again."

Brooke's eyes light up. "Oh, Kev, does that mean you…I mean, we can try again for a baby?"

Kevin freezes. Brooke watches his face morph from concerned to tense and back again.

He squeezes her hand, looks her in the eye, and says, "Baby, of *course* we'll try again." He yawns. "But for now, let's focus on today. The beach is right outside our door. Shall we get up and get some sun?"

Brooke wants to curl up under the covers and never come out.

"Sure, Kev. Breakfast out on the deck first?"

He grins and leans in for a kiss. "That's my girl," he says, his voice growing husky. He moves his warm hand from her tummy, slides it up to her chest, and gently cups her breast.

Brooke realizes she's not ready for sex yet. She's wounded in her soul, but also physically sore after that horrendous doctor's appointment, and after all the poking and prodding long before that.

"Kev," she says as gently as she can, "I have to run to the bathroom, OK?"

She doesn't want to upset him, to reject him. She's still attracted to him, just not right now. She slides out of bed.

– 15 –

Blue Blood

Kate

Kate hasn't seen Allison since this season's Upside Down's debut party. She finds herself once again wondering alone in arguably the most beautiful house on Nantucket. Jon is away for work *again* until tomorrow morning, and Kate has nothing to do but think and pace, but she never loses sight of the view outside. The towering cliff and seemingly endless ocean behind the lawn is enough to make her feel small, in a good way. It reminds her to keep her problems in perspective.

It doesn't always work. Last weekend's party has left Kate feeling anxious. Kate noticed that things have been different with Allison. But she can't figure out why. The tension between the two of them is affecting things with Marc, he is ghosting her!

Kate has been trying to stay busy. She saw friends for brunch the other day and had a lazy lunch with clients earlier today, but while she was "on" with all of them—and with everyone who stopped by her table to greet her, as is customary whenever she and Jon are out alone or together, because anyone who's anyone wants to know the Gibsons—she was left feeling empty every time.

Kate roots around in the fridge and decides she's had enough champagne for the week.

She pads to the wet bar overlooking the breathtaking pool and whips up a fresh lime margarita with the artisan sour mix the staff hand-squeezes a few times a week.

She knows what's getting to her today, what's making her melancholic and crave oblivion through alcohol, but she can't grasp how to solve it.

How do you solve a problem like Allison?

Allison's quaint little party in her fun beach house over in Cisco is happening tonight, and Kate is expressly forbidden from attending.

She's not sure how it happened, but in one snap of an invisible finger she and Allison seem to have gone from close friends to frenemies this summer. Or at least they're on that path. Kate knows Allison made a point of avoiding her at Bartlett's, and Kate knows she's not welcome in her home tonight, and it makes her feel more estranged from her close friend.

Kate understands why she can't go to this party. It's bad faith to break the rules their group agrees to live by, the guidelines that are designed to keep things from getting complicated. It's safer that way.

At the same time, she doesn't understand why she should have to sit home on a Saturday night in this huge house, alone, thinking too much and missing out.

She wishes Jon were here. Not because she's desperately pining for him, but because they'd be welcome to attend the Evans's party as a couple. She would never admit this out loud, but Jon is not the love of her life.

Kate was married once before, a long time ago. She and Chris were high school sweethearts. They were the first couple to marry from their high school class which, at the time, seemed like a cool thing to do: get engaged, wear a rock on your finger, plan a wedding, invite all your friends.

But in the end, it became obvious they married too young. They had a false sense of adulthood because of the family money Chris had inherited at a young age. With a honeymoon pregnancy, Kate gave up a college degree for a family. While all their friends were busy making new ones and leaving town to head back to college, Kate and Chris were decorating their new home and planning for a baby, pretending to be grown-ups. And when they woke up one day with the realization that this was their life, everything fell apart.

Kate gave birth to their daughter Caroline just months before she discovered Chris was cheating on her. Of course, her hormones were raging and she was beside herself with anger and grief, and when it got too much, Kate nearly poisoned her husband in his sleep.

She knew better than to Google home-made poisons and leave a trail, so she went old-school. She made a pitcher of margaritas sweetened with antifreeze, made a platter of tacos, and then came to her senses just as Chris was commenting on the oddly deep, darker color of the margaritas.

She'd whisked the pitcher away, apologizing for using a cheap mixer. *I'll only use fresh limes from now on,* she'd sworn, then dumped the poisoned cocktail down the kitchen sink. To this day, she cannot believe how close she came to poisoning her ex-husband.

For Caroline's sake, Kate never said a word about Chris's betrayal.

She did, however, cry herself to sleep every night. Eventually Chris's sex life became the topic of their small-town gossip mill and Kate couldn't bite her lip any longer. If she had nothing else, she had her pride and she could turn a blind eye no more.

All Kate cared about in the divorce was having primary custody of Caroline. The money mattered to her at one point, but look where it had gotten her. Chris fought her with all the resources he had; he swore he still loved her. *What you did isn't love.* Kate shot back and went forward with the divorce. Luckily for Kate, her friend was a divorce lawyer who charged her a nominal fee, and they kicked Chris's ass all over the courtroom. Kate got a large settlement, and then she went out and earned her realtor's license.

As soon as Caroline left for college, Kate jumped right into the dating scene. There was a lot of time to make up for. Kate spent her first year back in the game trying new things socially and romantically. She had only ever been with Chris, so she started out slowly.

But it didn't take long for Kate to feel comfortable as a free, young, attractive woman, and she was soon seduced into trying some experimental relationships. After a while, though, the excitement of her single life wore off, and she started to get the itch to settle down, so she pulled away from that scene. She knew she could never really love again, not the way she loved Chris. And she could never trust another man again.

She met Jon online. He was a successful architect and full-time resident of Nantucket, and Kate soon figured out that Jon Gibson comes from generations of hard-earned money. His family has been on the island for hundreds of years, and rumored to be related to one of the original explorers of Nantucket.

Their relationship started with emails, then progressed to phone calls, and after a few weeks Jon invited her to the island for the weekend. It was instant chemistry. After a year of dating, Kate was spending so much time on Nantucket that she started to develop strong friendships. She was happy. With winters spent in Aspen and summers on Nantucket, living in the homes Jon designed himself was a blissful luxury.

But Jon came with his own baggage, and as it happened, he handed some of it to her. He's the reason Kate is in this situation—for better or worse. It started when he shared with her that he'd been married before for ten years, and Kate thought, *Great. Here's a guy who can commit.*

Then he dropped the bombshell: Most of that marriage was spent as an open relationship.

Kate and Jon were still trying to figure out where their relationship was headed at the time, so they hadn't talked about it much. But Kate couldn't help but wonder if Jon was treating their relationship the same way. Jon told her that all open relationships are mutual, and that he would not pursue this with Kate unless she was on board.

She wasn't. Not for a while.

Finally, she began to see the upside, and agreed to give an open marriage a try.

Now she's alone and bored on a beautiful summer night. She shouldn't go to Allison's party; she *really* shouldn't show her face.

Kate wanders to her walk-in closet and idly paws through a selection of sexy summer dresses.

She shouldn't go. *You can't go,* a little voice reminds her.

She reaches out and grabs a red number.

– 16 –
Nantucket Reds

Carla

Carla sends the kids out to dinner so she and Lawrence can relax and have a pre-game cocktail. As soon as they're gone, the two dive into their favorite local drink, a Nantucket Red. A twist on a Cape Codder calls for Triple Eight cranberry vodka from the Cisco brewery mixed with soda water and a generous squeeze of lemon.

Carla leans over the kitchen island to kiss her husband between sips of her drink. His eyes fall to her cleavage.

"No kids around anywhere," he observes. Then his voice changes. "I want you in the shower. Now."

He takes her by the hand, her drink still in the other, and pulls her toward the bedroom. They shower together, and as he soaps her body she feel like the most desirable woman in the world.

I'm back, Carla thinks. *Maybe my little slip was the best thing that could've happened to this marriage.*

An hour later, slightly tipsy and strolling arm in arm with Lawrence, Carla holds tight to a bottle of her favorite champagne. Walking in sexy heels after two strong vodka drinks is no easy feat.

They make it to Allison and Marc's house in once piece, and as Allison throws open the door to greet them, Carla is surprised to find they're the first guests to arrive. She's secretly relieved; she's been feeling more and more nervous about meeting a bunch of new people at once.

She is so curious to meet Allison's husband. She has seen him from afar pacing on the beach path, the best place for cell service. According to Allison he has been preoccupied working on a high-profile case for days. Suddenly, he appears.

Carla's eyes go wide. Marc Evans looks shockingly like the baseball coach from home, and she feels that now-familiar twinge of guilt and thinks, *Why is everyone looking so attractive all of the sudden?*

They make a stunning couple. Allison's toned runner's legs are on show in a short halter dress and five-inch espadrilles. Carla catches Lawrence giving her a subtle once over. She can't blame him.

"Carla, Lawrence—this is Marc," Allison says, taking her husband's hand.

Marc raises his glass. "So pleased to meet you both. I've heard you've been spending a lot of time with Allison and the girls."

Carla nods. "Speaking of which, where are yours this evening? Don't tell me you got them to bed this early."

"Ha, not at all," Allison smiles. "They're at a sleepover. We find it best to keep curious eyes and ears entirely out of the mix. It's more relaxing that way." She winks at her husband.

Carla blinks but quickly recovers. *How wild can a little party like this get?*

"Well," Carla smiles, "It's been such a pleasant surprise to find such charming neighbors."

"We're thrilled to have you all next door, too," Marc replies, eyes twinkling. "Let's get some fresh drinks. Follow me."

As the four of them head to the fully stocked bar, Marc says, "Lawrence, I hear you're quite a surfer. Maybe you can teach me."

"Sure," Lawrence agrees. "Your daughter is already really good."

Allison asks Carla, "What are you drinking?"

"We made some Nantucket Reds before we came over," Carla tells her.

"Ooh, a brewery fav!" Her host replies, watching Carla comfortably move behind the bar and start fixing four cocktails. As Carla adds ice and instructs Allison to squeeze a few lemon wedges, she notes Marc and Lawrence seem to be hitting it off.

"I'm golfing in the morning," Marc is saying. "Do you play?"

"Not very well," Lawrence admits. "I'm a much better surfer."

"If I'm honest, none of us are that good," Marc laughs. "But we have fun. It would be great to have you as a fourth. How about I grab you at seven tomorrow?"

Lawrence doesn't hesitate. "Why not? Thanks."

Carla and Allison hand their husbands their drinks.

"Carla made some Nantucket Red cocktails," Allison says, taking a long sip. "They're *divine*."

In no time, they're all drinking and laughing as if they've known each other for years. They're on their way to getting tipsy when the doorbell chimes. From there, a stream of guests begin to pour in, leaving Carla and Lawrence to watch their hosts welcome sun-kissed friends, all of them couples, Carla notes.

She and Lawrence wander over to a table laden with a selection of gorgeously presented but notably light platters of nibbles and apps. No heavy artichoke dip, no sliders, nothing fried. Crudites, hummus, scallop skewers, even gorgeous lobster lettuce wraps that must have cost a fortune, and lots of sushi.

After enjoying some appetizers, they find themselves alone by the pool, crystalline under the night lights, and Lawrence leans in for a kiss. "This is the life," he says, and Carla has to agree.

She says, "I feel like we should mingle a bit. I really want to meet some friends on the island. Families we can trust, and hopefully watch our kids grow up with. You know?"

"I do," Lawrence nods and kisses her neck. "Let's go."

They wander inside and find the party is in full swing. When Allison sees them, she embraces them, and Carla and Lawrence are introduced to Nantucket society in a whirlwind of greetings.

Carla is too loopy to remember everyone's names, but she manages to hang on to some details: There's the island's most beloved yoga instructor, a member of the town's governing Select Board, and a few Boston-based lawyers whose names she's seen in the news over the years.

Carla can't believe their luck ending up with such perfect neighbors. She's looking at Allison in a new way, and has to admit she's developing something of a girl crush. Which is confusing, because she's also still tingling from meeting Marc.

She turns to Lawrence. "I need another drink," she says.

– 17 –

Breaking the Rules

Kate

Kate twirls in the full-length mirror, her bare feet sinking into the plush carpet in the main suite, regretful that she's the only one around to appreciate how perfectly this red Valentino crepe couture fits her.

But if she goes to the party, what will she say to Allison?

Kate pads back to her closet to find the perfect sandals. There *is* a loophole she could try to exploit to attend the party with impunity: She could stroll in with a bottle of champagne and play the unicorn card.

She'd been one before. After her divorce, a married couple enticed her to become the unicorn in their relationship. Kate had reluctantly accepted. She told herself it was a safe way to be wild, which is, of course, an oxymoron. And at first, she loved being the single woman, almost a plaything, visiting with this committed marriage from time to time. She was romanced by this happy couple who were looking to spice up their love life. Kate felt like a part of their family and grew close to them; maybe *too* close. Eventually the tides began to turn, and Kate noticed her involvement was starting to tear their relationship apart.

She decided it was best to bail out of that situation and go back to more traditional ways. She met Jon a week later, thrilled to find a mooring, relieved to be going back to monogamy. Little did she know what was bubbling under Jon's Old Money, family man veneer.

Kate met Allison during the second summer Kate and her daughter spent living with Jon on Nantucket after Caroline's junior year. Caroline had pasted flyers all over town in search of babysitting work, and Allison was the first to call. It was an instant fit, and Caroline spent most of her summer watching Savannah and Abigail over in Cisco.

Allison was a good influence on Kate. Kate became much more aware of what she was eating because of Allison's health-conscious lifestyle. She began working out again, and cut back on booze. Feeling more energized and confident than ever, she also found a renewed passion for her real estate career.

Kate, however, was a bad influence on Allison. But she preferred to look at it as balancing each other out. The two became inseparable, and they stayed that way all summer long.

This summer they seem to be drifting a bit, and Kate needs to make sure it doesn't get worse. Allison is the only true rock in her life. And while Kate will tell everyone that she doesn't need anyone or anything, she has found that she does need Allison.

If Kate drifts away from her rock, God only knows where she will end up. She fears she could sink fast, maybe all the way to the bottom of the ocean if she's not careful.

– 18 –
Party Crasher

Allison

Allison is hyperaware of Carla and Lawrence's presence at the party, even as the house fills up with guests. Marc is mingling in the kitchen, and their neighbors, left on their own, seem relaxed and enthralled. They're enjoying their drinks and chatting intimately with one another, and Allison must admit they're looking extremely hot while doing it.

She's about to grab herself a fresh drink and take a breather when she hears someone turn the knob on the front door. It swings open, and there she is, as predicted: tall and commanding of attention in a floaty new crepe dress and a glowing golden tan. This woman has an undeniable presence.

"Hello!" Kate Gibson calls as she steps over the threshold.

Allison feels her stress spike in a potent mix of anger, nerves, and new pangs of jealousy that have come out of nowhere this season. She resets and puts on her hostess face with a big, welcoming smile as she hurries across the room to welcome Kate with a hug.

"I thought you weren't coming?" Allison whispers as they embrace.

"Did you think I would miss seeing you and meeting your new friends? You spoke so highly of them at the last party." Kate replies with a coy smile.

"Jealous?" Allison purrs in her ear.

"You could never replace me," Kate murmurs back.

They pull apart, and Allison takes Kate's hand as they weave through the room to make introductions.

"Carla and Lawrence, this is our dear friend Kate Gibson," Allison smiles when she finds them. "Kate, these are our new neighbors, Lawrence and Carla Rossi."

Kate extends her slender arm. "It's a pleasure. I've heard so much about you." She stares into Lawrence's dark eyes, and Allison can see this move is not lost on Carla.

"Very pleased to meet you, Kate." Lawrence takes her hand. When he lets go,

Carla leans over and hugs Kate. Meanwhile, Kate never takes her eyes off Lawrence.

"Drink?" Allison asks.

"The sooner the better," Kate smiles.

Allison leads Carla, Lawrence and Kate back over to the bar, secretly fuming, thrown, and trying to keep her hostess face on. Even though she knew it could happen, even though she said it to Marc earlier that Kate doesn't follow the rules if they don't suit her, Allison is still caught off guard.

So Kate is playing the role of unicorn temporarily tonight, even though she's married, even though her husband is part of their group. This kind of surprise attack is not in the rules.

"How did you two meet?" Carla asks them.

Allison watches Kate, who doesn't flinch. She's sipping

champagne and waiting for Allison to answer. That's the moment she knows Marc was right; it's too soon to bring Carla in, too soon to let on about their lifestyle, let alone commence the recruitment phase.

Allison replies, "It's nothing too exciting, I'm afraid. We connected when Caroline, Kate's daughter, started babysitting my girls."

Carla opens her mouth presumably to press for more details, but Allison's saved by the arrival of more guests. A stunning couple glides into the house, arms linked, and Allison watches everyone's head turn.

The woman has long, thick black hair and big eyes and looks red-carpet ready in a plunging, white, see-through top and black mini skirt. Her partner has equally dark hair, slicked back and parted to one side, and a short, sculpted beard outlining a sharp jawline.

Allison steps away from her little group and waves the couple over. She greets them with a kiss to each cheek, as does Kate. Then Allison introduces them to Carla.

"Carla and Lawrence, this is Logan Williams and Alexa Barlow."

As Carla extends her hand Logan gently pulls it to his lips and kisses it. "The pleasure is all mine, Lady Carla," he says.

Alexa leans in, places a soft kiss onto Carla's cheek and says softly, "You are perfection, just perfection."

Carla blushes and offers a bashful smile. Allison smiles, too, because it appears her friend is enjoying the attention. She watches Lawrence observe these sensual greetings, his eyes about to pop out of his head.

"Lawrence Rossi," he says, taking care of his own introduction and extending a hand to Logan.

Lawrence grips Logan's hand tightly and shakes it, then leans in for an air-kiss with Alexa.

"I'm happy to meet more of Allison's friends," Carla says. "Where are you from?"

"I'm originally from England, but Alexa and I currently live in New York City," Logan replies.

"Good to know," Lawrence replies. "I grew up in Brooklyn. It's nice to meet some New York fans in this land of Patriots!"

"Well, Gisele and I have worked together. We both came of age in the New York fashion scene. And I absolutely loved Tom when he was in Boston," Alexa adds.

Lawrence's eyes are bulging, and Allison shoots a look to Carla to see if it bothers her to see her husband so obviously mesmerized by Alexa. Doesn't look like she is—because Carla appears equally interested.

"That's amazing," Carla says. "Are you still modeling?"

"I retired when I hit thirty," Alexa shrugs. "I didn't have the passion anymore. Then I met this charmer, and he tamed me."

They all laugh, chat some more, and Allison moves on to mingle and check on her guests. Midnight isn't too far away, and she trusts her more conservative, less adventurous friends to leave in plenty of time.

Around eleven-thirty, Allison pours herself a glass of champagne and prepares to drop her hosting duties. She's ready for some fun. Not long before midnight, she heads out to see who's still out on the deck, and sees Carla standing alone overlooking the ocean.

"You have the perfect life," Carla says to Allison swaying slightly.

"Whoa, let's get you back inside," Allison says, realizing her new friend has had too much to drink, catching Carla around the waist as she falters. Carla leans back into her for a moment.

Then Allison sees Carla taking note of the Evans's high-end beautiful watercolor painting of a summer pineapple upside down.

"Whas that?" Carla slurs. "Is that supposed to be upside down? Sorry. I think those drinks were stronger than I thought."

"It's nothing," Allison smiles to herself, and is relieved she sees Lawrence on his way to them.

"I've got her," he smiles.

He says to his wife, "Time to go, honey. Let's get you to bed."

"Oh hi, honey," Carla says, teetering on her heels and smiling at Allison.

"Look! It's your friend Kate. Hi, Kate!" Carla calls as Lawrence helps her make her way to the living room and out the door.

Kate smiles enigmatically as she watches the new couple leave.

Allison views this with interest. *If Kate really wants to play,* Allison thinks, *Let's play.*

– 19 –

Upside Down

Kate

Kate has been waiting impatiently for the Rossis to leave. She wants to get the real party started.

Catherine, the smug yoga instructor, is rooting around for her keys in her clutch. She sees Kate and winks. "I've got to get going before I turn into a pumpkin," she says, sliding past Kate to get out the door.

"Indeed," Kate replies.

She focuses again on the Rossis. They're an undeniably hot couple, but there's no way they're going to join in on the late-night fun she and her friends partake in. She could see it from the moment Carla blushed over nothing, and the way Lawrence clung to his wife.

As soon as Kate sees the door shut behind them, she corners Allison.

"I can certainly see what you mean about them," Kate says. "They're a gorgeous couple. They'd fit right in. But there's no way you're going to get them on board. Trust me."

"I take that as a challenge," Allison replies.

"Do you?" Kate asks sharply. "Are you no longer satisfied with our little group?"

Kate doesn't wait for Allison's response; maybe she doesn't want to know the answer. "OK," she goes on. "What if you *do* draw them in and then things don't work out? They live right next door. You surprise me, Allie."

Her friend takes that in, and Kate can see the doubts flicker across her face.

"You're probably right," Allison concedes. "I got caught up in the moment when we were running last week and I invited them. I've never recruited anyone before…I don't know what to look for. How can you predict who will actually try something like this?"

Kate jabs a finger at her friend. "Exactly. I have a ton of experience bringing couples on board, and I say they're out. And you really shouldn't be bringing them to a swinging party if they're not aware of our lifestyle. You know the rules."

This riles Allison up. She fires back, "You're talking to *me* about rules? Where's Jon tonight, Katie? I don't see him anywhere. I wouldn't be throwing rules in my face if I were you."

Kate has never seen this side of Allison before, and she's oddly turned on. She decides to ignore the topic of rules entirely and focuses again on the neighbors.

"I'll tell you one thing and we can leave it at that: you are never going to get Lawrence to swing."

Allison tilts her head and has a devilish grin on her face.

"I wouldn't try something so clumsy," she says. "If anything, I'd start Carla and Lawrence with a ménage trois. That's how you brought Marc and me into this."

Oh, Kate recalls it well. She feels a tingle at the memory.

Allison keeps on talking, clearly on a mission. "You're up next for hosting, but I want to have a say in the guest list."

"Fine," Kate agrees. Now, let's focus on the present. The night is still young, and you're getting me in the mood for a group romp. Speaking of which, where's that hot husband of yours?"

Allison checks around at the party, now reduced to a dozen guests spread out around the house, and says, "I've been wondering the same thing."

With Kate at her heels, Allison walks out through the kitchen, then back through the party room and out to the pool.

"There you are," Allison says. "Kate and I were just looking for you."

Allison has the seductive look in her eyes Kate has come to recognize.

Marc saunters further out onto the deck. "You found me," he says.

He stretches out his arms, looping one around each woman's waist.

Then he reaches towards the back of Allison's neck as he sweeps her blond hair behind her, twisting it as he licks just below her ear. Kate pushes her groin into his leg and starts to move up and down against his crotch.

She traces a long red polished nail over his bulge, and her hand meets Allison's. Together they caress him, and Kate and Allison lock eyes with desire and they begin kissing, tongues twirling and dancing.

Marc cups Alison's full breast and pulls down her tank dress.

Releasing her with his hands, he takes her into his mouth and gently bites her nipple causing her to growl.

"Ladies," Marc says gruffly. "Let's take this to the pool."

– 20 –
Buzzed

Carla

Carla removes her heels and hands them to Lawrence, who's already supporting her weight as she walks. She's giddy, drunk, and for the first time in a long time she truly feels utterly carefree.

"Oh shit," Carla hiccups, then laughs. "I left my clutch at Allison's. I'm sure it's fine. Oh, maybe you should go back and get it?"

Lawrence smiles and nods. "Of course. But let's get you to bed first."

Lawrence squats and his hiccupping wife hops on for a piggyback like their ten-year-old loves to do. He carries her into the house, then upstairs, and lets her off on the bed. As she strips, he heads into the bathroom and emerges with a glass of water and some ibuprofen.

Carla really is lucky. He's one of the last true family men, if her circle of friends back home is anything to go by. They've had a hell of a time with divorces, cheating, and dissatisfied couples barely tolerating each other in some marriages.

Carla never had reason to distrust Lawrence, and once again the guilt crawls back, though it grows more impotent each time now, especially when squelched by five Nantucket Reds. What's done is done, and so far, she's only reaped benefits from that one moment.

She watches her husband head out to get her purse, though all he wants to do is crawl under the covers and get some sleep before the kids wake up.

Lawrence is the ultimate sportsman and gentleman, and men and women flock to him with his pleasant smile, easy-going attitude, and positive personality. His clients are loyal because they trust him, which is the same reason Carla has loved building a life with him. The fact that he spent his most recent quarterly bonus to buy her a new, fully-loaded Range Rover is only a sideshow.

One thing she's not sure of: is he as unsatisfied with their once-a-week sex life as she is? She's afraid to ask. He's still attracted to her, she can tell, but is it work, family or a loss of interest that brought the frequency down from the once-a-day sex they had until a few years ago?

Carla fades, then snaps awake—she must have passed out for a bit because she jolts awake when she hears the front door slam and footsteps coming upstairs.

When Lawrence enters the bedroom, she's got one leg hanging off the bed and is unmotivated to move. The room is spinning.

"Hey…" she drawls, her voice cracking.

"Hey," he says, and with that, she tries to shake off the bleariness. Something in his tone snapped her to attention.

He's distracted, taking his watch off, his brow knitted. Carla blinks and sits up, holding her head and moaning.

"Sweetie, you gotta sleep it off," says Lawrence, who had been so attentive on the way home is now all business as he takes off his shorts to reveal his boxers.

"Oh, and your purse is in the kitchen," he says, and heads into the bathroom, shutting the door behind him.

Even in her state, his abrupt change in demeanor is noticeable. *What possibly could have happened in the ten minutes he was gone?* She wonders before she passes out for the night.

– 21 –
Freedom

Brooke

Brooke wakes and blinks in the sun peeking through the cracks of the beautiful white window shutters. She can smell the ocean air through a half-open window. She thinks maybe Kevin was right, that even though it felt soon, the fresh air and beautiful surroundings have begun to heal her.

Kevin wakes, yawns, and reaches out to rub her arm.

"Morning," she smiles. Ever since they arrived on Nantucket her husband has been staying by her side. Their days have been filled with barbecuing, playing in the waves, and relaxing on the beach. She is beginning to think she's ready to start trying again. Maybe tonight, even.

Kevin glances at the clock, squinting in the sunlit room.

"Oh, *shit*," he moans. "I'm late."

Brooke sits up, confused. "For what?"

"I have an eight o'clock tee time with some of the guys."

He bounds out of bed.

"What guys?"

"You remember my client, Jon? You've met him once or twice

before, maybe a few months ago at some client dinners."

Brooke takes that in, and tries to remember which client is Jon.

"I manage a shit-ton of this guy's assets," Kevin explains. "I'm sorry, Brooke. It was last minute. Jon texted me on the later side last night that the guys needed a fourth. You had already gone to bed and I thought you might like to have some quiet time to yourself today. Do you mind?"

Brooke is fully awake and alert now, and she knows *Do you mind* isn't a real question, not with Kevin.

"Of course not," she replies.

"Great," he smiles. "Do some shopping, have some fun. I'll be back early afternoon and we'll hit the beach together. Oh, wait…we only have one car. Would you run me up to the Nantucket Golf Club real quick?"

He races off to shower and grab his gear.

Brooke throws on a sundress, slips on a pair of sandals and freshens up in the bathroom. She emerges and grabs the Jeep keys. "Ready?"

Kevin crosses the room and kisses her hard on the mouth. "You're my dream woman, you know that?"

When Brooke pulls the Jeep up to the club's entrance, she sees a few people standing outside chatting, and they all turn to see who's arrived. Kevin leaps out and races around to the back to grab his clubs.

Jon waves and jogs up to the car.

"Hey, Brooke! Thanks for letting me borrow your husband."

Brooke steps out and gives Jon a loose, polite hug. "Of

course," she smiles. "It's nice to see you again."

Now she remembers. Kevin dragged her along on one of his client dinners a few months ago and Jon, who she thought was attractive and perfectly pleasant, was the only one who didn't bring a significant other.

Jon says, "You know, if you're free this morning, you should catch up with my wife Katie. I am sure she would be happy to show you around the island. I believe she's heading into town a bit later for lunch, maybe you can join her. I'll get your number from Kevin and have her call you."

"Thanks," she smiles, and as she does, she sees the one woman in the group break away. She heads toward Brooke, smiling and extending a hand.

"I'm Allison," she says. "Welcome to Nantucket."

Allison is athletic, tanned, and has straight blond hair pulled back in a sleek ponytail. Brooke, with her wild curls, feels pasty and messy in comparison.

"I'm Brooke. We just got here," Brooke smiles. "We've been here before but never in our own house. It's so beautiful here."

"It's a piece of heaven, isn't it?" Allison nods toward Kevin, who is out of view but can be heard rattling around in the back of the Jeep. "You drove your husband, too, huh? Marc and our neighbor, Lawrence, plan to have a few drinks on the course and didn't want to drive." She rolls her eyes as if to say, *Boys will be boys.*

Kevin slams the back door shut and comes around, baseball cap and sunglasses on, already rushing away. "Sorry I'm late!" He calls to Jon.

"Kev, honey, come meet Allison," Brooke calls to him as he

strides quickly away so they're not late for their tee time.

"Hey," Kevin whips around and waves, putting on that big smile he uses so well on potential clients. "Great to meet you, Allison," he says extending a hand. "Sorry, I'm running late, but really—nice to meet you."

Brooke turns back to apologize to Allison for her husband rushing off. When she does, she finds the woman staring at Kevin with an odd look on her face. Brooke can't see her full expression under her dark sunglasses, but her brow is furrowed, and her mouth is set in a hard line.

As the four men disappear into the club, Allison seems to snap out of it. "I'll have to meet him another time," she says, her face relaxing a bit. "Well. Gotta get back to my girls. Enjoy this beautiful day!"

Brooke, as a social worker who regularly deals with people at their most vulnerable, knows forced frivolity when she sees it.

She's done it herself a million times.

Brooke shrugs it off as she slides back behind the wheel. She pulls out and cranks up the radio, singing along all the way back to the beach house and thinking for the first time in months that she might be able to acknowledge how traumatic her battle with infertility has been, and then set it free.

– 22 –

Main Street

Carla

Carla treats her girls to a gourmet brunch at her favorite luxury boutique hotel, the White Elephant. As she sips her mimosa, she marvels at the resort's view of Nantucket Harbor. After they finish, they take the short walk into town to do some shopping. Carla soaks up the sun while walking with her two girls, one on each side, holding hands and swinging their arms. As they approach the cobble stone streets, she is reminded that some of her favorite stores are all at her fingertips. This adorable town has put her in the mood to shop, and to spoil the girls while she's at it, which means starting with *their* favorite store.

"Who wants to hit the candy store?" she asks, knowing the answer will be a unanimous *yes*.

"I do!" Marley grins ear to ear.

"Whatever," Gabriella replies.

Carla furrows her brow. "What's going on with you? You know I don't like that word. And since when don't you wanna go to a candy store?"

"I'll go," Gabriella says.

The streets are too crowded and noisy to get into any type of serious conversation now.

They find the candy store and Marley stops at every bin, overthinking every purchase but having a blast, and Carla watches her baby fondly. *This stage won't last forever*, she thinks as she watches Gabriella, picking through the selection without cracking a smile.

Once their white paper bags are filled, they head back outside. Carla suggests they walk down to the wharf and find a bench to people-watch and nibble on some of their treats. The girls agree and they head down Main Street, but soon Gabriella lags behind. Carla turns to see her looking into the window of a high-end clothing store featuring a skimpy outfit on a mannequin.

"Do you like that, mom?" She asks.

"Sure…for maybe an eighteen-year-old…actually, no," Carla changes her mind mid-sentence. "Maybe for someone in their twenties. Not appropriate for you though, sweetie." Carla says it as gently as she can.

"*Mom*," Gabriella snaps, whirling on her. "When are you going to realize I'm growing up? I'm a teenager now for god's sake!"

Where did this sudden sass come from? "Gabriella! Watch your mouth, young lady."

Carla realizes her mimosa-induced buzz is now completely gone.

"Well, I am," Gabriella adds. More calm now, she asks, "Can we just go in and look around…please?"

Carla wants to feel connected to her girls, so against her better judgment, she opens the door and leads the way inside.

"What about this, mom?" Gabriella picks through the clothes

to find some cute outfits, and Carla is forced to admit to herself she's struggling to let go. Gabriella even picks out a few dresses for Carla to try on.

They leave the store with a new dress for Carla and some fun new outfits for Gabriella. She finally sees the smile on her daughter's face she has been looking for all morning.

As they step out onto the cobblestone sidewalk, they literally bump into Kate. It takes Carla a second to place her from Allison's house the other night. But Kate clearly recognizes Carla right away.

"Carla, dear! How are you?" Kate holds out her arms and moves in for two cheek kisses. "These must be your beautiful daughters. Hi, girls, my name is Kate. How old are you?"

Before the girls can answer, Kate continues, "Is that a shopping bag from the Toggery? That's my daughter's favorite store! I'm so glad I ran into you, Carla. I'm having a party July 30th. Book your sitter because it is going to be a must-not-miss soiree. The same people you met at Allison's will be there, plus the sweetest couple I know you'll love. Kevin works with my husband Jon, and his wife Brooke is just a doll."

Kate leans in and whispers as if Carla's daughters won't hear, "Poor Brooke, she just lost her baby and is an emotional wreck, so we need to cheer her up."

Carla stares dumbly at her, unsure if she should be hearing this kind of deeply personal gossip. But Kate continues, unfazed.

"I'll be sending you an invitation with all the details, so keep an eye out for it. Bye, all." She waves, and off she goes.

Carla realizes after she's gone that she didn't even get one word in.

"Who was *that?*" Gabriella asks. "Do you know her? She didn't even wait for you to introduce us or anything, and then she just walked away."

Carla got a funny vibe from the encounter, but she downplays it. "I'm sure she was just in a hurry," she says to her daughter, not wanting to get involved in island drama while she's still trying to fit into the social scene.

Sanity Check

Brooke

After dropping Kevin off at the golf course, Brooke heads back to the house and puts on a pot of coffee. The scent of the ground beans brewing immediately relaxes her. She grabs a paperback beach read she bought at the airport while waiting for their flight back in Boston. Kevin was so kind to have bought her some books for this trip, but she would never read what he picked out. Doesn't he know by now what she likes to read?

She sprawls out on the deck lounger with her book and her coffee, and just as she's getting into it, her cell phone rings from inside the house. She reluctantly puts her book down to go in search of her phone.

She finds it on the counter by the coffee pot. Heading back outside plays the recent voicemail from a number she doesn't recognize. It's a woman named Kate. The voicemail explains that she's Jon's wife, and says that Kevin supplied Brooke's number. She wants to do lunch today.

Brooke has mixed feelings about the message. A part of her is flattered to be invited out to lunch. But a bigger part of her dreads having to make small talk with a new person. She knows deep down that she has no choice, she can't say no to a client of her husband's, however she doesn't have to say yes quite yet. She tucks her phone in her bag and picks her book up again.

If only she could lie on the deck all day and not speak to anyone. She wants to be swept away by her fluffy novel and get lost in other people's problems. Then she remembers her new resolve to let the fertility issues and her pity party go. She slowly reaches back into her overly stuffed Saint Laurent straw tote and digs for her cell.

Before she can change her mind, or Kate makes other plans, she types her reply:

Hi, it's Brooke! Thanks for reaching out. I look forward to getting together for lunch, just let me know when and where and what you'll be wearing so I can find you! ☺

Which reminds Brooke she now must decide what to wear for her Nantucket lunch date. It's been a while since Brooke truly cared about her appearance. She never had to put in much effort to look good, and everyone hated her for it her whole life, including her own friends. Kate texts back with all the details. It takes tremendous effort, but she manages to drag herself off the sun lounger and head inside to shower.

One hour later, Brooke feels like a new woman. She's dressed in an aqua-blue maxi dress and strappy sandals with a slight heel. Her hair is freshly blow-dried, and she carefully applied makeup to cover the dark circles leftover from everything she has been through.

She drives into town and easily finds a parking spot. Taking a deep breath, she steps out of the Jeep, ready to go find a woman in yellow at a restaurant down by the wharf.

– 24 –
Let the Games Begin

Kate

Kate was running a bit behind for lunch with Brooke and was speed-walking down the crowded sidewalk in town when she bumped into Carla and her daughters. Carla reminds Kate a little of herself last summer. There's something fresh and wholesome about her, but she also emanates a sexual energy that can't be ignored.

Oh, let's call it what it is, Kate thinks as she approaches Crue on the wharf. *Carla glows like she just had an "O" every time I see her.*

Kate is glad she saw her, though. She is feeling back in control with her spontaneous invite to her epic soiree, something she decided to do despite telling Allison that Carla and Lawrence were not welcome. Kate would have stayed and allowed for a proper introduction to Carla's girls, but she didn't want Brooke to have to wait for her. Based on what Jon told her about Brooke's fragile state, Kate feared Brooke might change her mind and leave, and Kate was desperate to connect with some new people.

When Kate arrives at Cru, she scans the room for a blonde woman with sad eyes sitting alone. Brooke is an easy target to find.

"You must be Kate," Brooke says as she stands up from the outdoor couch by the host's station.

Even as early as noon, the hostess is busy taking names and sharing the bad news that it would be an hour or longer wait time for walk-ins. Good thing Kate is connected and could reserve a harbor view table for two on the porch outside the hopping spacious indoor/outdoor bar.

Kate is surprised at how beautiful Brooke is. She wasn't quite sure what she was expecting, maybe someone who looked more battered from all that Brooke has apparently been through. Aside from a hint of sadness that Kate could see in her eyes, Brooke is a gorgeous, radiant woman with to-die-for thick and long wavy blonde hair, perfect (*and probably real*) boobs, and the most beautiful aqua-blue eyes she had ever seen, matching her dress.

"What can I get you, ladies?" The waiter, Craig, greets them with a friendly smile. Kate adores him—he's the one who hooks her up with ocean-view tables when she needs them.

"The usual for me," Kate says, then turns to Brooke. "The bartender makes the most delicious seaweed martini. I know it sounds god-awful, but there is some secret ingredient that mixes with the salty seaweed and dials down the strong tequila. If you ask for extra limes, you'll love it. If you like salty lime drinks, that is."

Brooke hesitates, then comes to a decision that Kate approves of. "I'll have the same," Brooke blurts.

Kate thinks she might have found a new friend—and maybe

even a new playmate. Brooke seems to be coming alive before her eyes in the trendy, bustling restaurant.

"So, Brooke," Kate says languidly. "Where are you and Kevin staying while you're on Nantucket?"

– 25 –

Here and Now

Carla

As Carla steers the SUV toward home, she finds herself floored that she's looking at *their* beach house, a gorgeous property with gables on the roof and a mahogany deck that spans the whole front of the house. She also notices something missing: Will's surfboard isn't there.

"Girls," Carla says as she parks in the gravel driveway, "we're going to the beach. And we need to hurry."

Carla can hear the stress in her own voice, betraying her calm exterior. She doesn't want to frighten the girls. Will is sixteen, but those waves scare the crap out of Carla. Gabriella and Marley are all too happy to oblige, and they race inside to hustle into their suits and grab their boogie boards and their Mom's chair.

Gabriella yells from the lower deck, "Mom, we got your chair! Don't forget our drinks and snacks!"

Carla yells back, "Got it, thanks! Go on down, I'm right behind you, and girls…up to your knees only until I get there."

Carla walks briskly down the path with her beach bag and small cooler. She makes it to the top of the stairs leading to the beach and sees her girls jumping in the surf up to their knees. Will is out where the waves break looking for the next perfect set to roll in.

She lets out a long, relieved breath and takes in the stunning view. There is a spectrum of rich color, from the deep, bluish-green of the ocean to the whites on the waves cresting, backed by the bright blue sky.

The girls spot her and race to grab their boogie boards now that they don't have to follow the knee-deep rule.

Carla settles into her chair and watches her children frolic in the water, catching waves, laughing and playing. She reflects on how easy this is, and how it wasn't always this way, especially when the kids were young. Mondays with Gabriella when she was two years old were spent at a large mommy-and-me playgroup in town that Carla was never quite comfortable in. When Will was two years old, Carla wondered why she was still so exhausted all the time. It took her three months to realize she was pregnant again.

She remembers the stress she used to feel making sure dinner was on the table at six sharp, because her husband walked home from the train and would arrive starving.

Carla loves Westbury. Her neighborhood in the Boston suburb is quintessential New England, filled with expansive Colonial homes surrounded by rolling lawns for the kids to play.

She knows she's lucky, but she still has some nagging regrets. She and Lawrence hardly had any time alone together before home and kids became her whole life. Carla wasn't always present with the children when they were little; she'd often daydream about what it would have been like to be the corporate attorney she planned on being, making upwards of $500,000 a year like her old law school friends who went for a career *and* a family.

During the hardest times, the most exhausting moments, Carla leaned on other young mothers in town and finally realized many other women were in the same boat as her. They all had to make choices—in her circles, they were fortunate enough to *be able* to choose—but it felt like they were always giving something up.

Carla was drawn to others who held a post graduate degree and the potential to have roaring careers, but who chose family full time. Eventually, she found her place in Westbury. Carla loves her children fiercely. Although she battled her own demons about what she had sacrificed, she wouldn't change it for the world.

All she needs is right here on this heavenly beach, she reminds herself.

The only thing still bothering her is that Lawrence has seemed perfectly content with missionary sex once a week, and she isn't. Carla looks much younger than her thirty-nine years, and she still turns heads. Doesn't Lawrence see this?

Case in point: Will's Baseball coach, Tom, the one she slipped with, the one she confided in Allison about—except she hadn't revealed the whole story. Tom is recently divorced and seemed to be on the prowl. All season Carla wondered if she was imaging the smoldering glances he sent her way at the games. She only hoped she wasn't obvious with how those glances made her feel. The intense exchanges left her so turned on that she began going home and jumping Lawrence's bones after the games were over.

Carla suddenly feels that pit in her stomach again. It seems like a bad dream, what happened with Tom. She *wishes* it was just a bad dream; she has so much to lose if this gets out.

It happened after one of Will's last games of the season. They stood at the edge of the field and her son asked her to take him over to a friend's house for a swim because his car was in the shop getting new breaks. Carla was happy to drive to him.

Carla's mouth dropped as the coach was suddenly there stepping out from behind Will.

"Hi, Carla," Tom said, gazing into her eyes. "It's fine with me if the boys want to hang out. I'll see you in a bit."

Carla had no idea Will's friend was Tom's son. With a flash of a flirty grin, the coach was off collecting equipment.

By the time Carla arrived at Tom's after stopping at the house first, he was outside, shirtless. My God he was sexy: long, lean, and cut. Flustered, she wondered where is this going.

She had to check herself. *Stop it, Carla.*

Will grabbed his towel and went out back towards the pool. Tom sauntered over to her car, leaned in, and asked, "Would you like some lemonade? I have a fridge in the garage stocked with this killer artisan stuff."

Lemonade sounded great after a hot day in the sun.

"Sure," Carla replied. "Is it spiked?"

"Follow me and find out." Tom replied with a hint of flirtation.

Carla followed him into the garage. If only she'd said, *No thank you.* If only she'd turned down his offer and driven away. As soon as she rounded the corner into the dimly lit garage, Tom moved his body into hers, hot from coaching in the sun, laying his mouth on hers. She didn't pull away. He pushed her back against the door with a bang that sent a shiver through her.

Pinning her arms on either side, he took and took, and she let him. When he slid one hand to her voluptuous breast and slid his other up under her sundress, quickly moving her thong aside to slip a finger into her, she moaned.

"The way you look at me on that field makes me crazy," he'd groaned into her ear. "I can't concentrate when I see you."

He took her mouth once again and without any warning, she had an orgasm.

"Oh my god," she cried. "What am I *doing*? I have to go."

She ran out of the garage, dizzy from the coupling and the surprise orgasm.

All the way home she could taste Tom on her.

She was utterly confused by dueling emotions: The high of the sexiest encounter she's had in decades and the shame of betraying her family.

She reminded herself that there were only two weeks left of school. She could just avoid him. No more baseball for her; get these kids through the next two weeks and she was home free, as the season would be over.

What was wrong with her? How could she do that to her family? Carla pulled into the driveway and saw Lawrence and the girls playing in their soccer uniforms in the front yard. As she stepped out of the car Lawrence approached her asking about the game.

Carla prayed he couldn't smell that encounter on her.

Lawrence looked at her strangely. Carla braced, closing her eyes, feeling like he could read her mind. But no. It was something else entirely.

"I need to see you alone, upstairs," he said. He turned away.

"Hey, girls, go play in the yard. Your Mom and I need to make some plans. We will be back out in thirty minutes."

He marched her upstairs, and when they reached the bedroom, he asked, "Where have you been? I have been waiting for you. I'm in the mood."

Carla avoids his question and instead asks one of her own. "When did you get home? I had to run out and drop Will off at Josh's house."

Lawrence grabbed her and led her towards the bed. With lightning speed, he was naked and hard. He loved showing off, and she loved drinking in the sight of him. Before she knew it, Lawrence was tearing off her clothes like the world would end, and they had what was quite possibly the best sex of their lives.

Just thinking about it on the beach now is making her hot. Both events of that day, together, created a lasting memory she can't shake.

Then the pit hit her stomach hits yet again as she thinks about the downside of the cozy town they live in, which is the vibrant gossip mill that thrives within it.

Carla has already planned her response if rumors ever do start circulating: It's called the Deny Everything Defense.

Just then, Lawrence, stinking of booze and cigars, pulls up a chair beside her. He leans down and kisses her hard on the mouth, sliding his tongue in. Carla pulls back.

"Lawrence! What are you doing? We're at the beach and you're drunk."

"Yes. Yes I am," he mutters. He plops down in the chair so clumsily that his feet fly up, almost tipping him over backwards.

Carla shakes her head. "Oh, dear…"

"Those guys are crazy," Lawrence grins. "I had so much fun at the golf club, I feel like I'm twenty again!"

"Well," she says, amused to see him letting go to this degree, "I'm glad you enjoyed yourself."

Carla pauses, then asks, "How was Kate's husband, Jon? What's he like? I haven't met him yet."

"Oh, Jon is a wicked pissa," Lawrence says with his best Boston accent. "He's a scratch golfer, a ball buster, and he can probably buy this island. I liked him a lot. There's something very genuine about him."

Carla adjusts her sunglasses and decides to admit her reservations about Kate. "I'm not sure about his wife," she says. "I bumped into her today in town, and she just talked right over me and the girls."

"Really? Maybe she was in a hurry," Lawrence yawns. "I think she was going to meet up with Kevin's wife for lunch."

"Wait—who's Kevin?"

"Our fourth," Lawrence says. "He joined at the last minute. He's another finance guy, actually. He's quite a character."

"Ah, that makes sense," Carla nods. "Kate invited us to a party and said something about wanting us to meet 'Kevin and his wife.' I guess they've been having a hard time."

Lawrence cocks an eyebrow. "You'd never know it hangin' with Kev. That guy can party. And I think he's a bit of a show-off, but whatever. Would you believe he asked the server on the course how much it would cost for her entire drink cart—and gave her five-hundred bucks to stay with us for the first nine holes. Unheard of." He shakes his head, smiling at the utter audacity of such a move.

Lawrence reaches for Carla's hand, lays his head back, and lets out a long breath.

Carla keeps her eyes wide open to monitor the kids playing in the rough surf and thinks, *Buying this house might have literally saved our marriage.*

– 26 –
Darling

Kate

"Hello, darling." Kate greets Jon, who reeks of cigars and expensive whiskey, as he walks into their gourmet kitchen.

"Well, hello my dearest wife," he replies, giving her a once-over and swaying ever-so-slightly. "You're looking incredible, as always."

"Why thank you," she smiles. "I went to town and met up with Brooke. What a lovely woman. And I do feel terrible for what she's been through, but I didn't say a word, per your request."

Jon nods. "I know Kevin wants her to put it in the past and not dwell on it. This trip is really important to him."

Kate feels a pang; what she heard from Brooke was a story of a loving relationship and a dedicated husband, and today's awkward chat in her own kitchen reminds Kate of her own faltering union.

She says, "Brooke did tell me he's been really attentive to her lately, and it sounded like a welcome change."

Jon's eyes widen and his eyebrows shoot up. "Oh? Well, uh,

between you and me, let's just say Kevin won't be winning any husband-of-the-year awards anytime soon. He works his ass off and entertains a lot of heavy hitting clients. He's big into… *socializing*."

"Whoa. What are you saying?" Kate asks. "That he's been 'socializing' with other women?"

Jon opens a cabinet, pulls out a glass, and fills it with filtered water from the fridge door.

"That's exactly what I'm saying," he replies. "But she has no idea, so please don't say anything to Brooke. Promise?"

Kate snorts. "Oh, I get it," she says. "He's one of those assholes who does what he wants while the wife stays faithfully in the dark." She turns away from him.

"Easy does it, Kate," Jon hits back. "You're getting personal about this, don't you think? Just because your first husband cheated, don't take it out on Kev. Honestly, I bet you'll like him. He's a lot of fun."

"I don't know much I can like someone who's cheating on a woman as lovely as Brooke," she says. "But if you're talking about bringing them on board, I would only consider them if Brooke was up for it. And I am not getting that vibe from her."

"Well, my love, we'll have to work on that," Jon says, sliding around the corner of the kitchen island with its deep blue granite and custom shape that mimics the cliff overlooking their private beach. He inches closer to Kate and changes the subject.

"Do you feel like taking a swim?" Jon pulls her to him. "We can go over a few things about our upcoming event."

"I could be convinced," she relents. "I do hope our new friends join the fun."

Jon leads Kate out towards their infinity pool overlooking the Atlantic Ocean from the cliffs of Sconset. He tosses his clothes as he strolls towards the pool's edge. By the time they walk under the rose-covered arbor to the pool, shielded by a ten-foot privet hedge, they are both naked.

Their bronzed bodies show no signs of tan lines as they dip into the pool and enjoy the amazing view overlooking the ocean. "We should have the party around the pool at sunset. It'll be lit up with candles—and of course we'll have Bridget's people cater," Kate suggests. "We can do a raw bar with oysters, clams and lobster tails, then move onto hot passed food like their lamb kabobs and chicken satay."

"Oh, yes," Jon, still buzzed from the golf day, says, moving toward her. "Order some mini beef Wellington too, won't you? Oh, and make sure they have a full bar. I hate when we attend a party and it's just beer and wine. I'll have a scotch and cigar bar from my collection as well, so make sure there are plenty of mint bowls."

Kate wraps her arms around Jon's neck.

"Perfect! Now the hard part. What about our guest list?"

Jon laughs, "What about it?"

"Well, we have the usual crowd," she says, "and then we have the newcomers and a few other neighbors we can't leave out."

Jon shrugs it off. "People are going to talk no matter what," he says. "We'll have our usual crowd on best behavior until late night, and if you stay past midnight, all bets are off."

Kate figures it was his relaxing golf day or maybe being around Kevin, who sounds rather oversexed to her, but for the first time in weeks, she and her husband come together in the pool and for a brief moment, it feels like they are back in sync.

– 27 –
Baker's Dozen

Allison

Allison has been in the kitchen all afternoon prepping for their big Sunday feast, a tradition in the Evans house. The girls have even pitched in and baked some of their favorite whoopie pies.

When the kids have headed back outside, Allison is left alone to face her thoughts about some dark memories from her past. Something she saw today has her shaken.

After her hot encounter with Marc on the streets of Boston, when he offered to break up with his girlfriend for Allison, things turned awkward for a while. On a whim, Allison took off for Nantucket after finishing her MBA at Northeastern. She told people she needed to figure out what she was going to do with the rest of her life.

When she returned to Boston in the fall, Marc had dropped out of the running group, and Allison fell back into her relationship with Billy. When Billy was offered a job in Pennsylvania and begged Allison to go with him, she couldn't think of a reason to turn him down. With Marc out of the picture, Allison worked up some excitement about starting a life with Billy; after all, he adored her and would do anything for her. When she left Boston, Allison thought she'd never see Marc again.

It was the worst decision she ever made, and what happened in Philadelphia changed Allison forever.

She's blocked out much of what occurred with Billy in Philadelphia. But there are rare moments, like now, when she can't forget no matter how hard she tries. This new woman she met outside the golf club, this friend of Jon and Kate's, seemed haunted to her. And when Allison saw her husband, something about him triggered her: His gait, his manner, his voice, his build.

She isn't sure why that at a time when she's meant to be enjoying the entire holiday week with her family, she's letting herself get dragged down into the past over a moment that was probably nothing.

As Allison begins cleaning the kitchen and fills a pot with warm, sudsy water, she reminds herself to focus on the beautiful parts of her past. Because as much as she wants to forget Philadelphia, she clearly remembers the night she was reunited with Marc about two years after she first moved there with Billy.

She had fled back to Boston, after losing all faith in men. Allison's best friend welcomed her into her back-bay condo until Allison could find a job and get back on her feet. Job one, though, was to reconnect with the few people who were left from her old running group.

Marc's roommate, Jerry, still ran with the group, and although Allison didn't know it then, Marc would often go out for a drink with the gang. One night Allison showed up and Marc was there. The instant she saw him, the tallest in the group he was hanging with at the bar, full head of dark brown hair, charming scruff on his face, she was overcome with lust again—but what really hit her was how it was mixed with a feeling she was *home*.

And then…*she* appeared. Allison remembered her name was Sara, and she was still as pretty as could be. Allison's heart had sunk to the floor.

She assumed any rekindled love affair was over before it started, but then Allison saw Marc's face. He wasn't even registering Sara, who was standing right next to him. But he was staring at Allison like she was his long-lost love, his eyes smoldering. Instead of feeling stifled by his strong reaction, she felt woozy with excitement and promise.

Allison and Marc ended up talking as much as they could that night, picking up right where they left off as if two years hadn't gone by. By the end of the night, they both realized how much they'd missed each other. Although Allison never told Marc (and still hasn't to this day) what happened with Billy, she did tell him they were finished. Marc insisted he wouldn't leave the bar until Allison agreed to go out with him that Friday night. Allison asked about Sara and Marc told her that was over too, and that he would break it off as soon as he could. The very next day, he did.

Less than a year later Marc got down on one knee and proposed. Allison accepted.

As if on cue, Marc walks in as she's hanging up a dish towel.

Allison smiles at her obviously buzzed husband. "Hey babe, how'd you hit 'em?"

She leans in for a quick kiss and smells the alcohol and cigars. Before he can answer Allison, Abigail runs to Marc for a hug. "Daddy!" She cries, wrapping her little arms around his waist.

"Why don't you both join Savannah out on the deck?" Allison suggests. "I'll bring out some appetizers."

The girls have set the table with a cobalt blue pitcher of lemonade and tumblers that match the yellow-and-blue plates. Allison made tuna tartare for her and Marc, and the girls are digging into their favorite chicken quesadillas. The sky this time of day is brushed with pastel yellow and orange hues as the sun shifts westward, and the ocean breeze is a welcome relief from the hot, late-day sun.

"How was your day?" Allison asks between bites. "Let me guess, Jon won again?"

"Of course," Marc laughs. "He's a scratch golfer. Lawrence and I made our way up together. Thank god someone is finally worse than me. He had this one shot that hooked so far left he landed on the next fairway. I have no idea how many balls that guy went through—at least a dozen."

"So, Dad, are you better than Mr. Rossi?" Savannah asks.

"Absolutely," Marc says. "Now, tell me girls, what's on the menu tonight? It smells delicious."

They all enjoy grilled swordfish and filet mignon with Allison's signature béarnaise sauce. It's an agreed-upon fact that Allison's talents in the kitchen are one of the many reasons Marc married her.

After dinner, the girls tear off after Marley and Gabriella, who are just now coming off the beach. Marc and Allison take in the sunset of rich pinks and deep yellows as the electric ball of fire begins to dip below the ocean's edge.

"It's nice that the girls have made fast friends," Marc observes.

Allison shoots him a knowing glance. "Speaking of fast friends with our neighbors, did Lawrence say anything to you about what happened at the party?"

Allison had seen Lawrence come back that night, but a part of her hoped he hadn't been able to take in what was really going on at their after-party.

Marc shakes his head. "Are you sure he saw us? He acted totally normal today…then again…he *was* asking some questions about our marriage. But that was only because Kevin was talking about his. He and his wife are going through something, apparently, but I'm not privy to exactly what it is."

"I can't be a hundred-percent certain, but it looked like he definitely saw us in the pool," Allison says. "And Alexa told me she was, shall we say…*flirty* with him when he came back to fetch Carla's purse."

Allison never wanted either of the Rossis to find out about their lifestyle this way, so she hopes he couldn't see in the darkness around the pool what was actually going on with her, Marc and Kate. Allison had been watching them go at it for a moment when something beyond the pool caught her eye. She moved toward it and squinted into the darkness. That's when she saw Lawrence move closer to their house and walk to their front door. Allison heard the doorbell ring from her spot in the pool.

Allison was frozen in place. *What to do?* The small after-midnight crowd was taking up various rooms in the house, including the living room. She had no chance of getting to him from the pool, nor did she want to call attention to the threesome currently happening there.

And then Lawrence turned toward her. She couldn't see his expression, but he stared for more than a beat. She panicked and ducked into the water.

Alexa told Allison later that she'd let him in from the lower deck and beckoned him in, thinking he was in on the late-night party dynamics. Alexa happily confessed to coming on to Lawrence, and reported that he was, in spite of himself, clearly entranced by her—until her hands ran over his crotch and he seemed to snap out of it, grabbed his wife's purse, and raced home.

But if Lawrence wasn't going to bring anything up about the afterparty, neither was Allison or Marc. Not yet anyway.

Now, as the sun is about to make its last gasp of blazing color, Allison asks her husband, "What do you think the odds are of getting the Rossis on board?"

"After what happened, who knows," Marc shakes his head. "You obviously have the best shot at convincing Carla. If I even approached it with Lawrence, I worry he'd tackle me. I'm not sure he's the type who'd take kindly to a neighbor expressing sexual interest in his hot wife. Although…he seemed pretty interested in Kevin's shenanigans during golf today. That guy was sharing some graphic details after one too many scotches."

"Like what?" Allison is intrigued.

She's convinced herself she overreacted when she met Kevin. He didn't show a flicker of recognition upon meeting Allison, and even though his face was mostly obscured by the rim of his baseball cap and dark sunglasses, she still would have known if they'd met before. *Wouldn't she?*

"Uh…I don't think you want to know." Marc makes a face. "It's pretty bad."

Allison leaves it alone and ponders who has a better chance of getting the Rossis on board, feeling a frisson of excitement as she does. Allison loves trying new things with other couples. Even adding Kate into their sex life opened so many possibilities she and Marc had never considered before.

When Allison and Marc made the decision to swing, it was strictly to enhance their own sex life, which rapidly declined after the children came along.

Marc takes a sip of his wine and regards her with one raised eyebrow. "Are you planning on giving Carla and Lawrence a heads up before Kate's party?"

Allison pauses as she watches the sun sink toward the horizon and sips her wine. She inhales, then lets her breath out before responding.

"I'm not sure," she says. "I guess I was hoping Carla and I would have a moment like Kate and I had. A sort of natural progression to ease into it. I haven't had that perfect moment yet."

"It *was* pretty shocking when I opened the laptop and found all your so-called research," Marc laughs. "I have to say, swinging is nothing like what you hear about. It's like learning law. You read all the definitions and hear the cases and other people's feedback or experiences, but you can never know what you're in for until you actually try it."

"I almost forgot about my research!" Allison giggles. "You're right, though, it is baptism by fire."

"I'm not sure you should tell Carla," Marc says seriously. "They're a really nice family and I'd hate to see this screw them up."

Allison sets her glass down, upset by his statement. "So you think this has screwed us up?"

"Well, ahhhh, I mean…" Marc is stuttering. "I'm just saying…"

"Marc!" Allison sits up and grabs his hand. "Saying *what*? Do you think the choice we made to do this has screwed up our relationship? *Do* you?" Allison is on edge now, waiting for his answer, almost not wanting to hear it.

She can see Marc has picked up on this. He holds her hand in his and says carefully, "I guess…well, if we're being honest, I think it has changed our relationship for both good and…not so good. Don't you?"

Not until this very second. Where is this coming from? She thinks.

"Well," she begins, trying to stay light and calm. "I think it's been mostly beneficial, especially sexually." She strokes his arm lightly.

"Obviously I have to agree with that," he smiles. "But has it ultimately brought us closer? Or has it planted some doubts?"

"Do *you* have doubts?" She pulls her hand away.

Marc shakes his head. "Not doubts, exactly. Look, Allison. I think it's a good thing we're finally talking about this. It's the thing with Kate, OK? Whenever she and I are alone I feel like you hate it, and you're bitchy for days afterwards."

"You know I hate that word!" She shouts back. "I can't believe you said that to me."

Allison puts one hand over her mouth and the other on her stomach, stands up, and races into the house. She bounds up to their bedroom and locks the door.

She flops down on the plush white bedding and sobs into her pillow. She's gone from feeling utterly connected to her husband to deeply hurt and alone in the snap of a finger. For the first time since they joined the swinging lifestyle, she wonders if they made the right choice.

Hearing her soulmate waver shook Allison to the core. She never had any regrets. Well, maybe one or two fleeting moments of jealousy…and maybe she wondered once or twice if Kate and Marc were having unprotected sex, but she didn't dwell on it.

And certainly, she's never *bitchy* because of these thoughts, is she?

She feels like she's going to be sick. Obviously, Marc must have regrets, or he wouldn't have mentioned it.

Marc is her rock, her everything. They need to make this right before it spirals out of control.

– 28 –

Unconditional Love

Brooke

Brooke is lying on the deck losing herself in the rhythm of the rolling waves beyond. While she has her book with her, it remains closed on her lap. She has no interest in reading now. She's feeling a bit lightheaded from lunch, she can't stop thinking about Kate.

Brooke was surprised by how much she instantly liked Kate. It usually takes her time to warm up to new people, but Kate was so caring, fun, and flirty that she put Brooke at ease immediately. And now, she has a fancy Nantucket party to look forward to.

It was freeing to be out with a friend who doesn't know about her fertility problems. As much as Brooke longs for a baby with Kevin, she's finally realizing she needs to reconnect with herself—and *then* with her husband.

Brooke has considered more than once whether all this pain and anxiety about starting a family was happening for a reason. She'd always been a firm believer in fate.

She thinks about Charlie and wonders how he's doing. Brooke is the child's social worker, and as she does for all her clients, she tries to stay in touch even outside of work hours.

She picks up her phone and shoots him a quick text.

Hey Charlie, how's it going? I've gone away for a last-minute vacation, but wanted to check in. ☺

Brooke receives a response right away.

Ms. B how u feelin? Miss u! Glad Mr. K is treatin u right!

Brooke smiles as she texts back, *I'm good. Don't you worry about me! How is your mom this week?*

Three dots appear. There is a longer pause this time, until Charlie finally writes,

all good, Ms B. Have fun

Brooke is relieved, though she suspects he could be glossing over things for her benefit. She's crossed a line that social workers are encouraged not to: she's grown to love this boy, and she constantly worries the hand he was dealt in life is too much to overcome.

All the clothes and toys she and Kevin have bought for him over these months would not provide what he needed most, which is unconditional love.

Brooke hears the driveway shells crackling, and then seconds later Kevin's voice booms through the house.

"Brooke…Brooke!"

She can see him put his clubs down. "I'm out on the deck," she replies.

She hears rustling in the kitchen, followed by a loud *pop*. Kevin steps out with some Dom Perignon and two glasses.

"There's my angel," he slurs as he walks out to where Brooke is lounging, all sun kissed and grinning.

Brooke blushes, then stretches out like a feline across her

lounger and reaches for her champagne. Kevin leans down and plants a kiss on her lips. She doesn't know if it's the sun, the vacation, or her husband's good mood, but she's feeling ready for romance again. The procedure did a number on her, but she's officially been given the all-clear, and as her husband moves his hands down her body, she goes with it.

The cool breeze off the ocean is blowing Brooke's wavy locks. He scoops her up and carries her through the doors and into the living room, setting her gently on the sofa. He tastes like she remembers, like scotch.

Afterwards, Brooke and Kevin stay cuddled up in the living room enjoying the last bits of light reflecting on the clouds. Brooke's phone begins vibrating out on the deck where she left it.

Still dizzy from her tryst, Brooke pulls herself out of her dreamlike state and wanders out onto the deck, leaving Kevin half asleep on the couch. She picks up her phone and sees four missed calls from Charlie's new iPhone that she and Kevin had given him for his ninth birthday and still pay for monthly. The boy kept it hidden from his mother; it was their secret. Not that his mom would have noticed he had a phone. She's a drug addict who has never shown interest in rehab, not even for the sake of her child.

Brooke picks up her phone and listens to Charlie's voicemail. He mumbles, speaking under his breath, but she's able to discern he is with Mrs. Adibe, the woman who lives a few doors down from Charlie and his mother. Brooke feels compelled to call the boy to be sure he's at Mrs. Adibe's place.

Her guess is that the abusive boyfriend is back, or his mother pulled her disappearing act again. He answers on the second ring.

"Hi, Miss Brooke," he says in his sweet, high-pitched voice.

"Hi Charlie," she forces a smile. "Is everything alright? Are you okay?"

She is profoundly uneasy that she's not able to drive over and make sure he's safe.

"Oh, yeah, I'm fine," he says, but she can hear he's not. "I…um…I my mom has been gone since yesterday morning." His voice cracks. So does Brooke's heart.

"Charlie! Just a few hours ago you told me everything was okay!"

"I know," he replies. "I really am OK. I came to Mrs. Adibe's like you told me to when my mom doesn't come—"

Brooke interrupts, "Did you stay there last night?"

"No," he says, "because I didn't know she was going to be out all night. But when she still wasn't home when I woke up this morning, I decided I should come here."

Brooke is relieved he is so smart. "Good boy," she says. "Charlie, you did the right thing and I'm proud of you. Now let me speak with Mrs. Adibe."

"Hello?" Mrs. Adibe's voice is a welcome sound to Brooke, who feels far away.

"Hi, thank you so much for taking Charlie," Brooke says. "Is he okay with you until they locate his mother, or would you like me to have him placed?" Brooke asks as her anxiety spikes further.

"Of course I'll keep him," the woman says firmly. "You know I love this boy as much as you do. I don't want him shipped off, just to be dragged back here in a couple of days. She'll turn up, always does."

Mrs. Adibe is a savior for this boy, as much as she is for Brooke.

"Thank you, thank you." Brooke is choked up. This one has gotten to her, and if her supervisors knew how much, she'd be reprimanded—or worse.

"Brooke, you are spoiling that kid with his fancy phone, but I am sure glad you do," she says, and they both laugh.

"I'll send my colleague out to document tomorrow," Brooke assures her. "Call me if you need anything at all. I'm always here."

"Sure, darlin' get some rest. He's in good hands."

Brooke sits on the deck, watching the moon dancing over the water as Kevin snores inside, and she tries to push thoughts of Charlie out of her mind. She fails. Brooke regularly fights urges to scoop him up and demand to adopt him on the spot, but his biological mother remains in the picture, and the situation simply isn't right. Still, she can dream.

It occurs to her now that if she hadn't moved to Cambridge with Kevin, she never would have met Charlie.

Brooke and Kevin met in New York City when they were both pursuing masters' degrees. Brooke had quickly fallen for his school-boy good looks and charm, and only later did she learn that is his M.O. He's skated through life on those attributes. After graduation, they moved to Cambridge straight out of school so Kevin could take a job with a world-renowned investment bank.

Brooke got a job working for the state as a social worker and quickly found meaning in helping at-risk children; it was as if she was born to do this work. They were innocent children, and yet were treated like they were disposable. It was equally depressing and infuriating to Brooke.

She met Charlie when he was seven and she was called to do an assessment at Boston Children's Hospital. Brooke felt instantly connected to this boy with curly dark hair and big brown eyes, whose skull was fractured by an adult who'd betrayed his trust in the worst way. His father was listed as "unknown," and his mother, Darcy, was a meth and heroin addict after getting hooked on prescription opioids, then finding street drugs cheaper and more attainable.

That first visit was to determine the mother's neglect. There had been several complaints of yelling and screaming coming from their apartment over the years, all of which ended in a police visit. The result was usually to remove his mother's boyfriend. It was only when Charlie was seen by a neighbor at their apartment complex's playground, shivering without a coat in the middle of winter with blood pouring out of his ear, that an ambulance and DSS were finally called.

Brooke checked on Charlie until he healed, and even after that she was called to his mother's apartment several times when neighbors and concerned distant family had called child protective services to do a wellness check. His mother finally followed through with the restraining order against her boyfriend. She had to, or she would lose Charlie. Usually, Brooke was free anyway, as Kevin spent more nights entertaining clients as the months passed.

Brooke learned not to dwell on Kevin's insistence that they delay having kids. She never wanted to resent him for his demand to wait until his career was more established and secure. She pushed thoughts of wanting her own children to the back of her mind and focused on protecting the children who needed her in the moment.

The second time Charlie was admitted to the hospital, Kevin was once again working late, so Brooke visited at night when she knew Darcy wouldn't be there. She needed the real story. With his mother around, Charlie claimed he tripped and fell down the apartment stairwell. Brooke knew better, but she needed him to say it. When she arrived and saw the beaten boy resting in the safety of the hospital, she sat with him for a moment, hating to wake him. But she needed to get to the truth, so she gently touched his arm.

He bolted upright, screaming and protecting his face instinctively with two crossed arms. Brooke went into full lioness mode then. She would not rest until Charlie was safe. This time the boyfriend was arrested for violating the restraining order.

She went home that night and sobbed for hours. She felt powerless to help this child. All she wanted was for Kevin to come home and listen, hold her, tell her she was doing all she could. But he didn't return until after midnight—and he was hammered. Still, she tried to talk to him, and said she was ready to try for a baby. He was in no condition for a deep discussion about anything. He grabbed her, planted sloppy kisses on her, then bent her over the sofa and ravaged her while she cried. She doesn't let that memory come back much, but today it rushes back, and she's sickened by it. She knows it's not normal; she knows that's not how a husband treats a wife.

Now, with him snoring inside, Brooke enjoys the peace alone out on the deck, and clings to the good days they've had together recently. Kevin's finally growing up—she's sure of it.

– 29 –

Lucky Bitch

Carla

As Carla pulls on her running shoes on Monday morning, she glances up at the plaque gracing her foyer: *If you're lucky enough to be at the beach, you're lucky enough!*

How true, she thinks. This run is a fresh start from the weekend. Carla's summer goal is to get into the best shape of her life, but all the wine and rich foods aren't helping. She needs to be disciplined if she wants to look hot at Kate's party.

She bounds outside and takes in the sun rising over Nantucket Island, promising another glorious day. Allison is ready and waiting at the end of her driveway, but not looking like her usual bright-eyed self.

"Morning," Allison mumbles, sounding almost sarcastic.

"Hey, what's up?" Carla tilts her head.

"Ah, it's nothing." Allison waves her concerns away and plasters on a smile.

Allison starts to jog, and Carla keeps pace. They run straight up the beach road and out onto Hummock Pond.

"Feel like going on a *real* run today?" Allison asks.

Carla laughs, "I thought our last run was real. Or my thighs did anyway."

"This one will be a bit longer…and faster."

"Alright, I'm in. Working something out, are we?" Carla jabs.

"You could say that."

And she's off. Carla lags a good thirty steps behind as she follows her friend down Hummock for a few miles until Allison swings a right and heads through a quaint, well-kept neighborhood.

About four miles later, they run down a winding beach road and arrive on Surfside beach.

"How you holding up there, Car?" Allison smiles.

"I'm glad you're enjoying this." Carla bends over with her hands on her knees, then raises her hand like a stop sign as she gasps for air.

"We can take a break," Allison concedes, swinging her small pack off her back and handing Carla a bottle of water.

"Thanks." Carla chugs.

Allison, calmer now, admits, "I probably should have given you a heads up. I got out on the wrong side of the bed this morning."

Carla hands her the water back.

"Sorry for my shitty mood."

Finally able to speak, Carla dares to ask, "Do you want to share?"

Allison starts jogging in place. "I had a bad night's sleep—I get bad cramps," she shrugs. "Ready?"

Carla nods, though she wishes she could call Lawrence to come pick her up. She wasn't expecting such a tough workout.

Allison takes off, with Carla in her wake, trying desperately to keep up.

When they reach home, both out of breath and barely able to

talk, Allison is no more forthcoming, and they part ways with a wave and a promise to hang out soon. Carla hasn't known Allison long, but it's clear something's wrong. She hopes her new friend will feel comfortable enough to share with her at some point.

Once she's home, Carla drags herself into the outdoor shower, thinking about that brutal run. As the cool water runs over Carla's face and down her back, she looks straight up into the bright blue sky and sighs. Now that the run is over, she gives herself the credit she deserves for sticking through the pain. She did her best and held her own.

This is something she promised to do for herself this summer; to push herself and get into great shape. Most people are still sleeping, and Carla's already run five miles. She feels rejuvenated, both mentally and physically.

Carla turns off the shower and realizes she has no towel.

"Oh, what the hell," she thinks.

The only neighbor that could possibly see her would be Allison, and she wouldn't care. Carla wrings out her hair, attempts to hold her sweaty running clothes over her body, and races for the back door.

As she opens the door she hears a whistle. Carla stops in her tracks. She looks over her shoulder to see Allison drinking a tall glass of ice water from her deck. *And is that Marc in the chair behind her?* Feeling a bit delirious and loopy from her intense workout and the ocean air, Carla spontaneously gives her ass a quick shake to tease her neighbors, then ducks in the house as quick as she can, laughing all the while.

Carla pads up the stairs, still laughing, and heads straight over to Lawrence who is still in bed.

"Whoa. What's gotten into you?" He yawns and observes her blankly.

What's that about? She thinks. He should be drooling at the sight of his naked wife.

Carla towels off, and spoons Lawrence from behind. "I just went for a killer run with Allison. At this rate, I'm going to be a Victoria's Secret supermodel by the end of summer." She kisses his neck.

"Babe, you already are my supermodel."

He yawns again. Carla, full of energy, hops out of bed and struts over to the sliding glass door, whips it open, and gives her best hair toss. She places her hands on her hips, and with perfect posture she puts on her best pout. She works it across the room and back.

Lawrence smiles. "You're more beautiful than any of them. Oh—wait, what time is it? I have a quick client meeting, and then I want to hit the beach. The waves are going to be killer today."

Carla slips back into bed, suddenly feeling self-conscious, wondering how he could be so blasé in the face of her serving herself up on a platter.

Carla saw it on a talk show once: It doesn't matter how often a couple has sex. It just matters that they agree on how much is enough.

Lately, she and her husband haven't been agreeing. She's coming out of a lull as the kids grow up and she's feeling more attracted to her husband.

He still likes it once a week, missionary style.

That kind of "disagreement" led her to the baseball coach.

That is not enough for her.

Something has to give.

– 30 –
Forgive and Forget

Allison

Allison returns from her run flooded with endorphins, but they're not powerful enough to fully eradicate her foul mood. She hopes Carla wasn't turned off, but Allison wasn't ready to share something so personal quite yet.

She's dreading confronting her husband. Marc is impossible to argue with. He always slips into attorney mode, and he's a pro at pretending to listen while plotting his next important point to build his case. Every time they "talk," Allison ends up in tears, like last night.

As she tosses off her shoes and heads up to shower, she decides this is a conversation best had in a relaxed setting away from the house. She decides she'll pack up the car and they can head over to one of their favorite spots, the Fortieth Pole, at sunset.

The kids can have a nice day with the babysitter while she and Marc can have a chance at clearing the air over wine and cheese on a beach blanket. The last thing she wants is to have the kids overhear their conversation.

Allison still isn't sure how they got here.

It was all supposed to be so perfect.

Allison had never been a wild child, and while she always loved sex, she'd been monogamous for most of her dating life. But Kate. *Ah, Kate.* Elegant, beloved, envied, beautiful, wealthy— and Allison's close friend. Marc has worked with her husband Jon on and off, for years.

Last summer Allison and Kate finally really connected. In fact, they were inseparable. They spent more time together shopping in town, working out, doing yoga. Kate's daughter, Caroline, was going to be a junior at Boston University come fall and had been lifeguarding on Cisco for the summer. The waves on Cisco are the best on the island, and Kate would always go and keep an eye on Caroline as she rode the waves. Caroline also frequently babysat for Allison that summer.

Allison's daughter Savannah desperately longed to surf, but Marc resisted; if you get caught in the wrong wave, you can get tossed around like a load of dirty laundry in an industrial washer. But Caroline was a natural, and she began teaching Savannah a few tips to help her get started in a safe manner.

Those late afternoons together on the beach were a favorite time for both mothers and daughters. Kate confided in Allison that she became pregnant with Caroline at the end of her senior year in high school, and the floodgates had opened between them. No topic was off limits.

It was about six weeks into that summer when Kate revealed all. Allison now knows it was a deliberately long buildup, and on that day, fueled by Triple Eight vodka and dizzy with the sun,

Kate confessed everything. Kate had suspected that Allison noticed something going on at their parties and had decided it was time to come clean.

"I know you've been wondering about our parties and why I'm always having our driver escort you and Marc home early," Kate said. "I have to tell you it's not because I don't want you there. It's because we're part of an exclusive 'club.'"

Allison was a bit drunk and thought Kate was saying Allison wasn't cool enough for her rich friends, and she must have made a face, because Kate quickly added, "Believe me, I've wanted you and Marc to stay tons of times. Jon and I love you two. But we don't want to jeopardize our friendship, and Jon relies on his work relationship with Marc and doesn't want it to change."

Allison was growing more confused by the minute. "Kate, nothing is going to change our friendship."

Kate had smiled and stared right into Allison's eyes. "Good," she said. "Because once I share this with you, there's no going back."

And then she launched into it. "After midnight, things get a little racy at our parties. And if you don't want to partake, you leave before midnight. We never want anyone to be uncomfortable."

Allison pictured hard-core drugs or dirty dancing. She couldn't imagine what Kate was talking about. Then Kate finally spelled it out: "*Allison. We're swingers.*"

Allison wasn't sure if she heard her glamorous, high-society friend right. "You're *what?*"

"Swingers."

"Like put your keys in the bowl and see who picks them out swingers?"

Kate let out a little laugh, and Allison joined in nervously. She was furiously trying to picture what that would look like and tried to imagine which of Kate's friends were banging *their* friend's husbands. *How could she and Marc have been so clueless?*

"It's not quite like that. There are different scenarios, but I don't want to horrify you with the details," Kate said.

"No, no, no," Allison shook her head. "You've opened Pandora's Box. Now I need to know what you've been up to after we leave. We thought something was up but didn't quite think you were having some big orgy!"

"It's not that extreme," Kate had smiled. "You know what a ménage a trois is, right?"

"Of course."

"Well, that is one of the popular starters."

"Really?" Allison was floored. "I can't imagine Jon being too excited that you're involved in a ménage à trois. He's actually willing to share you?" In Allison's experience, most men dreamed of a threesome, but Jon always seemed possessive of Kate.

"That's not all that happens," Kate replied. "It depends on each individual couple's rules. It's important that the couple figure out what their boundaries are before they start participating. When Jon and I began dating, we talked about open relationships, which are very different from swinging."

"Really?" Allison was dumbfounded. "I never would've thought…I mean, he's never hit on me or even looked at me in that way."

Kate had frowned and shaken her head. "He wouldn't. Not unless we discussed it and I approved. Those are our rules and number one is, no friends unless it's mutual."

"But all your friends from the parties…?"

Kate shook her head again. "Those are *swinging* friends. All those who stay past midnight know the house rules ahead of time, and they all have their own couple parameters."

Allison's mind was racing with images of a few of the party guests, who, let's face it, neither she nor her husband would have been remotely attracted to.

"But, like…what if a really gross guy tried it with you? What do you do then?"

"Oh, sweetie, I am *very* picky," Kate assured her. "Just because you go to the parties and maybe sometimes you participate, you certainly don't have to join. You just have to be open to it. It's sort of like college: If you're into someone, you hook up. Sometimes I just hook up with Jon. It's meant to enhance your relationship with your partner. And trust me, it does."

Kate added, "It's not something you do in haste, Allison. It needs to be a couple's decision. I'd say more than half of the couples in our group are married. I think the lifestyle helps them the most. Gives them something new and exciting to spice things up after years of monogamy."

That did it. Kate had struck a chord with Allison by bringing up the monotony of a married couple's sex life. Allison had gone home that afternoon and couldn't wait to discuss everything with Marc—and as she suspected, he didn't take much convincing.

They started slowly, trying out a threesome with Kate. Allison laughs looking back now because she never thought she'd be sitting here thinking about having the same talk with her neighbor.

After her shower, Allison walks out onto her deck wrapped in her favorite satin robe. She looks over to Marc who's sipping on coffee while reading some pleadings in a big case with a pending deadline.

He glances at her. "How was your run?"

Allison is leaning against the railing, watching the whitecaps out in the vast ocean, and before she can answer, she catches sight of her neighbor. She gives a loud whistle letting Carla know she has been spotted.

Allison bursts out laughing when Carla shakes her booty as she dashes from the shower into her house. "Ah…sorry. Did you see that?"

Marc smirks, "Clearly you saw more than me. I only saw a flash of white flesh!"

"Ah, tan lines," Allison laughs. She's relieved that Carla's little show helped break the tension.

Marc clears his throat, "Listen, about last night…I didn't want to upset you, so can we forget it?"

Allison sets down her glass of ice water and sits on the lounger next to Marc.

She whispers so the kids can't hear, "Marc, you can't tell me to forget about it. You know me better than that. You must know this is eating me alive. I would never do anything to jeopardize our relationship or our family." Despite coming into the conversation with a calm mind, she hears her own voice rising. "You made me feel like that is exactly what I've done."

"Allison, I didn't say that," he says in a stage whisper. "You're overreacting. My point is that you should give Carla and Lawrence a chance to think about this lifestyle before—"

Allison interrupts, "Because you regret it!"

"You're putting words in my mouth again. I never said that. They deserve the opportunity to choose it, not be thrown into it."

"Well aren't you Captain Integrity today," she hits back. "So what am I? The evil villain trying to lure them into this shameful lifestyle?"

Marc lets out an exasperated sigh and raises his voice. "You know that's not what I'm saying."

Allison stands up. She wants to retreat—badly. She's always been more flight to Marc's fight.

"We need to take a walk on the beach," she yells back. "I'm not having this conversation here. Get dressed and I'll meet you on the path."

She storms off, determined to finish this discussion with her husband. She realizes she always runs off and then everything gets swept under the rug. But Allison is not going to allow that to happen this time. This is too monumental an issue.

Allison waits by the beach stairs in her bikini and a sheer coral cover-up with a large bottle of water and her Kindle. She doesn't intend to return from the beach for at least a few hours; she is shaken and needs some space. Marc is wearing swimming trunks and a white T-shirt outlining his broad shoulders.

He places his hand on Allison's cheek. "I love you," he says.

She doesn't react and instead turns to make her way down the rickety wooden steps to the beach. She turns right and walks fifty paces, then spreads out her towel.

Marc sits next to her, uninvited. She flinches. He puts an arm around her. She melts then, and lets him hold her for a long while as they sit silently, listening to the waves.

After a few minutes, she knows it can't be put off any longer. Allison breathes deep and begins. "Marc, you know you're my everything," she says. "Since last night I've had a pit in my stomach knowing you have regrets. I feel responsible for all of this."

Marc keeps an arm around her. "Look, Allison, I'm an adult. I made the choice, we both made the choice, to swing," he says earnestly. "Now we've seen behind the curtain. When we were on the outskirts, it was fun and exciting to wonder what they were all doing and why they were so happy doing it."

He stares out at the endless ocean in front of them. "Now I'm starting to see some cracks. Cracks in *us* that have never been there before, Allie."

Allison's lip starts to quiver; she wants to talk but the lump in her throat stops her. She tries to swallow hard. She grabs her water and takes a long sip to help her catch her breath.

"I thought this was exciting," she says, her voice cracking. "I thought it took our sex life to another level."

"It has," he agrees, and she believes he's sincere. "There have been some amazing things about it. But now…I worry you and Kate are an explosion waiting to happen, and I'm right in the middle of it."

With the mention of Kate, Allison's white-hot anger returns. "That's because we *are* an explosion waiting to happen! I'm sick of her acting like she owns us. Owns *you*. She brought us into this lifestyle but she doesn't want to share us with anyone else."

Marc pauses, and she looks over at his face, and she sees the pain there. Maybe he's finally getting it.

"Do you want us to break things off with Kate?" He asks.

"Hell, I'll break off this whole thing right now if it's causing you stress or worry. You know you're my love, my wife, and my heart."

Allison hopes this really is the end of this fight. She's beyond stressed. "Do you mean it?"

"I do," he replies without hesitation. "What did you think? That I'm falling for Kate?"

Allison offers up a melancholic smile. "I guess I was getting a little jealous. It started to look like maybe it was more than sex between the two of you."

Marc sighs. "This is the problem with swinging. This is where we were always going to trip up. It's biology. Men can *just* have sex and women cannot understand it. They assume there always has to be some underlying feeling lurking in there." He strokes her head.

"You're not wrong," Allison admits. "But I'm not sure getting out entirely is the answer. I'm starting to think if we just take a break from Jon and Kate..." She trails off. "I'm excited about Carla and Lawrence, you know? But you're right, they should know about everything ahead of time. Why don't you have a talk with Lawrence?"

"Whoa, whoa, *me*? Why me? I thought you and Carla were going to chat about it."

She looks up at him, gives him a gentle play-slap on the cheek with an open palm. "We need you to put the 'it's just sex' spin on it that clearly, I cannot handle."

Allison sees no reason to confront him with what's really bothering her, because she knows it shouldn't. She heard something between Marc and Kate the last time they were together, something she'd kept buried deep, telling herself it was all part of the lifestyle.

She knows what happened at the party Saturday night was no big deal and she should just let it go, and so she does. For now.

She scrambles to her feet, tears off her cover-up, and races towards the water. Marc chases her down and they fall into a crashing wave tangled up in each other.

– 31 –
Tall Tales

Carla

Carla has shaken off her husband's lack of interest in her naked form and is currently relaxing on the beach with him pretending nothing happened. The pair of them keep sharp eyes on the girls as Gabriella surfs and Marley builds a sandcastle. Will is still in bed.

"Did you sleep this much when you were sixteen?" Carla asks Lawrence. When she went to ask her son if he was ready for the beach that morning, he was splayed out on his bed, face down and snoring.

"Absolutely," Lawrence smiles. "Especially in the summer. As long as Will's home by curfew and makes it to his job on time, I'm fine with him sleeping as much as he wants until school starts again."

He sits up and hugs his knees. Carla knows he wants to get in the surf and catch some waves, and wonders what's stopping him.

Then Lawrence turns to her. "How are things going with you and Allison?"

She lets out laugh of surprise. "Uh, good? Great, I guess. Why do you ask?"

He's gazing back out to sea.

"Well…there's something I didn't tell you about the night of the party."

Carla sits up. "What? Tell me!"

He has an odd expression she can't quite read. "I…you're not going to believe this, but when I went back to get your clutch, some stuff happened."

Now Carla is starting to freak out. *What stuff?* And why is he waiting until now to reveal it?

"Tell me," she commands.

"Promise you won't be mad…"

"You know I can't do that until I know what it is. You're not getting blanket immunity. Now spill."

"When I got there," Lawrence begins slowly, "I could just make out in the moonlight that three people close together in the pool. Kate and Marc were making out, and Allison was watching. Then I saw her grab Kate's boob."

Carla takes that in.

"*No way.*"

"Yes, way. It was definitely them. I saw it clear as day. And… there's more," he says.

"I figured. What's the part I'll be mad about?"

He meets her eyes, and Carla can see how nervous he is. "Alexa—remember her, the model? —well, she opened the door as I came up the stairs," he says. "She offered to help me find your purse and then she…well, she groped me and tried to kiss me. I pulled away, of course, but I knew you wouldn't be thrilled it even got that far. I promise you, Carla—I didn't react. I stopped it immediately. Hand to God." He literally holds up a hand.

Carla prays he can't read her expression, because she's feeling that creeping guilt again. He did what she couldn't. What she *didn't*. When a gorgeous member of the opposite sex came on to her, she succumbed. But her husband didn't.

She pushes those thoughts away, though, because there's a bigger headline here: Her new best friend has *orgy* parties?

"But they seem so normal," she blurts.

"I guarantee you there are a lot of 'normal' people in your life who have, shall we say, wild proclivities."

Carla is learning that's true in more ways than he knows.

"Come to think of it," she says, "there *were* some strange things going on that keep coming back to me." She twists her hair with her fingers.

"Like what?"

"I found a bowl of condoms in the drawer next to the bar." As she says it, it dawns on her that should have been a major clue. "I was looking for matches and thought it was an odd place for twenty condoms."

Lawrence jokes, "No wonder they were all so happy!"

"You seem pretty intrigued by the threesome," she says. "Are you trying to tell me something?"

She'd never told Lawrence because he's so traditional, but she'd done a little experimenting in college.

He strokes her leg and says nothing. "You know," she adds, "I had a little brush with my roommate and my old boyfriend once."

Carla shoots him a sexy look. Lawrence's eyes all but fall out of his head. "Which roommate?"

"Leslie," she says. "The hot one."

Lawrence squeezes his legs together, trying to hide a growing erection. "Let's talk about this later," he says, and Carla is happy to oblige to let him calm down so the beachgoers don't notice his excitement.

– 32 –

Separate Ways

Brooke

Brooke wakes up on the sun lounger, freezing, and it takes a moment for her to realize she'd spent the remainder of the night outdoors.

Her husband is standing over her and grumbling.

"Charlie, Charlie, Charlie," he says, scrolling through her phone. "What is that kid draggin' you into now?"

Brooke sits up as Kevin puts her phone on the charger. "What are you doing going through my phone?"

She's barely awake, still in a haze, jarred by this man who she'd had reconnection sex with a few hours ago.

"What are you doing sleeping out here?" He ignores her question.

"Well, right after we made love you passed out, so I came out onto the deck," she says, not intending to let him off the hook. She grabs her phone. "I must have fallen asleep from sheer exhaustion. And if you must know, Charlie's mom disappeared again and he's staying with Mrs. Adibe. It's my job to make sure he's taken care of."

Kevin sighs and begins to soften. "That's not unusual, is it?"

"I don't expect you to go through my phone," she says, now ignoring *his* question. Brooke doesn't usually press him like this, because it's always easier to gloss over his moods and missteps, but she's beginning to feel a change coming. Something feels like it's shifted in her, and she's going with it. "You either trust me or you don't. If you have something to ask me, ask it. Otherwise, I expect you to trust me as I've trusted you."

"Fair enough," he replies, but his eyes are hard and he can't quite bring himself to say the words *I'm sorry*. No one ever said Kevin didn't have an ego.

Baby steps, she thinks, and lets it go.

"I have a bad feeling this time," she says. "And I need to ask you something. Here—sit down with me." She pats the spot next to her on the lounger.

He sits.

"If Charlie ever needs to be placed in another home," she says, looking him dead in the eye, "I'd like to take him in."

Kevin takes a sharp breath. She can see his mind working.

"Brooke," he says after some thought. "You know how many times his mother has done this to him. She'll come back eventually, and he'll go running back to her to make sure she's OK, and it will never change. I wish we could do more, I really do. I hate seeing you get your hopes up about this kid time and again. But you know how difficult the system is, and she does care for him. I mean, not like we would care for him, but in her way, she does her best."

Brooke furrows her eyebrows, her expression darkening. "Since when are you so forgiving? She's a meth addict, for god's sake. She's been offered help tons of times but doesn't want to go to rehab. She doesn't *want* to get better—even for her own son."

Brooke is suddenly up and pacing around the deck. She should have known. "This isn't about his mother, is it, Kevin? You don't like kids. Fuck, you don't even want to have them, do you?"

Kevin remains surprisingly calm. "Easy does it, Brooke," he pleads. "Don't take this out on me. It's not my fault his situation is horrible."

"Let's say his mother *doesn't* return. Then what?"

"Brooke, I think you're jumping the gun." Kevin is losing his cool again; she can see it in his clenching jaw. "There's no point discussing something that hasn't happened yet."

He moves inside the house and heads upstairs. She follows, calling to him from the living room.

"What are you doing? Are you leaving? That would be so typical of you!"

"I'm changing my clothes. I thought I should go for a bike ride and give you some space to become rational," he replies, and disappears at the top of the stairs.

Brooke's mouth is agape. She calls after him, "Rational? Rational! Really, Kevin, maybe I should be more rational when you stay out every night of the week entertaining clients. Maybe I should jump the gun then, huh?"

Kevin reappears at the top of the stairs, clearly shaken, and Brooke waits for him to hit back.

He doesn't. He disappears again, and two minutes later he races down the stairs in his workout gear. He grabs his phone and wallet and storms out of the house.

Aiding and Abetting

Kate

Kate watches her husband doing laps in the pool as she slices lemons at the granite island in their chef's kitchen. She's been craving sangria, so she's brought out all the fruit in the house to add to the pitcher.

Jon's toned, tanned back glistens in the water with every stroke, and Kate almost nicks her finger with the paring knife as she watches through the picture window.

She thinks about what would happen if she went out there.

If she slipped into the pool with him, if she swam up to him, if she wrapped her arms around his waist.

But lately, without other people in the mix, their sex life has been awkward and seems to happen only in fits and starts.

Jon takes a breather and Kate goes back to slicing. When she looks up again, he's out of the pool and frowning at his phone. He dries off, then heads to the gate. *We're not expecting anyone today*, she thinks, and wonders what's going on.

Jon walks back toward the pool on the balls of his feet, the decking clearly hot on his soles, now with a very good-looking man in tow.

Curiosity gets the best of her and she steps out of the kitchen with a welcoming smile plastered on her face. "Sweetie," Jon says when he sees her. "Meet Kevin Doyle, Brooke's husband. Kevin, this is my wife, Kate."

Kevin, who possesses a full head of brown hair highlighted by the sun, smiles and leans in for a kiss on the cheek. "You're everything he said you were."

"Aren't you sweet. Can I get you a drink?" She offers.

"Kevin's only staying for a minute. He's got a plane to catch," Jon answers.

"Ooh. Sounds serious." Kate winks.

"Nah," Kevin says, "just some business we have to discuss."

Kate knows he's lying. "Well, I'll leave you to it," she says.

She turns and heads back towards the house and stops just inside to the right of the open door, where she can't be seen. She's heard a lot about Kevin's marriage with Brooke, but she needs all the information she can get if she's going to lure them into the life. She stands still, flattened against the wall, and listens.

"She's so angry lately," Kevin is saying, with zero empathy in his voice. "She's never let on that she might know something or acted suspicious of me before. Do you think she knows? I mean, you don't think Kate would have said anything to her, do you? I know they had lunch…"

Kate feels sick to her stomach. He really is a liar and a cheat. She barely knows Brooke but wants to tell her everything.

"Of course not," Jon says firmly. "I haven't told Kate anything. But Kevin, if you leave the island now, Brooke will definitely suspect something. Are you sure you want to risk that?"

"I can't deal with these mood swings," Kevin says. "I think we need a little space."

"By 'space,' do you mean one of your…special friends?" Jon asks. Kate is impressed he's trying to call his friend out, even if subtly and carefully.

"I can catch the eleven a.m. flight," Kevin replies. "I'm not saying I'll see anyone, but…"

Jon sighs. "Do what you need to do. But that wife of yours is a gem, Kevin. I hate to see you lose her."

"I won't lose her," Kevin says. "As far as she knows, I could have gone to the mainland to get her a present to make up for our fight. In fact, maybe I'll pick something up to create a good cover story."

Kate goes back to making sangria, smiling to herself.

She now has a way of approaching Brooke to begin coaxing her into the group.

In the meantime, she can help teach that Kevin a lesson, too, in more ways than one.

– 34 –
Would She

Carla

Carla glances away from her family riding the waves and spots Marc further down the shoreline, emerging from the water, slicking his wet hair back with both hands. Her cheeks flush with embarrassment as she remembers getting caught running naked from the shower that morning.

She can finally admit to herself she has an attraction to her new friend's husband, especially after what Lawrence told her about the pool scene. Carla's hormones are flaring like she's seventeen again, and this burgeoning attraction is part of it.

It occurs to Carla it's possible Lawrence made it all up—that's how out of left field it seems. Was he drunker that night than Carla realized due to her own inebriated condition? Did the threesome by the pool really happen? Did a hot former model *really* grope her husband?

Seeing Marc now as he grabs a towel off his sun lounger, Carla struggles to imagine Allison and Marc in a threesome with Kate. Carla tries to picture herself in Kate's place, the third person with Allison and Marc, multiple sets of hands caressing one another.

Would Allison melt under her touch? Would Allison want to watch Marc pleasure Carla with those powerful hands? Carla tries to picture if she could handle the reverse, and closes her eyes, lets the sun bathe her, and fantasizes for a moment that Lawrence is with Allison while Carla is with Marc. Allison's long outstretched legs twisted around Lawrence's neck. That vision is harder to imagine, her husband with another woman. Would that turn her on? Or make her jealous? It's hard to know.

Fantasy is one thing. Real life is another.

Carla is fascinated as she imagines how the swinger world turns. What are the rules—and how can they really protect everyone from crushes and drama and jealousy? She thinks about the baseball coach and it occurs to her she's halfway there. She isn't such a prude that she wouldn't consider joining the group…or at least dipping a toe in. *If* she were invited.

What seemed so shocking this morning seems suddenly plausible now. Marc is undeniably handsome. Carla thinks back to when she first met Marc at their party and how he reminded her of the baseball coach, only better looking.

It doesn't hurt that Marc and Allison are a hot couple. She loves Marc's broad shoulders and Carla always notices Allison's long, lean legs on their runs. She starts to find herself, once again, picturing herself with Allison.

Carla laughs to herself. It's not like she hasn't been there before. But that was in college, in a wilder time, on one drunken night or, maybe it was two or three. Then there was the time it was just the girls. The memory of her threesome experience is a bit blurry but the girls-only night she will never forget. It's a wonder she remembers the threesomes at all. But she does remember how sweet it was to kiss another woman in a way she wanted to be kissed. The overwhelming desire she felt and the craving for more had shocked her. She discovered she enjoyed it more than she should have for a heterosexual woman…if that's what she is.

After that first time with her boyfriend and Leslie, she avoided her boyfriend for days. She and her roommate never discussed it. Maybe Leslie didn't remember anything from that night. It was like the encounter never happened…until it happened again. Carla suppressed the details deep in her memory, chalking it up to college experimentation. God, she hasn't thought about it since…well, college. And now it seems that's all she's thinking about.

She wonders if Lawrence would like to be that lucky with her and Allison one night. Maybe she'll simply ask him. It certainly would make her feel better about her baseball coach transgression. But would she be able to endure watching her husband make another woman quiver as he does to her? Her stomach turns with a mix of guilt and confusion.

She suddenly bursts out laughing. Her emotions are all over the place. But she can't ignore the tingling she is feeling throughout her body.

– 35 –
Tell Me

Allison

Allison is relaxed and optimistic as she heads back to the house to organize lunch for her hungry crew. Clearing the air with Marc lifted a huge weight off her shoulders. She's been so wound up over everything lately, more than she cares to admit.

As Allison approaches the house, she sees Abigail and Savannah on the top step of their deck, bathing suits on, slathering suntan lotion on themselves. When she reaches the door she observes their two Vineyard Vines beach bags packed and ready with towels, hats and water bottles.

I've taught them well, Allison smiles to herself.

She calls out, "Nice job getting your lotion on, girls. Your dad is at the beach waiting for you."

Allison hears her cell phone ringing in the distance, and races up the stairs to catch it. It stops as soon as she hits the top step. She spots the device sitting on the quartz island where she must have left it earlier this morning. Anxious to get back on the beach, she gets lunch going before checking who called.

With a cooler full of sandwiches, chips, veggies and drinks, she finally grabs her phone. Her stomach flutters as she sees a missed call and voicemail from Kate. Why does she feel anxious? She takes a deep breath and listens to the voicemail.

Allison, it's me. Listen, we need to talk. I'm working on the guest list for my party, and I'm having second thoughts about your neighbors coming. I don't think they are a good fit for us. Call me.

Allison shakes her head as if someone is around to sympathize with her situation. *Is Kate serious?* She stares at the phone as if it holds all the answers. Who is *Kate* to decide which couples are a good fit? She's learning her friend is a control freak when it comes to newbies. Or maybe she's only a control freak when it comes to Allison and Marc? Plus, her party isn't until the end of the month.

Kate knows that Allison and Carla have been seeing each other every day for their morning runs, time on the beach and grilling at each other's homes. She is obviously jealous of her new friendship with Carla.

That's going to make things even harder. As it is, Allison has been trying to take it slow so she doesn't risk blowing it with her new neighbors.

Allison desperately wants to prove to Kate she can get Carla and Lawrence on board on her own. She's also feeling in the mood to play. There's nothing like the build-up to a first hook-up. She still has her hopes up for Kate's party, and had been growing more excited by the prospect of new friends in the group—until this call.

Allison has already imagined wrapping her legs around Lawrence and giving him the night of his life. She's always had a thing for guys like Lawrence, strong and well-built with some meat on their bones. She also wouldn't mind getting Marc excited by playing around a bit with Carla. She knows Marc would thoroughly enjoy getting in between the two of them. And now Kate is trying to take this potential party away from her.

Allison has a plan, though. She's saving it for when the time is right. She makes a last-minute decision to leave her phone behind and heads out with the packed cooler.

On her solo walk back to the beach, her mind continues to drift. She's gotten some hints Carla might be open to something like this; like kissing that baseball coach and the many times she's made comments about how hot Allison's legs are. But she must wait for Carla to open the door. And when she does, Allison plans to kick it wide open.

Her thoughts switch back to Kate. Allison knows she should return her call, but she's not up for a confrontation right now, especially the slick, passive-aggressive kind Kate is so fond of.

She thinks about asking Marc to talk Kate down, and for a second it seems like a brilliant idea—and then it hits her she doesn't want the two talking. At all. She's already suspicious of Kate's intentions with her husband. Damn, it turns out Marc was right: Allison *is* jealous. When did things get so complicated with Kate?

She can't seem to think straight anymore. This was supposed to be fun. It all started out so easy and innocent.

Marc isn't a talker during sex, and never has been—with Allison. But with Kate, he opened up, and Allison had to listen to her make demands of her husband: *Tell me. Tell me!* She'd said it with increasing urgency so that Allison knew something happened between the two of them when they were alone in a separate room.

Here and now, walking alone on the narrow path, Allison decides it's time to revise their rules back to same-room sex only. Who talked her out of that rule anyway. She never should have moved to that next stage. The rules became too loose. Maybe that is when all the trouble began.

Get a grip, she thinks. *This is what we wanted. It's just sex.*

That's what Marc told her earlier. As she reaches the beach, she decides to put her focus back on getting Carla and Lawrence into the mix.

– 36 –

Falling for Kate

Brooke

Brooke is in shock, standing alone in the kitchen of the house Kevin rented for them, unsure what to do with the rest of her day.

She finally stood up to him.

It's been building for a long time. She has no will left to keep their secrets and their mistrust buried any longer. Ever since she arrived on Nantucket, she has felt a bit of her old self bubbling under, and she knows there's no going back to the way things were. She doesn't want to.

It's been painful and exhilarating to let herself start to feel again. Brooke's struggles to have children with Kevin left her on a bumpy roller-coaster that she hasn't been able to get off until now. She's ready to exit this damn ride and find a new one.

Kevin walked out in the middle of their epic fight and took his cell phone and wallet, so God only knows how long he'll be gone. Brooke briefly entertains the thought that maybe he'll never return. Kevin has been breaking her heart since the day they met, but Brooke lived in denial, telling herself that all relationships have their ups and downs, and things would get better, especially once they had children. But . . . they don't have children.

And their relationship isn't getting better.

Feeling reckless, she grabs a bottle of Dom Perignon they were saving to drink in bed with a platter of chocolate-dipped strawberries. *Right. The strawberries.* She opens the fridge and grabs those, too, and heads upstairs. She and Kevin had planned to lounge naked in bed and take in the views of the vista from their suite.

Screw you, Kevin, she thinks as she pops the cork and fills her glass. Instead of reconnecting with him, she's had an epiphany: She's reconnecting with *herself.*

She drains her glass and picks up her phone. She finds Kate's number and dials, gritting her teeth, nervous because it's possible this upscale, classy woman was only being polite when she told Brooke to call her anytime.

Kate answers on the second ring. "Brooke! It's lovely to hear from you. You have *perfect* timing. I need to run into town to pick up a few things for our party and I'd love to see you. Care to meet me?"

"I'll be there," Brooke smiles, ends the call, and jumps into the shower, taking her second glass of champagne with her.

They meet in front of what Kate called her favorite boutique, and as Brooke gazes through the window, she says, "I've been thinking about your party. I have nothing fancy to wear. Will you help me pick out a dress?"

"You've come to the right place," Kate smiles, and ushers Brooke inside the store.

The two of them shop for hours, with Kate picking up some party essentials along with a new dress and Brooke buying some new beachwear for sunbathing and many pricey new garments so she has options for Kate's party. Their purchases complete, they head towards the harbor for a drink.

Brooke feels the weight of her shopping bag as she hangs it on a hook under the bar. Hell, if Kevin is going to walk away, she's going to spend his money. She sits comfortably in a high-back bar stool with a pink cocktail in hand.

Kate holds hers up. "Cheers," she toasts Brooke. "It's five o'clock somewhere!"

Brooke toasts back, "Cheers, to a celeb!"

Kate tilts her head. "What?"

"You remind me of Kate Hudson, my favorite actress," Brooke, buzzed and being herself for the first time in ages, explains. "You kind of look like her and you draw attention everywhere we go. Every store we were in people were staring at you, whispering to each other like you're famous. They either know you already or they want to know you. You have this ability to light up a room."

Kate lets out a shy little laugh. "Well…thank you, sweetie, you are such a dear to say that. We need to hang out more. You're good for my ego!"

She leans over and plants a kiss on Brooke's cheek.

Brooke blinks in surprise…and feels an unexpected frisson of excitement.

Kate goes back to chatting, but Brooke stops listening. She finds herself watching Kate's lips as she talks. Her beauty is distracting: her flawless tanned skin, her bright, clear, knowing eyes, her perfect white teeth, even her hair falls like silk onto her bare shoulders. Brooke has never felt so completely at ease in another person's presence.

"Hello? Earth to Brooke," Kate smiles. "Those drinks are a bit strong, aren't they?"

Brooke looks down at her near-empty glass and giggles. "Oops, I should probably slow down," she says thinking about the champagne she consumed before coming into town.

"Hey, do you want to get out of here?" Kate asks. "We can go for a swim at my place."

– 37 –

Perfect Ten

Brooke

Brooke follows Kate's Porsche to her cliff-side mansion. She pulls her rented Jeep into the circular shelled drive lined with cobblestones and hydrangeas. She is in awe of the size and beauty of Kate's home with its stunning landscape. Her eyes drift to the climbing roses flourishing in the corner and rose covered arbor large enough to see through to a magnificent view of the ocean that stretches out forever beyond the cliffs.

Brooke exits the Jeep and follows Kate to the grand double front doors. The home is enormous, tasteful, stunning. *She even lives like a celebrity*, Brooke realizes.

She notes an oversized copper knocker in the shape of an upside-down pineapple. Kate lets them into an imposing foyer with ceilings two stories high, leading to an immaculate, spacious living room beyond it.

"Let's change in my suite," Kate offers, and leads her upstairs. "We can christen the new suit you bought today."

Brooke changes in the plush bathroom while Kate heads to her walk-in closet the size of most bedrooms. Brooke tries on the gold bikini Kate picked out for her and finds her heavy breasts show some trendy under-boob.

When she emerges, she calls Kate's name, but hears nothing, so she finds her way back downstairs and outside to the sprawling deck and crystalline infinity pool.

Kate and Jon are already in the pool. Still buzzed, Brooke doesn't even greet them; she catwalks to the edge and hops into the deep end. As she surfaces like a rocket, she revels in letting go, exhilarated by releasing her inhibitions.

She slicks her hair back and rubs the water out of her eyes and finds her hosts next to her in the shallow end hooting and clapping.

"*Brooke*," Jon says and then whistles.

"Work it, girl," Kate smiles.

Brooke is floored at how far she's come since meeting Kate. She soaks in this awakened carefree feeling. Kate has been so kind and inviting. But her happy bubble is suddenly popped by a stab of sadness that her own husband can't be here. That he can't be a better person.

Her eyes begin to tear up and Brook shakes her head, trying to get a grip. Her emotions are all over the place. Jon notices and immediately his face softens as he moves toward her in the water.

"Whoa, hey. Are you OK?"

Brooke takes a deep breath and lets it out. "I'm good. Sorry about that. I'm having a strange day. It's been an emotionally exhausting time for Kevin and me."

She watches Jon's expression. "Oh…" Brooke breathes. "He told you."

Kate steps up and gives her a wet, skin-on-skin hug. "He did, but only in the context that he was worried about you and wanted to do everything he could to make you happy," she says when she pulls away.

Brooke shakes her head. "I can't believe he did that. I swear—"

It occurs to her these people are business contacts, and she's suddenly embarrassed and has no desire to unload her screwed-up marriage on Jon and Kate. She smiles, throws her hands up, and dives back into the deep end. *Peace.* She wishes she could stay under forever.

When she surfaces, they're both lounging on floats and holding onto the side, bobbing and taking in the sun. Brooke swims up to them.

"Let's have some fun," she says brightly, "and forget about all this."

Jon raises his eyebrows. "I think that's a wonderful idea." He slips off his float back into the water and reaches out to give her a squeeze around the shoulders.

She finds his bright green eyes and kind, dimpled smile reassuring. He is, Brooke must admit, highly attractive to her.

"Kevin doesn't know how lucky he is to have you," he says. "You're an amazing woman. Not to mention stunningly beautiful."

Brooke shoots a questioning look to Kate: *Is this kind of talk OK?*

Kate quickly agrees. "He's right, Brooke. Kevin is missing out. He should be here with you. To walk out on you like he did is despicable."

Brooke gives little thought as to how they knew what Kevin did earlier that day. She replies, "Let's not talk about Kevin anymore. I was just starting to feel better."

Brooke looks over at Jon and admires his fit, tanned body. She locks into his green eyes and quickly forgets about Kevin. She can't remember the last time anyone looked at her this way, right into her soul.

Kate leaps from the pool and sashays toward the diving board. "OK, loves, be my judges. One to ten, rank my dive." And off she jumps, sky high, and performs a flawless dive into the pool without a splash. Everything Kate does, she does with perfection.

Jon and Brooke look at each other. "TEN!" They both shout in unison and start laughing. They hold each other's gaze longer than they should.

Kate surfaces after a few seconds and her bikini top is missing. Brooke turns towards Jon, looking for his reaction. He laughs as his eyes connect again with Brooke's. She starts to tingle with desire. She tries not to stare but is distracted by Kate's tanned and perky breasts.

"Oops!" Kate giggles and dives back under.

Brooke hops out next, wanting to join in the fun, and asks for her scores as she dives off the board. When she hits the water, her bottoms slip down and she decides not to pull them up. Jon is underwater watching her. He swims up to Brooke and when they've both surfaced, he puts his hands around her waist.

"I think you're missing something, Brooke." He smiles.

"I know!" Brooke giggles, drunk on alcohol, sun, and Jon.

The next thing Brooke realizes, she is into a series of long, deep kisses with Jon. Their tongues feel their way around: exploring, intense, and wet.

Kate swims up behind Brooke and begins caressing her breasts, telling Brooke how sensual and sexy she is. Brooke is overwhelmed with pleasure. Kate confesses she has wanted to touch Brooke since the moment she first laid eyes on her. She spins Brooke around and they briefly lock eyes. Brooke leans in and kisses Kate. As Kate responds, Brooke is overwhelmed at how different this is from anything she has ever experienced.

Brooke has never kissed another woman. Not like this. The kisses are velvety and fulfilling. While gentle and sensual, Kate's attention gives Brooke a sense of freedom, releasing all her anxiety.

"Mind if I join in?" Jon asks as he gives a soft kiss to Brooke's shoulder. He hears no complaints.

Since Brooke has never pulled her bikini bottoms up, Jon runs his skilled fingers to her inner thighs and makes his way up to where they meet. Completely aroused, he wraps his other hand around her waist and pulls her against him. The pressure of his taut chest against her back and his erection through his suit is nearly enough to unravel her. She gently moves against him wanting more, needing him to give her more.

And then she comes to her senses in one quick burst. She's about to be carried away past the point of no return.

Whether or not her husband is an irredeemable prick remains to be seen. Whether she is going to leave him is up in the air. But one thing is for sure: She made a vow, and she intends to take care of unfinished business before she starts doing the things she despises him for doing.

She pulls away. "I can't," she cries, suddenly panicking, feeling crowded and claustrophobic and guilty. She wriggles away, breathless, grabbing her suit bottoms and slipping them back on.

"Hey, hey, hey," Jon says, backing away and trying to calm her at the same time.

"*Brooke*," Kate says carefully, also giving the woman her space. "No means no. Stop means stop. You're OK…this is OK. Let's get out of the pool and talk it through."

"I—I—" Brooke's teeth are chattering though it's eighty degrees outside and the pool is heated. "I…it's nothing you did. I was loving it, honestly. But I'm a married woman. And if I'm going to be with anyone else—of any gender—I have to make things right with my husband first. Whatever that looks like."

Jon and Kate exchange slow, meaningful glances.

"What?" Brooke asks, utterly confused, but also very, very curious.

"Brooke," Jon says gently. "We need to talk."

– 38 –

My Turn

Brooke

The three of them sit inside, dried off and sipping champagne. Brooke assumes she was offered a crisp glass of Bollinger to ease the sting of what they're about to tell her.

"Your husband was here this morning," Jon begins.

"Oh?" Brooke hides behind her glass as she takes a long swig.

"He was very upset about what's been happening with you two, and—"

Brooke almost chokes on her champagne. "Whoa, *wait* a minute," she cries when she's swallowed. "He told you about our personal business? Oh, my god, I'm horrified."

Kate steps in and rubs Brooke's shoulder. "It's nothing to be embarrassed about. Jon and I have both been married before. We've been through it. All couples go through rough patches and some end up moving on for the better."

"So…wait. Back up. Do you know where he is?" Brooke asks.

"He flew to Boston," Jon replies. "He swore he'd be back in a few hours. I'm sure you'll hear from him soon."

"*Boston?* Are you serious?" Brooke has suspected *something* for a long time, but to actually fly off the island, leave her behind without so much as a text to check on her, is shocking to her. "For what?"

Jon winces.

"Ohhhh…" Brooke breathes. "A girlfriend?"

Her new friends exchange glances again. "Just tell me. I can handle it. I'm a big girl."

"Brooke," Jon says. "Have you ever suspected he was up to something? I mean, from what I can gather, you're not completely in the dark about his…wild side."

Brooke shakes her head. "I don't know what's going on with Kevin," she admits. "I know in my heart something isn't right, and I know he loves to party and entertain clients. He never really grew up. It was cute at first, but we're not so young anymore, you know? There are no obvious signs of other women, but he's clearly not telling me the truth. I don't know if he's been faithful to me. I guess the answer is…no?"

Kate says, "I've been there. Something happened to wake you up. What was it?"

Brooke glances at her new friend and nods at her incisive observation.

"Let's just say this week has been different," Brooke says. "*He's* been different. Sweeter. More attentive. The sex was great, gentle, and he was actually connecting with me."

She lets out a little laugh. "And yes, I'm aware that should be a good thing, but all it did was make me suspicious. At first, I chalked it up to us not having the baby pressure for once, but it was more than that. That's when I realized he must've been going elsewhere for it. Then the dots started to connect. The after-work events, the after-dinner runs back to the office, the hour and a half he would be gone to get takeout…"

She looks Jon directly in the eyes. "So, who is she? I assume you know."

"I'm not sure there's one *she*," he says gently. "I honestly don't know exactly what he gets up to. He doesn't confide details, but if I was a betting man, I'd say there's no love in any of it. It's strictly a game to him. Almost like an addiction. I say this because I know that *you're* the one he loves."

Brooke feels a shooting pain through her heart. "Don't make excuses for him," she says. "He's perfectly in control of himself. He chooses to be cruel."

One of the most infuriating things about this situation is she still loves the guy. It's ridiculous.

"Brooke," Jon says, "whoever he's with in Boston today doesn't matter. You two need to sort this out between you— everything else is a distraction. Take Kate and me. People aren't always who they seem. You saw that with us today. It doesn't mean we don't deeply love one another, but *because* we do, we're able to embrace our sexuality together. Our relationships with other partners only deepen our own connection. But we don't cheat, and we don't lie. There is a big difference."

When he puts it like that, their almost-threesome in the pool now sounds almost romantic, Brooke thinks. Confusion sets in, as does the exhaustion from her fight with Kevin. Not to mention all those drinks. She breaks down right there in their kitchen, and Jon leans in and holds Brooke as she weeps.

"Let it all go, Brooke, it's going to be okay."

Brooke pulls herself together, wipes her eyes, and breathes deeply. "Thank you both. It helps to have someone to talk to about this. Kevin has made me feel like I'm going crazy. He's a master at pretending everything's fine." She pauses but decides to keep confiding in them. "The past two years have been dreadful, and I'm dealing with a lot. I've turned a blind eye, too, because I wanted a baby so badly. But now I think I've lost my marriage."

"Oh, Brooke, don't say that," Kate says. "All's not lost. You're just a bit off course. You know Kevin loves you."

Jon is nodding along as Kate continues, "It seems to me the biggest problem is him not being honest with you. But what if you both started exploring other avenues…what if *you* also got to spread your wings? We find that as long as we have rules and boundaries with others, it's benefited us both. Kevin could stop hiding it and you could stop ignoring it."

Brooke is in shock. Did they just admit to being swingers? She thought they'd all been carried away in the moment, but now she realizes how naïve that was. These two are acting like they had a quick hug, not a steamy threesome that almost got out of control.

"Wait. Is Kevin involved with this…lifestyle with you?" Brooke doesn't know who to trust. "Are you somehow involved with his cheating, too?"

Jon puts his hands up. "Brooke, *no*. It's not like that. Kevin doesn't even know about our lifestyle. But I've attended enough events and heard enough of the rumors to piece his lifestyle together."

Kate takes over again. "You need to know we're here for you in any way you need. If you even want to stay here for a bit, we'd love to have you," she says. "You and I both know this needs to be settled between you and Kevin and no one else."

Brooke is in utter shock. She wants to be alone all of the sudden.

Jon's phone, sitting on the kitchen island between them, vibrates.

He puts a finger over his lips before answering: *Shhhh.*

The two women fall silent as Jon greets the caller on speaker.

"Hey, man, where are you?"

"I'm out on my bike, heading back to the house now," Kevin replies. "Do you know where Brooke is? She isn't answering her phone. Is she out with Kate again?"

"She's here, and she's doing fine, so please don't worry," Jon says sarcastically. "She is about to leave and head back to the house. She should be there in about twenty minutes. Oh, and Kev? Get your shit together, buddy."

Jon hangs up. Brooke, eyes wide, giggles. It's a new and exciting feeling to have a man like this, one so reassuring and kind who clearly respects her, stands up for her. Not many are brave enough to speak to Kevin like that.

She's picturing herself back in the pool with him—and Kate.

"Are you going to be alright, Brooke?" Kate asks.

"I'll be fine," Brooke assures them, knowing it's true. "Though I'm not sure where to start. I feel like I should confront him right away, but I just want to take a nap. This conversation has been sobering."

Jon smiles. "Then you should. Let him squirm for a bit while you take care of yourself."

"Something tells me you're going to handle yourself just fine," Kate adds, getting up off her stool. "I'm going to grab a robe, then I'll walk you out to your car."

Fire and Ice

Kate

Once Kate returns from walking Brooke out to the driveway, Kate and Jon head back out to their pool.

"I can't believe you told Brooke her husband is a cheater. Is there more?" Kate questions, taking a sip of the frozen piña colada their chef whipped up.

Jon shrugs from his sun lounger. "Yes, there is more. But what was I going to say to that poor woman? I couldn't tell her Kevin goes to strip clubs, orders the happy ending when he gets his massage, and visits his favorite hooker once a week. It's the weirdest thing, he's obsessed with his own wife, but he can't stop screwing around on her. And he secretly hates himself for it."

"He's stuck in an addiction," Kate guesses. "The guilt will always get you in the end."

"Maybe," Jon says. "Or maybe he's a really bad guy. You don't know the half of it."

Kate sits up, straw in her mouth. She slurps, swallows. "Wait—*what?* Tell me!"

"I had Jean-Pierre check him out," Jon says of his longtime security chief.

Kate learned early on in their relationship that when you have as much money as Jon and his family, and you're as well-known as they are, you always have scammers, con artists and people who wish you harm lurking in the background. If you're smart, you have a crack security team always on hand in the background, to do away with them. *Always.*

"But Jean-Pierre could only learn so much through official channels," Jon goes on. "The worst stuff came from Kevin himself. The stuff he blurts out when he's wasted is pretty bad. He's charming until about five drinks in, and then he turns into a babbling, aggressive frat boy."

"Is this really the guy you want handling your assets?" Kate asks him.

"Only a portion of them," Jon clarifies. "As a finance manager, he is so good I never considered moving on. But seeing his wife now—getting to know her—I'm not sure anymore he's the kind of guy I want to do business with. We'll see how the summer unfolds."

"You can certainly handle the ruthless kind like him," Kate points out. "That's how you got where you are."

"Ruthless in business," he corrects her, "but not in life. Not with family. Not an abuser of women."

"So what did he do?" Kate presses. "What could be so bad?"

"He told some of the guys one night about something in his teen years," Jon says, setting his drink down and squinting in the sun. "When he was seventeen, he says he nearly killed his best friend in a drunk driving accident. He tried to escape the guilt by moving to New York for college but it followed him there. He got big into drugs, drinking and clubbing."

Kate makes a face. "Wow, it sounds like he went off the rails."

Jon sighs. "There's more. He told us he likes it rough in the bedroom. And he hinted that the rougher the sex, the more satisfied he'll be. He described an encounter with a 'slut' that led to rape accusations. You should know that he denied it, Kate, before you freak out. He swears it was consensual and she wanted it."

"That's what all rapists say," Kate adds icily. "And any guy who calls any woman a 'slut' deserves more than just a side-eye."

"I'm not going to argue with that," Jon says. "But he obviously has issues from whatever happened. He says the accusation nearly ruined his life and he insists he never forced anyone to do anything. She went after him for a year and almost destroyed him."

"But what if this is truly who he is?" Kate ponders. "Why are we trying to get him into our group? I mean sure, the guy's hot and super charming, I'm not going to deny it. But if he's done what you think he did, shouldn't we get away from this guy rather than trying to pull him in?"

"It's a big *if*," Jon argues. "Jean-Pierre did investigate the accusation and there's no legal record of it, so he was never even arrested, let alone convicted of anything. He was wasted when he told us—for all I know *none* of it ever happened. I honestly don't know what to think. He's required to go through epic background checks and drug tests to have such a senior role at his firm. With him and Brooke, it's clear there's love among the dysfunction. That's none of our business. However their relationship proceeds from here, they need to give it a chance, or at least get real. That's not for us to say. In the meantime, maybe giving Kevin an outlet with our group could help."

Kate is listening intently, hearing some good points and some justifications that give her pause. Ultimately, they could use some new blood in the group and it's not like she's in any danger.

"The bottom line," Jon says, "is we found out today that sweet little Brooke is open to branching out. It's not the sex that's the problem," he adds. "It's the lying."

Kate considers that, but intends to have her own talk with Kevin before allowing him near her friends. Safety first. Total transparency. That's the only way this lifestyle can work.

Kate is relieved it's all out, and she's also noticing Jon is eyeing her in her bikini. They needed a reset in their sex life, and what happened today with Brooke has served to jumpstart them. She can feel it.

It's going to be OK, she tells herself.

She drops her robe and notices that Jon is immediately aroused by her cleavage popping out of her bikini top. She smiles as he joins her on the lounge chair and starts teasing her by gently massaging her breasts.

He grins as Kate responds to his touch.

"I adore her," he says, "but I'm glad she's gone. It's you I want, Kate. Always you."

Kate whispers, "Tell me."

Jon responds, "Kate Gibson, you are the sexiest, hottest, woman I have ever had."

He's kissing her neck and unhooking her top.

"And?"

Jon moans, "There's only you, and there will never be anyone else."

She straddles him and they have the best sex, just the two of them, they've had in months.

Jon kisses Kate as she lies back in her lounger. He stands up and dives back into the pool.

Kate watches him. She sighs, thoroughly enchanted with herself for seducing Brooke after only two meetings. She knows she's good at what she does, but this level of seduction is next level.

Kate longs to flaunt her conquest in Allison's face. She thinks she's going to bring Carla and Lawrence on board all by herself. Allie doesn't recognize they will never join their lifestyle, certainly not this early on and not with Allison leading the way. There's a difference between those who will experiment and get their feet a little wet versus those who commit to their way of life.

Kate still can't figure out what's been going on with Allison lately. It's driving her insane, making her realize just how much she misses her. Kate makes a promise to herself that she's going to get Allie back and get her back for good.

Brooke is a nice distraction and will be a fun partner to play with, but Allison is something more. Kate decides she needs to let Allie know she is hers, and she has the perfect plan.

Jon surfaces and hangs off the side of the pool with his elbows on the deck.

"I'm in the mood to go out," Kate calls to him. "How about we stop by the brewery? Maybe Allison and Marc will meet us."

"Sounds good," Jon says, then dives back under water as Kate sends a text to Allison.

– 40 –

Curiosity or Craving

Allison

Allison relishes the feel of saltwater pouring over her feet as she walks with Carla along the edge of the surf. Once she decided to have The Talk, she'd gone down to the beach, found Carla buried in a book on her sun lounger and coaxed her on a girls-only walk.

"I am absolutely floored," Carla says, shaking her head and giggling as they leave footprints in the sand. "You're this perfect all-American family by day, and you're having wild sex parties by night. Who knew?"

Allison can't be sure her friend is being polite or is hiding how freaked out she might be, but she instinctively knew this was the right time—possibly the *only* time—to spill every detail of her swinging, from her first experience to her last, which happened this past Saturday night.

Allison takes a breather from explaining everything and they walk in silence for a few moments. She realizes how relieved she is to talk this through with someone other than Marc, considering men have such a different perspective on sex.

They have a different perspective on everything, as far as she's concerned. For once, Allison is able to speak uninterrupted and uninhibited. All of her built up thoughts and feelings about Kate and Marc burst out like champagne from a shaken bottle.

When she and Carla find themselves all the way down at Ladies Beach, Allison continues, "It's not always perfect. If I'm honest, it hasn't been easy this summer with Kate and Jon so far."

She reveals the strange incidents and tension she's had lately with Kate, as well as her fears that Carla and Lawrence would be turned off or judgmental about their lifestyle.

Carla remains quiet, listening, nodding her head from time to time, but saying little.

Allison stops when she's done, then turns to Carla, not sure what to say. Carla smiles, holds out her arms, and hugs her. Her friend holds her for a long moment.

"Girl, you've been carrying around way too much stress." Carla pulls away and looks her in the eye. "I think you need to clear the air with Kate. It sounds like you have a deep bond and with the lifestyle you both live, it's bound to get blurry."

Allison sighs, relieved Carla understands. "I know I need to talk with her," she says. "I love Kate, I really do. I just feel like she's starting to come between Marc and me. And I don't know when things changed! Up until now, she only enhanced our sexual relationship. I think it's my own jealousy messing everything up."

"I think you're being a bit hard on yourself," Carla shakes her head. "Those feelings are normal. Marc is your husband and if you need a break from Kate, take one."

Carla turns Allison back towards Cisco and they begin the walk back home.

"What about Jon? Do you join them sometimes?" Carla asks.

"Well, yes," Allison says, "but he's not around as much as Marc, so the three of us spend more time together without Jon. It used to be that we'd just swing at our parties, but it got to the point where Marc, Kate, and I would go out for dinner together a lot. Afterwards, we would hit the beach for some stargazing and one thing would lead to another."

"So what's different in your threesome?" Carla prods. "What do you think is making this one spin out of control? You must have some idea."

"I guess I do," Allison replies, realizing that with Carla gently pushing her, she's finally understanding there's an answer she's unconsciously suspected all along. "Kate once told me she was a unicorn in another relationship, so I think she's used to being the other woman. But she told me that marriage ended up breaking up not long after she decided to stop joining them. She said she stopped because it was getting complicated, and she always wondered if she was the reason they split up. Now I am starting to feel that it's becoming too much for me and my marriage. I think Marc senses it too."

Carla turns to Allison with a knitted brow. "Wait, back up. What in the world is a *unicorn*?"

Allison cracks a smile. "It's when a woman has an exclusive relationship with a married couple. You're the third person in the group. That makes you the unicorn—you know, because an attractive woman who's willing to be the outsider is rare. Jon was always into open relationships and when he and Kate first met, she didn't want an open relationship. So instead, they discussed swinging. They started to recruit other couples on the island and that is how our upside-down pineapple club came about. Jon and Kate are the original ring leaders."

"Ah, the *upside-down pineapple*. Now it makes sense!" Carla giggles again. "I saw that picture on your wall."

"Exactly," Allison nods. She can feel Carla being reeled in, and her laughter reminds Allison what this is all for; it's supposed to be *fun* above all else. "It's our tradition to gift a portrait of an upside-down pineapple from a local artist to the newest couple to join the group. The new couple displays the painting in the home where it can be seen by their guests. This is a way for those in the know to recognize who is a willing participant."

"How clever," Carla says. "What other rules do I need to know?"

Allison stops on the sand. They're almost there, and she needs to know how serious her new friend is.

"Carla," she says, "before I go any further with this, I need to know how you feel about it. I mean, are you OK knowing we do this…but more to the point…could you ever see yourself joining?"

Allison feels herself literally holding her breath. This came about faster and more abruptly than she ever planned. But she also knows this is the best way for it to happen: Naturally, spontaneously, and with the fully informed participation of her potential new recruit.

"And of course," Allison adds before Carla can answer, "what about Lawrence? Although men are often easier to attract, there's also the constant worry they'll freak out when they see someone else touching their wife—regardless of who it is."

Carla's face doesn't change. She's not remotely upset by any of this, and Allison exhales.

"I don't know about Lawrence," Carla replies. "He seemed pretty turned on when he told me about seeing you, Kate, and Marc together. But he is such a straight family man. As for me…"

She blushes, and Allison jumps in to steady her nerves. "You don't have to answer now," she says, hiding her shock upon learning in this vague, roundabout way that her neighbor *definitely* saw their tryst by the pool that night. "I'll tell you a bit more about the rules of the game and you can take time to process it all."

As they weave in and out of the waves along the beach, Allison explains more rules, including how she and Marc aren't the only couple they know to carry on with threesomes on their own beyond the swinging parties, and in fact it's rather common for couples to continue long after they embrace the swinging lifestyle.

"That tracks with what I've heard about swinging over the years," Carla says.

"Here's something you might not know," Allison says. "You're not technically a swinger until you indulge in what's called a peak swap. In other words, when you have penetrative sex with someone other than your partner. This idea is *almost* the definition of what swinging actually is."

Allison snaps her fingers. "Oh! Remember James from my party? The short stocky guy with the Nantucket red shorts and golf shoes?"

Carla pauses as if trying to remember meeting someone of that description, and Allison isn't surprised. They all had a few too many cocktails that night. "Oh, right!" Carla says finally. "Yes, I remember…I was thinking it was goofy to be wearing golf shoes to a party."

"Well," Allison smirks, "James is a total exhibitionist. He and his wife were another one of the original couples in the upside-down pineapple group. I remember when we first branched out from our little safe threesome with Kate, we decided to watch first, and James begged to be in the group romp we were watching. He gets off on having others watch him fooling around. That basically explains exhibitionism."

Allison looks over to Carla to make sure she's not freaking out. "Our first group romp was the same. It took us a while to work our way up to the actual swapping of partners for full sex. When we finally did, we were together in the same room, so we knew how we were doing. But then Kate wanted Marc all to herself, and I was starting to get a little frisky myself, so I allowed separate room sex. From that point on the lines got a little blurry. I just decided we shouldn't do that anymore, and our personal rule now is to always be in the same room."

Carla is shaking her head. "I never thought about how many rules there must be in this kind of thing," she says. "It sounds like it can get pretty complicated."

"It does," Allison admits. "And believe me, I want you to consider our group, so I hope I haven't made you want to run into the dunes. I hope you'll talk to Lawrence, and that you'll still want to be friends with us no matter what you decide. We've grown to adore your family in such a short time. Every day here on the rock is like three days in the real world!"

Carla nods and smiles.

"Great," Allison says. They're almost home; she can see her husband in the surf up ahead. "There's one last thing I need to tell you."

"Oh?" Carla is clearly intrigued.

"Kate and Jon like to bend the rules," Allison warns. "They find a way to push you beyond your comfort zone. I'm not sure how they do it, but their charm can be dangerous. I want to make sure you know that going in."

– 41 –

Approaching Storm

Brooke

Not long after Brooke pulls their rented jeep into the driveway, she spots Kevin pedaling up to the house and feels a pang of disappointment. She was hoping for some time for herself before he came home.

She desperately needs sleep and time alone to process everything—including her imploding marriage *and* what happened with Jon and Kate in the pool. Her head is spinning, and it's competing with her heart, which holds a place for her husband despite everything.

As much as she wants to escape inside the house, she decides to wait in the driveway for him.

Brooke has no idea what her own husband has been up to for the past seven hours. It gives her some satisfaction to know he'd be shocked if he had any idea what she'd been doing. She notices a strange expression on his face as he approaches her, one she hasn't seen before and can't quite interpret.

"Hi," is all she can manage to squeak out.

"Hello," comes Kevin's one word response. He hops off his

bike and walks it to the garage, where he leans it against the wall.

The two of them stand in the driveway looking at each other like complete strangers, not knowing what to say.

Fine, I'll start, Brooke thinks. "Why did you take off on me? That's not acceptable, Kevin."

"Because I don't want to argue with you."

"That's not a valid answer. We need to start communicating like actual married people or this is never going to work," she says with a sigh. "Something's gotta give. I can't keep living like this."

"What do you mean 'if this is going to work?'" Kevin's eyes grow wide. "Are you thinking of leaving me?"

She crosses her arms and sighs again. She wants to tell him she can't imagine her life without him, that she's not ready to say goodbye, that she loves him. But that will open the door for him to slide in and use his charm to get away with everything.

"Let's not do this outside where the neighbors might hear," she says, and turns to walk back into the house. She runs herself a glass of filtered water, then grabs a throw pillow and sits on the living-room sofa, gazing out the French doors at the calm ocean.

If he wants to talk to her, he can do it on her terms.

He walks slowly over to her and wisely chooses to sit on a cushion two down from her.

"I do love you, Kevin," she concedes, "but I also can't continue with the way things are." Her voice quavers as she continues. "Neither of us has been happy together in years. I know it, and you know it. It's time to stop pretending otherwise. Life's too short to be miserable."

"I can't help but think this is all about the baby stuff," Kevin says.

"*Baby stuff?*" Brooke can't keep her voice from squeaking.

"Sorry, sorry." He holds up his hands. "All I meant was you've been through so much trying to have a baby, and it's been hard on both of us."

"Let's not blame this on trying to have kids." Brooke's voice is strong now. "We both know our problems go deeper than that."

"What are you saying?" He sits up straighter. She recognizes his defensive stance.

"I'm saying that our relationship has had its ups and downs since we first met," Brooke replies. "I figured all relationships do, but you know what else I know?"

She pauses. He blinks.

"I know you haven't been faithful to me."

She can't believe she had the guts to call him out specifically, finally.

Will Kevin admit to it or deny it? Brooke isn't sure which response she fears more.

She waits.

Bombshells at the Brewery

Allison

Allison's phone chirps as she and Carla approach their beach after their walk. She reads Kate's text and rolls her eyes.

"What is it?" Carla asks.

"Speak of the devil," Allison sighs. "It's Kate. They're heading to the brewery and want Marc and me to join." Her anxiety bubbles up.

"You should go and talk it out," Carla advises. "They're your friends and you've been through so much together. Tell her how you feel. You'll work it out."

They see their families still at the beach, and Lawrence waves to them.

Carla leans in for a quick kiss on Allison's cheek. "I've gotta run. This was a great and interesting walk. Good luck today. Let me know how it goes!"

She heads off to see her family.

Allison decides Carla is right. It's time she and Kate have a heart to heart. She texts back, *See you in an hour!*

Allison walks up the beach to collect her own family.

She spots her girls jumping into the waves with their father, a sight that fills her with contentment. It seems like yesterday they were babies, crawling in the sand. Allison decides life is too short for drama, and she runs into the water to join them.

After a few good dives into the waves, she asks Marc if he'd like to hit the brewery for an hour or so. She mentions a great fish and steak store as an added incentive, saying they can grab some fresh dinner on the way back from cocktail hour.

Allison heads up the beach path to home, then takes a quick outdoor shower. Once dried and dressed, she gets the girls settled with some drinks and snacks in the downstairs living room where the kids love to hang out after a day in the elements.

They cozy up on the blue sofa with comfy sand-colored decorative pillows. The seating is a perfect complement to dark brown hardwoods that warm the room. But everyone's favorite part of the room comes from the pop of color in the blue, yellow and red surfboard mounted over the flat screen, hand painted by the kids and Marc.

With big bowls of ice cream, the girls settle in and are instantly glued to the television. Allison loves how they have recently turned a corner and no longer worry about being left home alone.

"Hey Mom," Abigail says, "are we going to the water fight tomorrow morning?"

"Oh my gosh!" Allison cries. "Is tomorrow the Fourth already? It can't be!" Allison checks her phone.

"Can we make water balloons and fill the soakers with Marley and Gabriella for the water fight, then go to town with them and then go to the beach with them, then can we watch the fireworks together and make s'mores? Can we, can we, *pleeeaase*?" Abigail spits out all her questions without taking a breath.

Marc comes around the corner in his cargo khaki shorts, flip flops, and worn Cisco brewery T-shirt underneath a white buttoned-down polo with the sleeves cuffed. Tall and built with his blonde-streaked hair growing just a little too long, he is still so hot to her. It's distracting.

"Hey babe, you ready?" He smiles, and it reaches his eyes.

Marc turns to his daughters. "Girls, be good and don't forget to feed Reilly. Your Mom and I will only be gone for about an hour or two. I have my cell, so call if you need us."

Allison watches as Marc tells their girls, "Love you." He leans down and kisses them both on the forehead.

"Oh, and girls, no inappropriate shows!" Allison adds.

"Bye, love you!" They say in unison.

Marc and Allison jump in their old, but restored, green Land Rover with the top off.

She should be feeling nothing but happy and content, but once again, anxiety creeps in. First, she's having nagging regrets about spilling everything to Carla and second, she's nervous about telling Marc because they agreed to wait and tread carefully.

Allison sighs as she realizes the gravity of the situation. If Carla is turned off by their lifestyle, it affects the entire Evans family. Allison's gut told her Carla would be cool about it even if they were not into it for themselves, but only time will tell.

"What's the matter? Is it Kate?" Marc notes Allison's tension.

"Ha," she says wryly. "Oddly enough, it's not Kate. I had a long talk with Carla and really put myself out there. I filled her in on pretty much everything today."

"Oh? Wow," Marc says, taking his eyes of the road for a

moment to look her way. "That was fast."

Hint taken, Allison thinks. She pretends it's all fine. He seems surprised, but not annoyed, so she goes with it.

"How did it go?" He asks.

"It actually went pretty well, I think," she says. "But then I started to get a little freaked out back at the house when the girls started talking about the Fourth and everything they wanted to do with their new best friends, Carla's girls."

Marc shakes his head. "You know, I guess neither one of us really thought it through. We got so caught up in everything. The girls are all having a blast and getting along great with each other. It really would suck if things got tense with the Rossis."

"Marc, you're not helping! That's exactly what I'm worried about." She glares at him, but he keeps his eyes on the road.

The ride is short and they're out of time to continue their conversation. Marc slips the Land Rover into a tight parking spot, but Allison isn't ready to get out and face Kate yet. She feels the pit in her stomach grow.

Her husband pauses.

"You know what, Allison?" He says gently. "I think we need to sit back and take it all in. The Rossis know now, and if they're interested, they'll come to the party. If not, we keep it neighborly. I really believe they're good people. They won't hold it against us, and certainly not against the kids."

God, she loves him. With his support, Allison feels like she can face Kate now.

"You're right," she concedes. Marc gives her a look. "Yes, I said it," she adds wryly. "*You're right*, OK? I love you. Let's go have a drink."

– 43 –
Free Fall

Brooke

Kevin recovers quickly, as he must do at work when he has bad news for clients about their faltering portfolios.

"Brooke," he pleads, inching closer to her on the sofa. She hugs her pillow harder. "You know I love you, right?"

She says nothing.

"We've been through so much lately. I swear to you, I'd never want to hurt you." He reaches for her hand. She whips it away.

"Kevin," she says, "I don't have any patience for your lies. I've heard enough of them over the years: your work dinners, golf commitments, late-night client meetings. It's all bullshit, isn't it?"

That does it. Her husband's eyes widen, his lip quivers, and he leans in toward her.

His façade is collapsing.

"No matter what you think, it's *you* I love. It's always been you, Brooke." He starts to cry. "But yes…I've betrayed you. I fucked up. I fucked up *bad*. And you should hate me. I hate myself."

She is more shocked than she should be; deep down, she wanted to be proven wrong. She wanted to believe she was reading too much into everything.

But no.

She leaps off the couch and heads outside to the expansive deck, gasping for air. She hugs herself and stares at the vast sea. He follows, tries to wrap his arms around her, but she squirms away and faces him, jabbing her finger in his face and saying one word: "No!"

Kevin's breathing slows down and he dares to speak again. "I'm so ashamed. You deserve so much better. I want you to know I've been working on myself, trying to figure out why I do the things I do. I've been seeing a therapist for two years."

"*What?*" Brooke is shocked, and not sure whether to believe him. "What for?"

"I'm a sex addict," he says, facing her, arms at his sides, cheeks glistening with tears.

He lowers his head and sobs, and Brooke reaches a hand out, but can't bring herself to touch him, or console him.

She's done being manipulated.

Brooke can't believe what she's hearing. *A sex addict?* It hits her only now what Jon and Kate were hinting at the whole time.

Brooke knows her husband. Addiction is a disease, nothing to joke about and not to be minimized or mocked, but her husband is a master manipulator. She won't take anything he says at face value.

Is this really happening?

"I need some space," she says, and heads down to the beach, unable to look at him.

Kevin starts to follow her. "Brooke. Brooke! Please! Don't walk away. I need you."

This stops Brooke in her tracks. "Excuse me? You *need* me?" She lets out a harsh laugh. "I can't believe what a selfish bastard you are! Everything is always about you."

Brooke whips around and runs inside once again. But Kevin stays close on her heels; she can't get away from him no matter what she does.

"Kevin, stay back! I don't want to be in the same room as you."

She runs up the stairs, slams the bedroom door, and locks it tight. As she stands with her hand gripping the lock, she realizes how badly she's shaking.

Kevin follows and bangs on the door. "Brooke! Come on, let me in. I'm your husband! We've been through so much. Don't shut me out, don't turn away from me. Please, Brooke. I'm begging you."

As he bangs like a stalker, she wonders how she let this man suck her in years ago. If she's honest with herself, she knows the answer. The same way anyone gets sucked in when a seductive, successful, gorgeous human being targets them. It's that high of knowing she is special, that everyone wanted him, but he wanted *her*. The charm, which she didn't know then was superficial; the success, which she didn't know he was dependent on like a drug; the libido, which she didn't know couldn't be satisfied, ever, by one woman.

The pounding suddenly stops. "I'll never forget the first time I saw you," he says through the wooden door. "It was after a night class. You were this goddess with brilliant aqua blue eyes and a figure that put Marilyn Monroe to shame. You had hair like a princess—long, blonde, wavy, all the way down your back."

Brooke isn't feeling the way she knows he expects her to. His way of wooing her years ago now sounds outdated and sexist. He was always into her hair, and what used to feel like affection— the way he stroked it, smelled it, talked about it—now starts to smack of a fetish or obsession.

"I knew then I was a goner. I knew I'd do anything for you," he goes on earnestly. "I straightened my Brooks Brother's tie and sauntered towards you for an introduction. You agreed to grab coffee with me, and the rest is history."

"I thought you were a gentleman back then," she says quietly.

She thinks she hears a sharp intake of breath. That got to him.

Everything started off so well. Kevin graduated from undergrad with honors and went on to Fordham University for his master's degree in finance. Brooke dreamed of starting a family from the beginning, but Kevin pursued his career in Boston early on, and she agreed to wait as they adjusted.

Kevin was at the top of his game then, and he soared through the ranks at the firm, charming everyone as he went. He was eventually running his own hedge fund, and the money that was coming his way was beyond their wildest dreams as a couple.

Finally, when Kevin agreed to start trying for a baby, Brooke was ready. She did everything right: she charted her menstruation, ovulation, and temperature. She ate clean and took the right supplements. She exercised and greatly reduced her alcohol consumption to barely a glass of wine a week with dinner.

She believed Kevin was finally ready, and truly happy, to finally give her what she'd always wanted.

They'd always had a great sex life, but now it revved up even more.

And then nothing happened.

Brooke knew Kevin was growing impatient after months of trying, and she sensed a change in their relationship the longer they engaged in scheduled, mandatory, passionless, temperature-taking sex. That lasted for two years before they finally decided to seek help for their infertility.

Tests revealed no major problems, though they did discover Kevin's sperm weren't the fastest swimmers. This does not help Kevin's ego, but he took it in stride. The doctor recommended IVF, and they signed up to try it.

At the same time, things were going south at Kevin's job. World events were sending the markets into a tailspin every other day. The million-dollar bonuses the managers were so used to were starting to evaporate.

Brooke knows her husband grew exhausted by the whole thing. Her instinct was always to bounce back and try again. His was to move on, though he never explicitly admitted that to her.

Her dreams were crushed the day she went in for a routine ultrasound after arriving at her appointment high with joy and yet still anxious.

Brooke's heart raced as the doctor's face grew obviously concerned as he moved the wand. Several blood tests and two more ultrasounds later, the doctor broke the news: yes, she was pregnant, but the embryo implanted in the fallopian tube.

Brooke was beside herself. "Why, why, *why*? What does this mean, exactly?"

"It means the embryo didn't remain in your uterus like it

should have," the doctor explained. "If we don't operate immediately, you risk the tube rupturing and that's extremely dangerous. We have to remove it."

Brook stared up at her doctor, speechless.

"Brooke, we have to terminate. Your life is at risk. I truly am sorry. You can try again in a few months."

Brooke was in shock, knowing if she let herself process the news right then she'd lose it. She needed Kevin desperately, but instead of holding her up and supporting her, he unraveled, complaining loudly about the money they'd spent and how he resented the failure of their first attempt at IVF.

On the way home, Brooke cried. Kevin, having calmed down, took her hand and murmured platitudes about how it wasn't over and she just needed some sleep.

– 44 –

Their Happy Place

Kate

Kate emerges from the vodka bar at the brewery and almost slams into Allison.

"Oh, hello! Would you like a blueberry lemonade, darling?" Kate hands Allison one of the drinks she's carrying.

"Absolutely!" Allison grins and accepts it.

They embrace, then make their way over to where Jon is sitting at a table.

As Allison and Jon converge for a cheek-kiss, Kate asks, "Is Marc joining us?"

"He's here," Allison replies lightly. Kate looks for signs of tension or jealousy in her friend's demeanor but sees none. "He wanted to wait in the beer line while I came to find you two."

Kate scans the crowd again, then sees Allison has locked on to her husband. Allison smiles and points, "There he is!"

Marc walks by them three times as Kate, Allison, and Jon call out to him.

"Oh my god, he doesn't see us. What a riot," Jon chuckles.

They're watching him and laughing as he takes a sip of beer, looks around, and takes another. Kate finally yells, "Marcus!" and he whips around.

He saunters over, bobbing his head to the live band playing in the corner.

"Kate, Jon my friend, how are you doing today?" Marc toasts them all, then takes a seat in an empty chair. "Man, it feels good to kick back and relax in one of my favorite places."

It's not lost on Kate that Marc skipped any form of physical greeting with her, which is unusual. *Are there new ground-rules in their marriage?* Kate wonders. If there are, those two better be willing to share with her what's changed. Everyone being on the same page is one of the most important rules of swinging.

"Doesn't it?" Allison smiles and puts a hand on Marc's thigh, which irritates Kate, oddly. Allison adds, "Great idea to meet up here, Kate."

"I figured we haven't had our seasonal brewery kickoff yet with just the four of us," Kate replies. "Summer can't really begin until we do, right Allison?"

"What does *that* mean?" Allison retorts.

Kate decides to jump right into why she called them here.

"Look, Allie," Kate says, "the four of us *work*. We've been a well-oiled machine for a long time now. We understand each other, we have the same rules, and we're all about discretion."

Kate can see Marc and Jon tense up, but so be it. This needs to be aired out before it spirals out of control.

"I don't think your neighbors are a good fit for our group, and I don't think they should come to our party."

"Whoa, whoa, *wait* a minute." Allison holds up a hand like a stop sign. "First of all, *you're* the one who invited them in the first place."

"Be that as it may," Kate says, keeping her voice calm so that Allison looks like the irrational one, "I was being polite after meeting Carla in the street. I didn't realize at that point you were trying to get them into the after-midnight group."

Allison narrows her eyes, and Kate can read her mind.

Kate actually *isn't* sure of the timing of her invitation, but it *was* a spur-of-the moment one. She hadn't realized how close Allison and Marc would grow to the new hot couple in town.

The two men are hiding in their beers, unwilling to get involved, pretending they can't hear the drama going on at the table.

"You and Marc are welcome, of course, but I don't want your neighbors knowing about our lifestyle. Please respect that."

She's calm and cool even as Allison's face reddens. Kate takes a long sip of her refreshing cocktail and adds further insult to Allison's judgement, "You really shouldn't have invited them to your Upside Down party. And I know deep down, you would agree."

– 45 –

For the World to See

Allison

Allison doesn't know how to respond to Kate's brazen attempt to control her. She shouldn't have to explain herself and why she wants her neighbors at their Upside Down parties. No one has been following the rules lately, so, why should she?

"The thing is, Kate," Allison says, gaining control of her temper. "I already told Carla about our lifestyle. So technically I'm not breaking the rules by inviting them. If they're not down with it, they won't come. Nowhere in the rules does it say they need to partake. And who knows, maybe after being exposed and seeing how fun it is, they'll join."

"Wait a minute. Back up. You did *what?*" Kate leans forward, her eyes flashing with anger.

Allison knows her friend hates not being the one in control. She stands her ground.

"I told Carla all about it," Allison replies.

"That was not smart." Kate says it flatly, as if that ends the argument.

"Oh? How is this any different than when you told me about

214

swinging last summer when we were growing closer?" Allison shoots back.

Marc says quietly to Jon, "How about you and I get back in the beer line for another round?"

"Lead the way," Jon replies, and off they go.

Kate doesn't skip a beat. "Allison, you're crazy for moving so fast with them. If the shit hits the fan, you live right next door. Aren't your kids becoming friend? You know how things can get complicated."

"Yeah, like it's getting complicated with us," Allison says with more disappointment than anger now. "I don't know what's gotten into you, but you've been acting really strange lately. What did you mean the other night when you told Marc to 'Tell me, tell me'?"

It doesn't happen often, but Kate is speechless.

She soon recovers.

"I don't know what you're talking about, Allie," Kate says finally. "Don't try to change the subject. I'm hosting the next party and I don't want your damn neighbors there. You can invite them to your own parties if you must."

"Come on, Kate," Allison says, trying to ratchet things down a bit. "What's this really about? What's going on with you?"

For a minute, it looks like Kate might let her guard down and share what's driving her behavior lately, but as she opens her mouth to speak, the men return with their draft beers.

Allison knows their husbands can feel the tension that's thick as fog, dampening their sunny afternoon at the brewery. She says to Kate, "I'm almost ready for another blueberry lemonade. Want to hit the bar?"

Kate nods and the two women leave Marc and Jon to their beers and their people watching.

They make it to the bar and as they wait in the line, Kate touches Allison lightly on the upper arm.

"Allie, I'm sorry I've been so bitchy lately." Kate abruptly launches into an apology, and Allison is shocked by the sudden turnaround. "I think I'm just jealous of your crush on the neighbors. I don't do well with jealousy."

Allison melts instantly, remembering their closeness before things got weird. "I'm sorry too," she says. "I guess this summer just threw me some curveballs. I want us to be friends again. I mean good friends. Real friends."

They talk it out in line, end the conversation with a hug, and make their way back to Marc and Jon, drinks in hand. Before they reach their table, they hit a relatively quiet spot and Allison stops.

"Kate," she says. "You're friends with those renters, right? Brooke and her husband…"

"Kevin. Yes," Kate replies, pursing her lips before taking a sip of her drink through a straw. "He's one of Jon's asset managers. You haven't met them yet, I thought?"

"Just briefly when I dropped the guys off for golf," Allison replies. "Where are they from?"

"Boston," Kate says.

"Ah," Allison nods. "But he doesn't have any sort of Massachusetts or Boston accent. They must have come from somewhere else originally?"

Too many questions. Kate raises her eyebrows. "Why do you ask?"

"Oh, no reason." Allison says, starting to walk again. "He reminds me of someone I once knew, is all. She seems super nice."

The band strikes up a beach favorite, *Toes*. As they approach, Jon scoops up Kate and Marc takes Allie's hand, and the four of them twist and twirl toward the band.

Before long they're all taking turns dancing with each other and it's like nothing ever happened.

When it's time to go home and fix dinner, Marc gives Allison a boost up into the old Land Rover's passenger seat. She's feeling good again after clearing the air with Kate.

What a strange summer it's been, and it's only just begun. It's almost the Fourth of July, one of Allison's favorite days of the year and in her mind the official kickoff to summer on the island.

"I say we do the usual this year," she says as Marc drives towards the market to pick up some fish and steaks. "But should we include the Rossis? I'm sure Carla would love to run the Firecracker 5K road race. The girls have already asked if their new friends can come to town with us for the parade and water fight."

Marc sucks air through his teeth. "I do want to include them," he says. "It would be the neighborly thing to do, but I'm hesitant after you spilled your guts to Carla on the beach. Do you think we should put a little distance between us for a bit until that blows over?"

"What is there to blow over?" Allison is confused why Marc is being so reticent and, frankly, a bit cowardly. "She was totally cool about it. She had a ton of questions, almost like she was considering joining. I mean, I'm sure she was surprised, yes, but she didn't seem horrified or upset or anything."

The conversation ends when they arrive at the market, and they move on for the rest of the ride home without coming to any conclusions. They pull into their driveway and Allison steps out of the SUV to see what the girls are up to.

– 46 –
Sunset Grill

Carla

Carla and Lawrence load up the Range Rover to do some beach grilling at 40th Pole, arguably the best place on the island to watch the sun go down. Lawerence loads the cooler in last.

"Girls, we're ready. Let's go, your dad and Will are already in the car!" Carla shouts.

The girls bound out of the house, sweatshirts and sunglasses on.

Once on the road, Lawrence steals a glance over his shoulder to check on the kids. Will's eyes are at half-mast.

"Will, you alright buddy?"

"Yeah, Dad, I'm just beat."

Carla looks back. Her eldest doesn't look well. She makes a mental note to check in on him the next time they're alone.

Lawrence speeds up and takes the shortcut on Millbrook. The car is like a roller coaster over the dips and bumps. The kids whoop, but Carla's nauseated.

"Lawrence, go easy, you're making me car sick," she complains as he floors it over a big dip in the winding dirt road, jolting the Rover off the ground.

"You got it, honey," he grins. "Kids, you heard your Mom. I do not want any smiling, I do not want any laughing, and I definitely do not want to see anyone having fun!"

Lawrence grabs Carla's hand and squeezes it tight, and she smiles back.

As they fly past Dionis beach toward the 40th pole, Carla thinks about her conversation with Allison. She's conflicted. She can't imagine Lawrence being into it, nor can she imagine sharing him with anyone else. God, she loves him.

Things are also already on the upswing in their marriage without dipping a toe into a wild new lifestyle. Their sex life has been picking up lately, though it's occurred to her this is partly due to external factors like Lawrence seeing Marc fooling around with Kate and Allison, and, on Carla's part, the baseball coach who was turning her on for months before their illicit encounter.

The sex she and Lawrence had after that was next level, but how far did she want to take it? Watching? Threesomes? Even further?

Lawrence finds a perfect parking spot, and they all climb out.

The orange sun is hanging low in the sky with nothing but endless sea beneath it.

The girls make their way down the beach, their silhouettes dancing behind them as they run towards the sun. Carla sighs as she sits in her beach chair, warm and cozy in her sweats and black Versace shades. She takes a deep breath and watches the girls collecting shells while Will is glued to his phone.

"Look at our well-behaved kids," Carla says. "Why can't they be like this at home?"

Lawrence lets out a little laugh. "I know, right? Nah, they're good kids. We're lucky. I think they like it here. It's going to be great for us to keep coming back here anytime we want."

He hands her a glass of wine and she raises it. "To us."

"To us," he says, and leans in for a kiss.

They bask in the early evening sun, enjoying the last rays of the day.

"Look," Lawrence points. "There's the full moon."

"It's going to be a stargazing night," Carla observes.

Lawrence rises from his chair and lights up the grill. His favorite grilled corn takes a good twenty minutes. With the setting sun over the ocean as their backdrop, Carla sets everything up as they get ready for their dinner.

"I'll walk down and get the kids," offers Carla.

"The corn needs another a few minutes. Let's sit."

She holds out her wine glass and he refills it.

"So, are you going to tell me about your walk with Allison?" He finally asks. She'd been waiting.

"I have no idea what to even say."

"What do you mean?" Lawrence asks.

"I don't know, it's so shocking," Carla shakes her head. "I mean, I've heard rumors about people in town before, but this is next level stuff. I'm not sure you can handle it." She's half kidding.

"You might be surprised at what I can handle." Her husband is suddenly grinning like a schoolboy. "Let me guess: They're swingers, right?"

Carla's jaw drops as she tries to process that not only did her husband seem to already know about their lifestyle, but seems perfectly comfortable with it.

– 47 –
Screwed

Brooke

Brooke hears Kevin slump against the door, then hears his cheek slap on the slick painted wood.

"Brooke, please open the door," he cries. "I have so much I want to say to you."

"Screw you, Kevin. I can play games too, you know."

"*Broooke*," he moans. "I don't want to play games. I want to see your face. I just want to talk. Open up."

"No. Please, just go." She pauses. "Or I'll call Kate and Jon. They'll take care of me."

"What the hell does that mean?" Kevin snaps, his mood pivoting on a dime. "I'm the one who is supposed to take care of you. I'm your husband."

"You've been doing a shitty job of that though, haven't you?" Brooke feels a deep-seated bitterness crawling out of hiding. "Kate and Jon have done more for me in the last six hours than you've done in the past three years."

"And exactly what have good ol' Jon and Kate done for you?" Kevin's no longer imploring. He's turning angry again, and

Brooke knew it was coming, thus the locked door. "Open the goddamn door, Brooke. I'm not having this conversation with you from the hallway."

"Oh yes you are, Kevin. You're not calling the shots anymore. How does it feel?"

He's silent for a few moments, which makes her nervous, and when he speaks again, he's somewhere between tired and cruel.

"You're not the only one who can complain about our relationship," he says. "We've done it once since we got here, Brooke. *One time.* Every other time we've had sex for years now was about baby-making. It's vanilla. It's clinical. It's not what I signed up for. What did you expect?"

"I was just scraped out with a scalpel," she replies icily. "I thought it was finally my turn, but I got the worst news of my life. You think I should be begging for it days later? That's cold, Kevin. Ice cold."

She's past losing her cool with this man. She hopes so, anyway.

She can hear him pacing in the hallway. Brooke knows she triggered him by mentioning Jon and Kate; Kevin will hate that his work life is now mixing with his personal life.

"Brooke!" She says nothing, but he persists. "What the hell were you doing with Jon and Kate all day anyway?"

"It's none of your business!"

"The hell it isn't my business! Tell me right now, Brooke, or so help me God…"

"So help you, what? That sounds suspiciously like a threat, Kevin."

She can hear him sigh, then he snarls, "You want to talk about unacceptable behavior? You went crying to my biggest client about our personal problems."

Brooke flinches, even though she should be used to his shifting moods and demeanor, that charm he turns on and off like a faucet.

Kevin's voice is filled with rage again. "If you want to keep living this life, you better think a lot harder about who you badmouth me to. Do you know how unprofessional this looks? Do you know you've put my biggest client, and therefore my position at the firm and your credit cards, in danger?"

"That's just it," she says, ignoring the talk of money. "Right now, there's very little about this life I care to keep."

She hears him pacing.

"Fine, you wanna know, Kevin?" She asks. "You really wanna know?"

Brooke cracks the door open. "I was hooking up with them in their pool. Both of them. *That's* what I was doing with them, OK? Now, kindly go fuck yourself and leave me alone."

She slams the door in his face and locks it.

Kevin exhales and collapses again. Brooke hears everything, can tell he's sinking to the floor; she pictures him leaning against the wall like a rag doll.

"I don't even know how to respond to what you just said, Brooke. I am in disbelief. There is just no way. But I meant it about the therapy," he croaks. "I know I need it. I'm a sex addict. I try so hard, but I can't seem to stop myself. No matter how much I love you, this thing inside me won't let me go."

Brooke starts to tear up, then to cry, because this whole thing is such a rotten mess. He's taken her righteous anger and, once again, made it about him. He took away her right to be angry and to call him out on his shit.

"Brooke, please open the door. I love you. I need you, please."

Brooke takes a deep breath. Her head is throbbing, her mind racing. She blows into a tissue as quietly as she can.

"As far as I'm concerned, calling yourself a sex addict is just an excuse for bad behavior," she says.

"Actually no, it's a result of PTSD. You of all people know about Post Traumatic Stress Disorder."

"Yeah, I know what PTSD is, Kevin." She responds, then gentler, "I'm a social worker. Why didn't you come to me with this sooner? How long has it been going on?"

"Baby, I know you have a lot of questions, and I'm going to answer them."

"I have a right to know everything. And I mean *everything*."

"I know," he says. "Will you open the door, please?"

She cracks it open, checks his posture, and decides it's safe— for now.

He tries to kiss her but Brooke recoils. "You need to get help. Real help," she says.

"I know, I know. Baby…will you come with me to see my therapist? Would you do this for me?" He pauses, then ads, "I know I don't deserve it, deserve you. But if you would just hear me out."

"First I need to know if you're serious about getting real help," Brooke replies. "Do you think you can change in treatment?"

"I *am* in treatment."

"No, you're in denial, or at least you were. You need rehabilitation."

"*Rehab*?" He moves away in the hallway and is pacing again.

"What the hell are you talking about, Brooke? I'll stop. I can do it."

"Kevin, if you want me to go down this road with you, I'll seriously consider it. For us, and for our marriage. But only if you commit to getting the necessary treatment."

She's met with silence. But then, he comes towards her, nodding as he does, tears glistening in his eyes. He reaches out, and she allows him to hug her.

They both cry together.

Once Brooke has calmed and no longer gasps for air between sobs, Kevin carries her over to their suite and lays her on the bed. He gets in beside her, and they hold each other until they both fall asleep.

Awkward

Carla

Carla is curling her toes at the tension she's feeling. She shouldn't be too surprised that Lawrence made the leap from seeing the neighbors fooling around on the deck to assuming they enjoyed a full swinger lifestyle, but the gleam in his eye has thrown her.

As Lawrence pulls onto the dirt road on their way home from grilling on the beach, Carla thinks about how they're possibly going to act normal around the neighbors. Will Allison be sizing Lawrence up? Is Marc lusting over Carla, and will Lawrence freak out if he thinks Marc is fantasizing about his wife?

Lawrence parks in their driveway, winks at her, and hops out. The neighbors are in their yard, and Carla follows as Lawrence walks around the hedge, casual and confident as ever, and greets Marc, who sets down some hotdogs he was unwrapping to shake Lawrence's outstretched hand.

"Hey, man." Lawrence smiles.

"Hey, how was your night?" Marc asks, waving to Carla.

"Great," Lawrence replies. "We did some beach grilling and

watched the sunset at the 40th pole. The Land Rover had no issues driving over the dunes. Can't say the same about Carla."

"Very funny Lawrence," Carla interjects as she gives her husband a light punch on the arm.

So far, so neighborly, Carla thinks as she let's out a sigh of relief.

"It was spectacular tonight," Marc grins. "We saw it from the brewery." He picks up the meat again. "Hey, I've got to cook these girls some hot dogs. Do you want to come over and keep me company?"

Lawrence hesitates, and Carla braces for his answer. Finally he replies, "Uh…I need to unload the truck."

"Good," Marc says. "Unload, then stop over with Carla. I'm sure your girls will still be here."

Lawrence laughs when he sees his girls running around the Evans backyard, and he's hoping the neighborly chit-chat will dash the underlying awkwardness. "Fair enough. We'll come by and collect them in an hour."

"Great. See you then." Marc gets to grilling.

Lawrence and Carla head back to the car and unload wordlessly.

Once they're done and inside together, Carla, leaning against the island and nibbling at a hangnail, observes her husband. He grabs a beer from the fridge and seems to sense her looking at him.

"Well," he smiles, "that was a little awkward."

"It was, wasn't it?" Carla agrees. "You both seemed quite cool at first, but…"

"I know," Lawrence shrugs. "Marc must know his wife

propositioned you earlier today. I'm a little surprised at how well Marc acted like nothing happened."

"We should take their lead, I guess," Carla says. "We can always pretend it didn't happen and never speak of it again."

"I'm thinking seriously about that," Lawrence agrees. "But…"

"Aha!" Carla perks up. "But *what*? Are we seriously thinking we could try something like this?"

Lawrence pauses to take a long sip of beer. After he swallows, he says, "Nah. Let's forget this ever happened."

Carla knows her husband, and his delivery does not convince her. He's intrigued, and she knows it, and it's making her doubt everything she ever knew about him.

– 49 –

Family First

Carla

It's dark by the time Carla and Lawrence head to their neighbor's house to fetch their girls. As they approach, they smell a roaring fire. When they round the tall, lush hedges and into the yard, Carla's heart melts at the sight of their two girls with the Evans family sitting around the fire pit, roasting marshmallows at the end of long skewers.

She decides to keep things strictly friendly with Allison and Marc.

"Mom! Dad! Grab some sticks and get roasting," Savannah, a smudge of marshmallow on the corner of her mouth, calls out. "Mrs. Evans has the best chocolate for her s'mores. And a secret ingredient, peanut butter. I've already had two. But this is my last one."

Allison lights up and walks towards Carla and Lawrence. "Hey, you two! Sounds like you had a wonderful night at the 40th pole."

"It was spectacular," Carla smiles.

Lawrence walks over to Savannah and joins in the toasting.

"Wanna come inside for a minute while I get you two a drink?"

Carla nods and follows. When they make it to the kitchen, she asks, "How did it go with Kate at the brewery? Were you able to kiss and make up?"

"Actually, we did," Allison smiles, opening the freezer and grabbing a bag of ice. "Thanks for your advice."

After a long pause, Allison continues, "Listen, Carla, I feel a little weird that I unloaded all of that personal stuff on you at the beach earlier today. I…"

"It's fine," Carla smiles. "I've done a little thinking, and I've talked with Lawrence. I think maybe we should just pretend that never came up."

"I was just going to say the same thing!" Allison looks wildly relieved.

"Really?"

"Yes, really," Allison laughs. "I can't believe how much I told you. I feel like an idiot. It was way too forward of me. I was so upset with the way things were going with Kate, and you've become such a great friend, so I felt like I could share with you. But after we talked, I realized it was inappropriate."

"No," Carla shakes her head. "It was fine, I promise. So we're not on the same page with that. No big deal, right? We've enjoyed hanging out with all of you and we don't want to jeopardize anything."

"We feel the same way," Allison sighs. "So we can just pretend the whole conversation never happened?"

Carla reaches out to give her a reassuring hug. "Absolutely. I think that's a wonderful idea."

As they are in mid-embrace Marc walks in. "Hey, we need two ice-cold Cisco brews out there. If you can bring those, I'll grab some blankets for the kids. They're getting chilly."

Redefining

Allison

The four adults have drinks in hand, and instead of using the blankets Marc brought outside, the girls have gone inside to watch a movie.

Marc eases into a chair by the fire after the girls scamper inside. "Man, what a gorgeous night."

Allison notes the pause that follows and thinks the guys might not have as easy a time as the women moving on from the swinging revelations.

Marc finally asks, "What are you guys doing for the Fourth?"

"Not a lot," Lawrence replies. "We talked about heading into town. We heard about the water fight from the girls. Sounds like fun."

"The kids will love it," Marc confirms. "We need to get them loaded up with balloons and soakers beforehand. We'll show you how it's done."

Another quiet pause.

"We usually grill and do the traditional lobstahs and steamahs," Marc adds with his full Boston accent. "Then we sit at the fire pit from sunset on, if you'd like to join."

"We'd love to," Carla pipes up. "Well, four of us, anyway. I'm pretty sure Will is heading to some beach party."

"Uh oh," Marc warns. "You might want to remind him that the ferry brings over a boatload of state troopers to help the Nantucket cops patrol the crowded beaches over the Fourth. I can't tell you how many calls I get from stressed-out parents about their child being arrested and arraigned in Nantucket District Court."

"Thanks for the heads up," Lawrence replies. "Glad we have a lawyer next door. Will has a good head on his shoulders. I'm sure he'll be fine."

"Famous last words," Marc says under his breath.

Lawrence laughs and Allison notes he still doesn't seem fully relaxed.

Allison feels a sudden chill, so she reaches for one of the blankets and wraps it around her. She leans back in her chair and looks up towards the crisp, deep, dark sky. Suddenly she shouts out, "Oh! A shooting star!"

"Make a wish," Marc says.

Allison, now feeling the warmth from the plush fleece blanket sinks further into her chair. She closes her eyes and makes her wish. When she's done, her eyes pop open and they land on her husband. Their eyes lock and she can tell he is starting to melt under her gaze. She loves when she makes him melt; it doesn't seem to happen as often as it used to, but maybe that makes it more special, she tells herself.

Carla and Lawrence are holding hands across their chairs now, and despite her promises to Carla in the kitchen, Allison can't shake the feeling there's a smoldering chemistry between the four of them.

She shoots a look towards Carla and sees she's turned her eyes on Marc for longer than a moment. Allison isn't sure this issue has truly been put to bed, so to speak.

– 51 –

Divisive Daydreams

Kate

After leaving the brewery and saying goodbye to Allison and Marc, Kate and Jon head to Lola's Bar. For regular people, it's nearly impossible to get a seat without reservations. Not for Jon and Kate.

They're immediately escorted to the outdoor oasis, lit with propane-fired lamps for warmth and ambiance. They relax over sushi and seaweed martinis, and Kate is feeling particularly satisfied about clearing the air with Allison.

Jealousy does not suit her, she decides. It turns her evil, and she knows it. Not only that, she loathes the feeling. It reminds her of her insecurities all over again back when she found out her ex-husband was cheating on her all those years ago. Kate damn near killed him for it, and that same rage seems to resurface whenever she feels a loss of control which happens when she begins to care too much about someone.

Thankfully, the meeting at the brewery worked like a charm. Not only did she patch things up with Allison, but she also made headway with convincing her to *not* add Carla and Lawrence to their group.

Still….

Kate has a nagging feeling Allison and Marc aren't quite over their new neighbors in the way Allison claimed. A couple this hot is always going to be trouble, and Kate can see her friends' attraction to the Rossis.

"Jon," she asks, holding two chopsticks over a loaded piece of sushi, "what should we do about our party at the end of the month? It will be here before you know it!"

She picks up a piece and pops it in her mouth.

"What do you mean?" Jon asks.

When she's done chewing, Kate explains, "I mean, should we just make it a big bash and include everyone on our extended list? Then we could send a note to the upside-down pineapples about our midnight rule."

"I guess so," Jon shrugs. "Whatever you want to do, babe. Just find a way to get Brooke there."

"Oh, really?" Kate saw this coming, but it's interesting he's being so blatant about his strong attraction to the blonde. "You enjoyed our afternoon with her, didn't you?"

He appears to take this as a rhetorical question. Kate continues thinking aloud. "Only problem is, they're a bit of a mess. Why don't you text Kevin and see what the hell is going on with them?"

Jon raises an eyebrow and Kate continues. "You know I feed off drama, but the Doyles seem to be a ticking time bomb. Do we really want to be in the middle of that?"

"When has that ever stopped you before, Kate?"

She rolls her eyes.

"OK, OK," Jon relents. "I'll text him now."

While Jon taps away at his phone, Kate daydreams about the

possibilities for their party. She runs through her mental list of guests and which ones she wants to extend the after-midnight invite.

Kate's thoughts are interrupted by Jon's concerned voice. "Uh oh. It appears the shit's hit the fan with Kevin and Brooke."

He looks up at her. "He told Brooke everything. And so did she."

Kate covers her mouth. "*What?* You don't think she told him about the three of us in our pool, do you?"

Jon gives her a knowing look. "What else would he mean?"

"Did you respond? Is he pissed? Or... I mean...maybe he'd be happy?"

Kate, so relaxed a few minutes before, is now re-frazzled. Those out-of-control feelings are powerful and resilient.

"I have no idea," Jon shrugs. "There's one way to find out. Why don't we ask if they want to meet us in town after the parade for a Fourth of July brunch?"

"Shit, Jon." Kate tosses back the rest of her martini. "Do you really think that's a good idea?"

"You have a better one?"

Kate sighs. "No. I'll book my special table at Cru for the four of us."

Kate removes the olive from her glass and pulls it off the stirrer with her lips. She thinks about how this meeting with the Doyles could be exciting—or an unmitigated disaster.

– 52 –

Contentment

Allison

The Rossis are gone, and the girls are sound asleep before 11:00 p.m. Allison has a slight buzz leftover from the night and is happily snuggled up in bed with Marc. They ended the night on the earlier side because tomorrow will be a hectic day of getting ready for the big holiday.

"What a long day," Allison says. "But you know what? I actually feel good about how everything worked out. Kate apologized at the brewery for being out of sorts, and I cleared the air with Carla about how we didn't want to make them feel weird about our lifestyle."

Marc nods, seeming at peace with all of it as well. "Did Kate say why she's been acting so snippy?"

"Not exactly," Allison admits. "The main thing is she apologized, and we agreed it's all in the past. I think she was jealous of the Rossis."

Marc tries to appear supportive, but Allison can tell he's slightly dubious. She changes the subject. "Carla told me in the nicest way they're not interested."

"Really? I'm a little surprised," Marc admits. "I don't know about you, but I felt some vibes tonight. Are you okay with that?"

"Actually, I am," Allison says, almost believing it. "I'm relieved. I don't know what I was thinking moving in on them like that. I adore them, you know? But I've realized I can adore them without crossing any lines."

"That's great," Marc says. "All's well that ends well."

"Now I don't have to hide it," Allison goes on. "It's nice to be open and honest about it and have a friend to talk to who won't judge me. It couldn't have worked out better. Oh! And Carla is going to run the 5K race with me tomorrow."

She nestles into Marc's shoulder and he kisses the top of her head. "Sounds like a good plan," he says. "You know…maybe we should think about skipping the next Pineapple Express, he makes himself laugh out loud. Take a break from the drama."

"What?" Allison doesn't want to go that far. "We could also leave early, tell everyone that you have to get back to work on your case."

"That's a thought. But really, we can miss *one* party Allison.

"True, as long as we don't miss Kate and Jon's, right?" She looks at Marc and holds her breath.

"That is the one I am most afraid of," Marc replies.

"No, we aren't missing that one, that was the best party of the summer last year. I mean, Marc, come on—this is one of the most exclusive events on Nantucket's social calendar. Kate throws better parties than anyone I know. What if we go, but agree not to hook up with anyone?"

She can feel Marc shaking his head. "I think we need a lower profile, Allie. We don't need our island lifestyle following us home."

Allison sits up and leans against the headboard.

"Don't get mad," he says carefully. "But if I'm honest, I was nervous after you spoke with Carla. I know you needed to confide in someone, especially since you and Kate had your falling out, but we have to remember, that's how rumors spread."

"I wouldn't say we had a falling out," Allison counters. "Just some jealousy accompanied with her lust for you—*my* husband. When we started this, it was about us enhancing and experimenting. I didn't expect her to be so possessive of us."

"I don't think she expected us to be recruiting our new neighbors." Marc sits up too, and takes Allison's hand. "If only the older couple we saw touring the place had moved in, and not the hot one. Speaking of which, you think Carla and Lawrence are definitely out?"

"I do, and it's probably for the best."

"If you say so, but I saw you watching Carla checking me out tonight," he says with a cheeky grin.

"Oh?" Allison raises one eyebrow. "Maybe. But don't get a big head about it."

"And I think you have more of an effect on Lawrence than you know," he adds, ignoring her good-natured jab.

"What? No way." Allison has been so focused on not letting Marc see how attractive she finds Lawrence, that she hasn't paid as much attention to Lawrence's interest in *her*.

"Honey, he's a hot-blooded man with desires, and baby, you *are* desirable."

Allison rolls her eyes.

"You know it's true."

"Do I? Tell me more."

Allison, suddenly aggressive, rolls over and straddles him.

"I said *tell me*, like Kate makes you tell her!" Allison pulls his shirt up and bites his chest, then runs her tongue down his tight core. She yanks his boxers down. Marc is shocked and hesitates.

"Now!" She releases him as he quickly hardens under her demanding tongue. Marc looks down at her and relents.

"Allison, it is you and only you," he gasps. "You are so much sexier than Kate."

She whips off her negligée, then lurches back onto his naked and bronzed body. She looks him up and down, admiring his taut muscles.

The silence is cut with further demands. "Tell me, Marcus!"

Marc ravages her, grabbing her wrists and twisting them behind her back as she gasps with surprise and pleasure. He leans his strong broad shoulders down into her breasts and inhales the nape of her long neck.

She gasps again, this time softer, "Tell me."

After, when they're lying back on their pillows, Marc whispers in her ear, "You are the hottest, sexiest woman I have ever seen. I have never felt anything for anyone but you."

– 53 –
Restless Determination

Brooke

After a long, restless night of dealing with Kevin and his issues, Brooke is finally free of his grasp. She enters the bathroom and draws a hot bath, adding some sea salt and bubble bath from the Jacuzzi deck that the owners had left for their guests.

Brooke lets out a long breath, thankful for simple pleasures. Catching herself in the mirror, she frowns at her reflection, at her swollen eyes and dark circles. She heads to the kitchen for an ice pack and some green tea.

She manages to make it back to her oversized tub before it overflows, and quickly turns it off before locking the bathroom door. Brooke sinks into the hot, lavender-scented bath. She rests her weary head on the bath pillow, placing a wet cloth over her eyes along with some ice. She breathes deep; her mind is numb from the last twenty-four hours.

Of course she knew something was off with her marriage. She thought *maybe* it was another woman, but a sex addiction? She's angry and if she's honest with herself she's disgusted, but she also feels bad for Kevin and worries about him and his PTSD. Brooke reels off the rehabs in her mind that would be a good fit for him. She is unsure if Dr. Brown knows the depths of Kevin's problems. Brooke heard the doctor speak at a convention and knows of his excellent reputation, but does he know her husband is a sex addict?

Then the fury sets in. *What are you doing, Brooke? Do what you're always telling clients to do—break the pattern! You're not his mommy, you're his wife, and you've been treated horrendously.*

She sinks down into the bathwater and submerges herself.

Why? Why did he have to choose *her* all those years ago? What has she done to deserve this? Did she do something in a previous life? Reality seeps in, and she knows she cannot fix this. She cannot fix him. He needs to do it, not her.

She bursts out of the water and rubs her eyes.

She'll point him in the right direction, but he's going to have to do the work and if he doesn't, there is no marriage. She's not sure there's one regardless. She is profoundly and suddenly grateful there is no baby. A child would have complicated matters so much more. As Brooke breathes in the lavender scent floating through the room, she remembers that she has a core belief that everything happens for a reason.

Brooke decides it's time to focus on herself for a change. She knows as a social worker that the success rate for treating addiction is low, and she refuses to be a head-in-the-sand enabler. Unless Kevin goes away for inpatient treatment, there's no way he's going to be able to manage his addiction. And even then…

Using sex to alleviate stress and pain only leads to more shame and guilt. Brooke is not giving in to this. She will only consider standing by him if he does it right.

She sheds yesterday's worries in the tub and leaves them there; she emerges with unwavering determination and dries off. She decides to use the matching lavender lotion perched prettily by the owners.

As she begins to rub the lotion onto her skin, the tantalizing smell brings back the memory of her, Jon, and Kate together in the pool, and she thinks for a moment what it would be like to be done with Kevin once and for all.

– 54 –

Searenity

Carla

After some early morning surfing, Lawrence heads up the beach path, and Carla watches him from the front yard, where she and the girls have been practicing for the big water fight.

She's been up for hours, having joined Allison in the 5K early that morning. She's full of energy and thoroughly proud of herself for getting out of bed to run the road race. Sure, she nearly vomited in the field by the finish line, but she kept pace with Allison for most of the route.

"How was it?" Carla asks her husband, leaning in for a kiss. His lips are cold, wet, salty.

"Heavenly," he says. "It's so serene around here, don't you think?" He's gazing at the house with laser focus. "What should we name her?" He switches gears. "People around here like to name their houses. I was thinking as I walked up the path we should do that, too; what about Searenity, but spelled S-E-A?"

"I never thought about naming it," Carla replies. "But that's a nice play on words. I like it."

"Dad! Check it out!" Gabriella races into view and whips a water balloon at his board.

"Whoa!" Lawrence ducks behind the board and makes his way over towards the cooler full of water balloons.

Lawrence grabs two balloons and runs in the other direction, Gabriella and Marley tearing after him. As the girls squeal through the yard, he turns and lands both balloons. The girls have their soakers and shoot back, their aim precise.

Carla watches from a safe distance, loving how her family is able to have so much fun together, even with Gabriella entering her too-cool-for-school teen years.

"Not fair, he already has his suit on!" Marley yells.

Lawrence grins. "You have to get up pretty early to pull one over your dear old dad."

"Hey!" Marc shouts from over the fence, "I see the girls have shown you what we're up against today in town."

"This is awesome." Lawrence laughs. "We've never been to the water fight, but it looks like we're fully prepared, thanks to you."

Carla waves to Marc. "I think I'm going to stay out of it," she laughs.

"We're old pros at the Fourth of July water fight," Marc says, then, to Lawrence, "You may want to leave your suit on. We plan to leave soon so we can get a good spot. The girls like to wander around and get their faces painted before the fight begins."

"We can be ready to leave in twenty minutes." Lawrence glances down at his watch. "How about we meet at Murrays in an hour?"

"Perfect."

Carla walks toward the house and shouts, "Let's go, girls! We want to find parking and get a good spot for the parade."

She bounds into the kitchen and grabs a bag, throwing in a tube of sunscreen, and as she does, it occurs to her the reason she kept up with Allison during the race was that her friend purposely slowed down for her.

Ah hell, either way it doesn't matter, she thinks. She ran her butt off. For the first time, Carla feels like the running is getting her in shape.

All Carla knows right now is that when she is with Allison and Marc, she feels young and wild and free.

She grabs bags and towels and calls to her scattered family: "Let's go!"

For once, everyone converges without prodding, piles into the car, and they're off. Once they're closer to town, Lawrence carefully maneuvers the car through narrow streets packed with strollers and kids decked out in red, white, and blue, adults dressed ready for the water fight, various dogs, and other vehicles trying to do the same thing they are.

"We have time," Carla assures Lawrence, who's growing tense. They still have thirty minutes to meet the Evans in front of Murrays.

They reach the bottom of Main Street with no sign of an open spot. "Why don't I drop you and the kids off here and go find parking?" Lawrence suggests. "You can take the cooler with the water balloons and soakers in case I have to park far away."

"That's probably our best option," Carla replies. "Girls, hop out and help me with the cooler."

They unload, and off he drives. She knows he'll meet up with them eventually, even if he does park halfway back towards Cisco. At least he'll be doing all the walking. Man, her legs are tired from the race.

– 55 –

Anxiously Disillusioned

Brooke

Brooke finds Kevin in the kitchen with its multi-million-dollar view that she barely registers right now. He appears to be going through the motions of a breakfast of coffee and dry toast.

She feels her blood pressure spike looking at this man who's let her down so many times. She wishes she could forget about all of it for today; it's a holiday, and she agreed to go to brunch with Kate and Jon at a trendy restaurant.

Brooke had been too emotional to see straight when Kate's invitation had come in via text, and Brooke had reflexively said yes because she gets the sense you don't say no to Kate Gibson. Now she's not sure she can put on her game face, especially with her heightened feelings about her husband just now.

Kevin is freshly showered, sitting in his towel at the counter staring out at the ocean, looking catatonic.

"Happy Fourth of July," Brooke says sarcastically. She leans against the counter, blocking his view, and zeroes in on him.

He holds her gaze. "I don't know what to say, Brooke," he

croaks. "I've been in therapy with Dr. Brown for years and it's done nothing. God knows, I want to stop. I've even gone to Mass to pray for the urge to go away. I don't know what's wrong with me. When things get hard with us…"

"Uh uh," Brooke says, shaking her head. "This isn't *your* pity party. It was mine, remember? You're the one who brought us here to reconnect and get over what you like to call 'our' loss. Well, guess what? The party's over and you have some decisions to make right here, right now."

She can see Kevin's mind working. She swears she sees a twinkle in his eye emerge out of nowhere; he's going to try to charm his way out of this, the way he's always done with everyone in his life.

"Do not give me that look, Kevin Doyle," she orders. "It's not going to work. It's time to deal with this. If you decide not to get the proper help, we have no marriage. But if you do, it will be on my terms. Then, and only then, we can talk about staying together."

"So…what are the terms?" Kevin hangs his head.

Brooke responds without missing a beat. "You enter an inpatient treatment program."

"*What?* You know I can't do that. I have to work. Who's going to pay—"

"We can talk with Dr. Brown today and decide what's—"

"It's the Fourth of July, Brooke. He's not—"

Brooke interrupts one last time, her voice loud and final. "This is a crisis. Surely you have his cell. We'll talk to him today and make arrangements."

"What arrangements?" Kevin raises his voice.

"Hey. You don't have to," Brooke shrugs. "But it's this or I'm done."

Kevin crosses his arms over his bare chest and storms out of the room.

"That is just great, Kev, run away like you always do!"

"I'm getting my fucking phone and some damn clothes!"

Brooke follows quietly at a distance. She hears the rattle of a shaking pill bottle and wonders if it's something his doctor prescribed. She makes it to the landing and watches two pills tumble out onto his palm. He swallows them before she can check the label, and when she does, she's alarmed. He's taking benzos. Downers.

"Kevin, that's enough to knock you out," she says. "How long have you been taking these? That's too much to start with today. What are you doing?"

He exits the bathroom and heads to the closet, pulling on his red, white and blue rugby jersey and a pair of faded blue Vineyard Vines cargo shorts. He throws his phone into his pocket.

"I'll be fine," he says when he's dressed. "The doc gave them to me for times like these when the stress is overwhelming."

He reaches in his side pocket, holds up his phone, and shows Brooke the number on the screen for Dr. Lewis Brown. Kevin reluctantly makes the call and puts the phone on speaker.

Hello. You have reached Dr. Lewis Brown. If you are in crisis, please leave a message here and proceed to your local mental health facility. Beep.

"Lewis, it's Kevin. Would you call me ASAP? Thanks." Kevin ends the call.

"OK, done," he says to Brooke. "Can we go into town and walk around? Maybe get a bloody mary?"

Kevin tries to read her eyes, and Brooke throws him a bone. "I'm proud of you," she says. "That was a first step."

He looks into her eyes. "You're amazing, Brooke. I don't know how you put up with me."

"I don't either," she sighs and heads back downstairs.

– 56 –
Fire and Water

Allison

As the Evans family weaves their way through the crowded streets, Allison glances at her watch. "We better pick up the pace. We told them we'd be there in ten minutes. Let's go, girls!"

Allison whips around when she hears a voice over her shoulder. "Allie! Marc! Happy Fourth."

It's Kate. Allison feels that pit in her stomach again. *But why?* She thought she was over everything after their chat at the brewery yesterday.

Kate's wearing a fancy sundress and looks fresh as if she walked out of a hair and makeup session.

"I'm glad I ran into you, Allie," she says, her voice like honey. "There's something I want to talk with you about. Can you swing by my place after the parade and lunch? Say, two-thirty?"

Allison looks at Marc. He offers the slightest nod of his head.

"Sure," Allison says with forced enthusiasm. "See you then. Is…is everything OK?"

"Absolutely," Kate assures her. "Gotta scoot, running late. See you this afternoon." With that, Kate disappears into the crowd.

"What was that about?" Marc asks.

"Hell if I know," Allison replies, slightly down all of the sudden, the wind taken out of her sails. "But I do know one thing: Kate is simply not good for my health."

"Try not to worry. You know Kate. It's probably nothing," Marc assures her. "Maybe she wants you to come over and play with her in the pool." He inches closer and whispers, "Maybe I should come with you."

"Oh really? What about wanting to have a lower profile?"

"Private parties with the Gibsons don't count, babe," Marc smirks.

"You need to stay with the girls and get the lobster ready," Allison replies, too distracted to bite. "Don't forget the Rossis are joining us."

"All work and no play makes Marc a cranky boy." He puts on a pouty frown.

"Don't worry, hon, we'll have plenty of time for play," Allison placates him. "Kate's party is coming up. I know you want to keep a low profile, but who are we kidding? We're not going to skip one of her events."

Marc's playful look turns more serious. "Speaking of the Rossis, there's Carla." He waves her down. "Carla! Over here. Where's Lawrence?"

Carla's face lights up. "Oh, hi! Lawrence is trying to find parking. It's absolute chaos down here."

"This is nothing," Allison warns her. "You're going to wish you didn't wear that white sundress."

"Oh, no!" Carla laughs. "What was I thinking?"

"Here come the engines." Marc points to the ladder truck as

it pulls up to the top of Main Street, and all the vendors and face painters scatter. The vintage truck pulls about halfway up, and they can see it's loaded with kids squirting water guns and throwing water balloons.

"Lawrence better hurry up or he'll miss it," Marc says.

Allison spots Lawrence jogging up Main Street. "There he is!"

Everyone is waving and shouting. They watch as the crowd starts to take over the street and Lawrence is getting soaked by kids on both sides.

"Let's get Dad!" Marley yells.

The Evans and Rossi kids converge on Lawrence, pummeling him with balloons. He grabs one of their soakers and fights back. Onlookers provide open coolers filled with water to reload. Lawrence, in the thick of it, faces the crowd which consists of mostly kids. It's wall to wall from the first fire engine to the second. The ladder starts to go up as the *whoosh* of water is unleashed. Lawrence, resembling a post-apocalyptic action hero, looks up with his water gun in hand. A waterfall of water pours down from the fire truck and drenches him.

Marc, Carla, and Allison remain fairly dry standing by the steps of the Toggery store. They watch Lawrence lose this battle against not just the kids, but the fire hose. Eventually the trucks stop, but the kids go on until every last balloon is thrown.

"You lost that battle, buddy." Marc calls out as Lawrence makes his way through the crowd.

"But you sure looked good doing it." Carla leans over and smooches her dripping, wet man.

Allison is openly noticing Lawrence, dripping wet, tanned, energized, and oozing sex appeal. Lawrence catches her, but she doesn't look away. She gets a jolt she hasn't felt about another man, even at Kate's parties, in a while.

Carla reaches over and tugs on her husband's dripping shirt, pulls it over his head, and rings it out, revealing his tight muscles and the rippling abs that have only sharpened from the surfing he's been doing. Seriously, when she was younger, no one told Allison that nearly forty-year-old men could look like this.

Marc appears to notice his wife is all but drooling, and politely invites her to come with him to get some coffee.

"We're going to get some java, would you like anything?" Marc asks the Rossis as they walk toward Provisions.

"No, thanks." Lawrence responds.

"Keep an eye on the girls? We'll be right back," Marc says.

Allison steals one last glance at Lawrence in his khakis, which have fallen a little below his boxers. She can see the top of his hips and she takes a deep breath. She tries not to look at Marc for fear that her lust is obvious to him, which she suspects it is, as he's literally pulling her through the crowds and around the corner up one of the side streets.

Marc drags her into a small, uninhabited doorway. She is trapped in the small alcove as he presses his body into hers; she feels his erection against her leg. They passionately kiss, frantic, with uncontrollable lips and tongues.

"There is no way you are going to Jon's house like this." Marc whispers, "I want you now. You are so turned on, and I love it!"

– 57 –

Comfort Food

Brooke

Brooke and Kevin skip the holiday parade and head directly to Straight Wharf. As they walk closer to the restaurant, she feels a tightening in her chest and butterflies in her stomach from a mixture of anger toward her husband and nerves about seeing Kate and Jon for the first time since their pool romp.

Brooke cannot believe Kevin agreed to join them for brunch. She worries Kevin might be planning to confront Jon and Kate about their fooling around in the pool, but is afraid to ask.

Brooke feels her palms start to sweat the closer they get to Cru. She pulls her hand from Kevin's intertwined fingers and stops to look him in the eye.

"I don't know, Kev. Do you think this is a good idea?"

"What?"

"Our brunch with Kate and Jon. We have a lot to deal with, and..." Brooke stops when she hears Kevin's phone.

"Hello?" He answers, and the pause lasts forever. "Oh, hi, Doc."

Brooke grabs Kevin's hand and leads him over to a bench

facing out onto the docks. She sits next to him. Watching and listening intently, she tries to hear Dr. Brown speaking, but she cannot quite make out his words.

"Well, I guess I had a breakthrough. I told Brooke everything." Another pause. "Yes, we're talking about next steps. You know she's a social worker…right…she thinks I need inpatient treatment."

Kevin's knee begins bouncing up and down. "Really? I thought the two of us could work through it together with your help."

Brooke is imagining the doctor must be telling him how hard that would be—and that it's *his* problem, not hers.

"Alright, here she is." Kevin holds the phone out.

"Hello, Dr. Brown," she greets him.

"Hello, Brooke. How are you doing?"

"I've been better. I am glad Kevin has been working with you. I was at a Marriage and Family Therapy conference a few years back and heard you speak. I always remembered you, and in fact, when Kevin first told me about his addiction, you came to mind."

"Kevin is certainly lucky to have you," the doctor replies. "I know he would do anything for you. What do you want to have happen here?"

"I think he's looking for you to make a recommendation. He already knows mine."

"Ah, well," Dr. Brown replies, "he knows mine as well. Telling you about his addiction is a huge step in the healing process, but he has a long road ahead of him. I know of several reputable programs in the area that offer outpatient and inpatient options. I would ideally like him to do in-patient to start, but

I'm not sure he'll go for it. Right now he wants help, so if there is any chance he will, it's now. You know him better than I do. Do you think he's willing to admit himself to an inpatient program? As you know, it has to be his choice."

"That would be my preference too," she agrees. "I do understand he has work obligations and is concerned about who might find out about this. Do you want to ask him? Or should I?"

"Why don't the two of you discuss it and call me tomorrow," the doctor replies. "Either way he needs to start as soon as possible. I can make some calls tomorrow after you let me know what he's willing to do. There is a long wait list to get in, especially the in-patient programs."

"Thank you, Doctor. We'll call you first thing in the morning."

Brooke hits *end* and sighs.

"I am *not* doing inpatient with a bunch of strangers." Kevin leans over and runs his hands through his hair. "Knowing my luck, I will see a client there and in my business I can't risk my reputation."

Anger begins to creep in as Brooke wonders why it is always about Kevin, never about her and what she is going through. Thankfully, Brooke's crisis training takes over and she masks her resentment. She has her hand on his back as he buries his face in his hands.

"Kevin, you know I love you. For some reason I still do. But I hate what you have done. I'm willing to stand by you if you get help. You need to be honest with yourself. Do you think you can handle the outside world while you're in treatment?"

Kevin rubs his eyes. Brooke notices he's begun to sweat. He

jumps up and begins to pace the dock.

Brooke watches, resisting the urge to comfort him. She's not his mother; it's time he stopped treating her like his caretaker. Kevin reaches into his pocket for another pill.

"I don't know," he cries, popping a benzo. "Right now, all I know is that I cannot do this without you."

"I have an idea. Why don't we ask Doctor Brown if he knows of any option here on the island. And that way you can start right away and other than Jon, who knows everything already, you probably won't know a sole."

Kevin just stares at her. "I can't deal with this right now Brooke. We need to go meet up with Kate and Jon and I am getting really revved up."

Brooke sighs again. "Let's take a walk and calm down a bit."

Kevin looks relieved that she is not pressuring him for an answer. He takes her hand, pulls her soft hand up to his mouth, and gently kisses it.

As Kevin and Brooke walk along the docks, Brooke can't help but wonder how she's going to get through this. She's been through too much over the last few months. There's not much left of her.

She fears she won't have the strength to stand by Kevin after all, and if she tries, she might disappear entirely.

– 58 –

Something Sweet

Carla

Marc and Allison return with their coffee, and Lawrence, soaked to the bone and starting to shiver, gazes longingly at Allison's hot drink.

"Lawrence, you look like you could use something to warm you up. Here, have some," Allison offers.

Carla watches this and is still surprised at herself. Lawrence was gazing at more than just Allison's coffee a few minutes ago, and it didn't bother Carla. At all.

Lawrence gratefully accepts and savors a warm sip.

"Who's up for the candy store?" Allison asks.

"Force Five!" Carla's girls shout in unison.

"You know Force Five has a hidden candy section in the back? Most people think it's just a great clothing store." Allison seems impressed.

"We discovered it a few years back, it's one of our favorite places. We were there the other day!"

"I guess you know more about this island than I realized," Allison smiles. "I hope you don't mind going again. We always head there after the parade. It's our tradition."

Lawrence, still shivering, says, "Carla, why don't you take the girls to the candy shop while I go grab the car and pull it closer. I had to park about a mile out of town. I'm too wet to hang out."

"Works for me," Carla agrees. "Text me where to meet you when you get close. Oh, and hon, why don't you stop in one of the shops on your way and get yourself a dry Nantucket T-shirt?"

"Good idea. See you in a bit. And grab me a few peanut butter cups, will ya?"

Lawrence watches as his family and the Evans head toward the wharf, and Carla sees him wave before she brings her full attention back to Allison and the girls.

What a fun day.

Her mind begins to wander about the possibilities of what could happen at Kate's party. She finds herself picturing them out on her deck after the party, and she's suddenly turned on. She knows her husband is thinking about a three-way with Allison. No good could come of it, right?

Carla follows Allison and Marc, and everyone gets their candy and there's not a bit of awkwardness, and Carla prays it stays like this. So far, so good.

– 59 –

Nantucket Royalty

Kate

Kate and Jon walk hand-in-hand through the crowds towards Cru. If she didn't have her connection at the most exclusive restaurant in town, they'd have to wait hours for a table.

Kate has taken a liking to Brooke, so she made a call ahead of time to reserve a spot for the four of them. She called in a favor she'll have to repay at some point soon. But it's worth it.

Kate is on a mission to convince Brooke to come to her party. Brunch at Cru on the Fourth is as exclusive as it gets on this island, and Kate made it happen to impress the Doyles. It'll be a nice little taste of the fun they can have.

Her thoughts are interrupted when she sees a familiar face. She drops Jon's hand and stops to get a better look. She can't be sure, but from afar it looks like Allison is here with her family, and is that Carla? It is! *So now they're inseparable?*

Kate feels a pang of jealousy. Or is it anger? She has no idea anymore. How is it that Allie can get her to feel this way just by being with someone else? Kate turns her attention to Marc. He is objectively a good-looking man, and Kate has always thought

Allie has no idea how lucky she is.

Kate realizes Lawrence is missing and wonders why he isn't with them. She wants to go up and say hi and give Allison a big Fourth of July hug, but she can't bring herself to do it. Not with that Carla woman around.

Why did I invite her to the party? Stupid move. Allison's going to have to un-invite them and come up with a killer excuse, to boot.

Kate realizes Jon didn't spot them in the crowd, so she grabs his hand again and steers him away, continuing to fight the mob of wet, loud people migrating toward Cru.

Kate smiles again as she turns her thoughts back to Brooke. Then she remembers Kevin will be there too.

She says to Jon, "If Kevin gets out of control, you need to handle him."

"He'll be fine, Kate," Jon insists. "How much trouble can he really cause? We'll be in an upscale waterfront restaurant in the middle of the day."

"I know, but the way you talk about him makes me think he could cause a scene anywhere. You did say he's a bit of a hothead, right?"

"He can be, yes. But nothing I can't handle."

They make it to the restaurant and Kate revels in the power of being able to walk past the long line of hungry patrons waiting to be seated. The host leads them to a table in the exclusive back bar area facing the water. Jon makes sure Kate gets the seat with the view, as usual.

When the waiter comes, she orders a bloody mary with extra Worcestershire and a side of shrimp cocktail. "I'd like to start with a Mary and the boys, please." The bartender on Sundays makes them super spicy, just the way Kate likes them, so she hopes he's working today. Kate and Jon arrived early on purpose. They planned to chat more about her party and strategize how to persuade Brooke to attend, with or without Kevin. She can talk them into staying on the island longer, or maybe Brooke would just fly back here from Boston for the weekend.

Unfortunately, their drinks arrive at the same time as Brooke and Kevin. Kate forces herself not to wince; Brooke doesn't look so good. Her eyes are red and swollen. Kevin appears antsy and intense. Kate wishes she'd ordered an extra shot of vodka to handle this brunch. So much for strategizing with Jon before this couple showed up. Looks like they'll have to wing it.

Brooke smiles nervously. This timid woman is not the same Brooke who was at their house yesterday. Kate rises and gently kisses her on the cheek.

"Brooke, darling. How are you?"

Jon is on his feet and shakes Kevin's hand. "What's up, buddy?"

Brooke doesn't answer Kate but sits down beside her.

The waiter appears, breaking an awkward silence. "What can I get for you?"

Kevin asks for a $2500 bottle of Salon Champagne, the most expensive on the menu. "It's the Fourth of July, after all," he adds, as if to justify his extravagant order. "Bring four glasses, please."

He turns to Jon and Kate. "You'll join us in a toast, right?"

Jon nods while Kate shouts, "Yes!" a little too enthusiastically. Damn, this guy is making her uncomfortable.

Brooke looks over at Kate, and a little twinkle returns to her eyes. Kate sees her opportunity and pounces.

"So, Brooke darling, have you shown Kevin your gorgeous dress for our party?"

Brooke turns to Kevin, who speaks for her before she can even open her mouth. "Why no, Brooke, you haven't. You'll have to model it for me after brunch."

He gives her a seductive wink.

Kevin proceeds to take over the conversation. "Speaking of your party, what is the date?"

Jon chimes in, "It's the last Friday of the month. Will you still be on the island?"

Kevin and Brooke look at each other and there is a long silent pause before either of them responds.

"We aren't sure yet when we are headed back to Boston," Kevin eventually replies.

"Well even if you aren't, you must fly back. Cocktail hour begins at five-thirty. I have Summer House catering, and they do a phenomenal job. Jon and I will not let our guests starve."

Brooke seems to be trying to whip up some excitement about the party. "That sounds like fun, Kev, doesn't it?"

"We're going formal, but keep in mind that many of our guests end up in the steamy pool before the night is through," explains Jon.

"I've heard about your legendary parties," Kevin says. "I'm glad we're finally on the list."

Kevin looks almost manic to Kate.

The champagne arrives and Kevin makes a big show of checking the label, then nods to the server to pop the cork. The server pours, and Kevin holds out his glass.

"A toast," he says, as they all raise a glass. "To the Fourth of July on this beautiful isle, and to Kate and Jon's party!"

After they enjoy the smooth bubbly, Kate turns to Brooke. "I need the ladies' room. Care to join me?"

"Let's go," Brooke agrees.

The two women walk away from the table. Now that she's out of Kevin's earshot and away from his wild eyes, Kate feels like she can speak freely. But before she can get a word in, Brooke speaks.

"Kate, I'm excited for your party, but I'm not sure we're going to make it."

Kate takes a beat, then treads carefully. "Can I ask…did you tell Kevin about our impromptu rendezvous yesterday?"

Brooke pushes open the restroom door and says, "I did. I felt I had to."

Kate follows her to the mirror and whips out some lip gloss. She's trying to stay calm, but she's thinking, *Holy shit, Jon was right*. And now Jon and Kevin are alone at the table.

"Do you think that was such a good idea?" Kate probes as gently as she can.

"Well, it's a long story," Brooke replies. "Kevin and I had a heart-to-heart and I blurted it out. There are some things going on with him…"

"What exactly did you blurt out?" Kate smacks her lips together and pops the wand back in the tube of gloss.

"That I spent the day naked with you guys," Brooke says, casually applying some light pink lipstick. "In your pool."

Brooke's phone rings, she checks the caller, and raises her eyebrows. "I'm so sorry," she says to Kate. "I have to take this. I'll meet you back at the table."

– 60 –

With a Chaser

Kate

Kate returns to the table alone and sees the men chatting quietly. She figures it's a good sign Jon isn't on the floor; if Kevin suspected anything about Jon and Brooke, he would've decked him already.

As Kate pulls her chair up and takes a sip of her drink, Kevin says, "So, my friends…you might want to brace yourselves. Things might be about to change."

Jon swallows a sip of his drink and asks, "What are you talking about?"

"When I confessed to Brooke she completely overreacted. She wants me to do an in-patient program."

Jon side-eyes Kate so quickly Kevin clearly misses it.

"Kevin, cut the shit," Jon snaps. "That's not funny."

"Bro, I am not fucking kidding," Kevin shrugs. "I am hoping there's a long wait list."

"How in the hell did that happen?" Jon probes. Kate stays out of this one, which is fine, because Kevin barely seems to notice she's there.

"Let's just say I had a weak moment and told her everything," Kevin replies. "I know you know about Michelle. You both do, right?" He cocks his head to show he does, in fact, recognize that Kate has joined the chat. "Come on, Jon. You introduced her to me. Well, I've been seeing her pretty frequently. That's where I was yesterday."

"Whoa, whoa, *whoa*," Kate jumps in, holding up a hand. "Is Michelle the…the *professional* you mentioned to me, Jon? And Kevin, have you lost your mind? Brooke thinks you both came to this island to save your marriage. Not to mention, your wife needs to heal. I mean, a sex worker? Seriously?"

Kate is disgusted by Kevin's behavior, but she can see Jon is trying to keep the guy from getting spooked. They need him to keep talking so they're able to find out everything in the next minute before Brooke returns.

"Hey," Kevin hits back. "*I* need to heal too if we're going to have a marriage. This hasn't been easy on me, you know."

"Wait," Kate leans in. "Did you tell Brooke about Michelle?"

"No, not specifically, but she knows something," Kevin admits. "Even if it's not anything too specific. Women always know, don't they?"

Kate recoils as if she's been slapped, as if he was directing that at her. *Was he?* That stung more than she'd like. She wonders how much Jon tells his friends about her painful past and her trust issues.

"It all came out in that huge fight we had the day I went back to Boston," Kevin says.

"After you were with Michelle," Jon says darkly.

"I know it was stupid," Kevin says, not appearing the least bit sorry, "but whenever I get stressed, I need to blow off steam. I knew Brooke was on to me and I planned to tell her I had an affair and then…well, I don't know…"

"What do you mean you *don't know*? She's the best thing that ever happened to you. Why the hell would you risk blowing it?" Kate is disgusted.

"I'm a dumbass. I cracked." Kevin's voice quivers. "I couldn't take it anymore; I had to tell her. She bought all my therapist's crap about being a sex addict hook, line, and sinker. And she's going to stand by me. I can't even believe it. I actually feel pretty good…I mean, other than having to go through treatment, which she insists on, but I think it will be good for us."

"You really think you can quit the strip clubs and give up Michelle?" Jon deadpans.

"Jon, man, you know I love Brooke," Kevin says. "I'd do anything for her. I have to try." He adds through gritted teeth, "Don't get your hopes up, buddy. She's still mine. I don't know exactly what happened in your pool yesterday, but I don't think I want to. Let's just leave it at that for now."

Kate sees Jon's face flush, and with that she reassesses her feelings about this couple. Maybe she'll only try to recruit Brooke; maybe she's going to bring in a unicorn instead of a couple.

Both men suddenly straighten up, Kevin clears his throat, and they all greet Brooke as she returns to the table.

– 61 –
Another Round

Brooke

Brooke barely keeps a straight face when she watches the three of them paste on smiles and greet her with far too much enthusiasm. *Who do they think they're kidding?* She could feel the tension from across the room when she was winding her way back toward her table.

She was relieved on some level, though, because the call she took was from Charlie, who confirmed that all was well, at least for the moment.

The waiter returns and they order another round. Brooke can see Kevin is out to get drunk today based on his order of a double Kettle on the rocks with a twist. He is avoiding eye contact with her, and instead focuses on Kate. She's wearing a bright-red, silk scarf tied around her neck and low-cut white spandex top and pulls it off like a model in a Nantucket brochure.

"What are your plans to watch the fireworks tonight?" Kate asks trying to change the subject.

Brooke rolls her eyes. "I'm not sure if we will make it to the fireworks."

"Sure we will," answers Kevin with a devilish grin.

Jon jumps in and suggests, "why don't we watch them together?"

Kevin obviously feels his wife's stare and turns to catch it before he adds, "Are you able to see them from your pool?"

Jon and Brooke nearly choke on their drinks, but Kate doesn't skip a beat; Brooke senses she's been waiting for Kevin to make a comment. "Well, Kevin, you'll have to see for yourself tonight. It's going to be a spectacular evening with shooting stars and all."

Brooke should have known better. Her husband is never going to change. He can't even pretend to be the grown-up she needs him to be. She glares at her husband and doesn't care who sees it.

Brooke catches her breath and checks her new friend out subtly, under her eyelashes, and wonders what her game is. Kate must know Kevin is bad news—after all, his most recent behavior has eclipsed the Sexy Bad Boy vibe and gone straight to Sad Middle-Aged Loser, in Brooke's opinion. Kate's too smart to have missed that.

Is she trying to keep him at bay? Or…is Kate truly enchanted, the way many women are when the charming, attractive, successful Kevin Doyle first turns his charms on them? Kevin is now treating Kate to his famous schoolboy grin. Looking for one last hurrah before going into treatment, Brooke guesses. She's seeing her husband more clearly every day, but she knows the love—yes, true, real love—she has for this flawed man keeps a gauzy filter over her eyes. Even now.

Out of nowhere, Kevin stands so fast his chair clatters against the floor.

"Excuse me," he says. "I need to use the restroom."

He heads off and Brooke watches him grab their waiter and slip him his American Express. He continues out to the front bar, where she loses sight of him. She knows he's ordering another drink, which fills her with dread because benzos and alcohol don't mix.

Brooke, Kate and Jon chatter for a moment about who's invited to the party, the who's who of Nantucket society. She flicks her eyes toward the bar every few moments to check for Kevin, and the third time she does, she sees him standing at the edge of the patio watching them, a faraway look in his eyes. He staggers toward them and Brooke suspects they're going to have to make an early exit.

He arrives and extends his hand towards Brooke while looking straight at Jon. "Thank you both for meeting us for brunch," he slurs. Brooke is on her feet. *Time to go.*

She grabs his arm, pulling him close, offering him stability. "I guess those drinks hit a bit hard on an empty stomach," she offers as a weak excuse. "Let's go, honey."

"Kevin, are you alright?" Jon stands.

"Yup, all good."

"We'll walk with you." Kate hurries to Kevin's other side.

When they're on the cobblestones outside the restaurant, Kevin is even more wobbly. He's flanked by Brooke and Kate while Jon trails behind.

"What are you on, Kev?" Jon asks.

"I don't know…loraza something. Benzodoolozawhatsit…"

"Are you taking *Valium?*" Kate asks. "You know downers don't mix with alcohol, right? Have you taken it before?"

"He's having a tough day, Kate," Brooke answers, wondering why she's still defending this man. Yes, he's struggling. But most of his problems are self-made.

"I think I took four…" Kevin stumbles, and Jon lurches forward to help support him.

"I've got him," Jon says, gently pulling Kevin away from the two women.

"He'll be OK," Kate says to Brooke. "He needs a nap. For future reference, Kevin, don't take more than one of those if you plan on having a few drinks."

They approach the car and Jon and Kate help Kevin into the passenger seat as Brooke takes the wheel.

"Call us if you need anything," Jon says quietly to Brooke. "Anything at all."

"She doesn't need anyone but me," Kevin says, though Brooke might have been the only one to understand it as it came out as *Sheesh usn't meed anywhubume.*

"Thank you both," Brooke says, mortified. "We clearly won't be making it tonight."

Kevin waves out the window with his eyes half shut as Brooke peels out of her parking spot and out of town.

# – 62 –

On the List

Allison

The Evans family leaves the fish store with fresh lobsters and steamers, and Allison drops Marc and the girls at the house before heading to Sconset to help Kate with her party planning.

As she heads out of Cisco, Allison sees Lawrence behind the wheel pulling out of Bartlett's in his Range Rover. She feels an unexpected shot of adrenaline; the guy is truly handsome, and Allison can't help but picture him running around town earlier that day, drenched and steamy.

She realizes now that she's extremely attracted to him, having officially started fantasizing, which is always a sure sign.

What is it about him? For starters, the two of them have sizzling chemistry. Carla spoke of that same draw on the beach, and Allison realizes that while Lawrence is objectively attractive, he's also magnetic, and that's a dangerous package.

In virtually the same moment she acknowledges her attraction, she admits she needs to get over it. Lawrence and Carla are a close and bonded couple, and Allison wants nothing to do with disrupting that.

She knows all too well the double-sided coin that is the swinging lifestyle. Switching it up in the bedroom—and outside it—is meant to be a way to bring couples closer together. But she's seen first-hand how feelings can grow out of control like weeds choking a garden, how the balance of power in a relationship can tip like a seesaw, how the unexpected effects of so many unpredictable variables can collide in disaster.

Allison has seen how it pushes couples, and friends, apart. Carla told her Lawrence would never go for their lifestyle. Allison needs to cool it with the sexual thoughts.

Easier said than done. The long ride to Kate's 'Sconset compound gives her more time to imagine the possibilities. As much as she'd like to seduce the Rossis on her own, she knows that she'll need Kate on board. Allison approaches Kate and Jon's timeless mansion. The elegant entranceway never ceases to amaze her with its cobblestone circular drive and privet hedge trimmed and immaculate. She's been here dozens of times and viewing it on each occasion is as breathtaking as the first. The lush grounds covered in manicured grass and hydrangeas galore complement the meticulously kept home. The priceless view of the Atlantic Ocean behind the cliffs is untouchable in this tight real-estate market.

As she pulls in under the covered entrance, she admires the climbing roses draping the columns. She exits the car and takes a deep breath and knocks on the door.

"Hello, Allie." Kate hugs her warmly and strokes her hair. "You have no idea how happy I am to see you. You're a sight for sore eyes."

"It's nice to be here. It *has* been too long, hasn't it?" Allison feels the tension seeping out of her with the warm welcome.

"Oh, it has," Kate says in a tone that tells Allison she has gossip to spill. "You won't believe the drama we had today at Cru."

"Ooh, *do* tell," Allison squeals as she walks with Kate through the grand foyer and into through the sunken living room.

She and Kate could always find common ground in sharing and analyzing local gossip. God knows with so much money, power and beautiful people crawling around this island, there's always something scandalous brewing.

Jon is already bustling about grabbing wine glasses and an ice-cold bottle of crisp unoaked Chardonnay. He pauses to greet Allison with a brief hug and a kiss on the cheek.

"I nearly lost my connection at Cru because of Jon's colleague," Kate moans. "Granted, we've had our share of naughty behavior in town, but usually not at a civilized brunch!"

"No! Anything but that," Allie replies, only half-kidding. "What happened? Weren't you meeting Brooke and her husband? Kevin, right?"

"Yes, Jon and I met up with both of them. So there we are at brunch on the busiest day of the year. Anyone who's anyone is there," Kate says as Jon pops the cork. "Kevin shows up half in the bag. Meanwhile, Brooke, who of course is a stunning woman, looks like death warmed over. Puffy eyes, dark circles, you name it. She's not herself."

"Ugh," Allison winces. "I hope it's nothing too serious…"

Jon pours the wine and slides two glasses over to them. Allison dives in.

"Kevin was loopy from the minute he shows up," Kate goes

on. "Talking too much, too fast, checking me out in front of his wife. It only gets worse from there. He's drinking champagne and then straight double vodkas."

She takes a beat and sips some wine, savoring it, then setting her glass down.

"Before we can even order the main course, Kevin is a total wreck. He nearly fell into the table. If it hadn't been for Brooke springing into action and holding him up, I'm convinced that man would have toppled right over." Kate is shaking her head as if visualizing it all over again. "One minute he's OK, the next he's slurring and can barely walk."

Kate lowers her voice as if they're still at brunch and she doesn't want the other society types to hear. "Turns out he was mixing alcohol and benzos! I mean, that stuff can kill you if you're not careful."

"Oh, I know," Allison says. "Marc said he was pretty hardcore during golf, something about paying the drink cart to follow them. But I didn't realize he was *that* bad."

"He was a mess," Kate says. "They've been having some fertility problems. Well, and…some other issues." Kate pauses for dramatic effect. "And by other issues, I mean problems that go beyond cheating on his wife."

"Beyond cheating?" Allison's glass is nearly empty. She wants Kate to keep talking, to give up more details on Kevin. She can't quiet visualize the man she met in the golf club parking lot; he reeked of morning-after scotch, barely said two words to her, and had his face covered with a hat and sunglasses. "I don't understand that mentality. If couples want to expand their horizons, all they have to do is be open and honest and join our club."

Allison smiles and they both giggle, and she realizes she really has missed Kate.

"Kevin was a disaster," Jon confirms from his seat across the room, where he's half listening to them, half reading the *Boston Globe*. "Way worse than Marc or me after our longest day at the brewery."

"That's pretty bad. Where did you say he's from?"

"I didn't," Jon says. "I'm not sure where they were before Boston."

"Well, anyway," Allison says as if she doesn't care about the answer, "Kate said something about prescription drugs?"

Kate drains her glass. "I think he recently started on some meds and didn't know his limits," she says after she swallows. "I, of course, gave him a few pointers. A glass of vino and a Valium: not so bad. Several Valium, champagne, and vodka straight up: very, very bad."

Jon notices their empty glasses and brings his own over to where they're chatting at the kitchen island. He drains the bottle refilling all three glasses.

"Oh!" Kate's eyes gleam, and Allison senses a change of subject coming. "Remember the time we had that sex toy party?" Kate raises her eyebrows, and they all burst out laughing.

"Yeah, we had to call cabs for half the guests," Jon recalls.

"Yeah—because a certain person was adding vodka to the champagne punch." Kate side-eyes Jon.

"Wasn't me, I swear," he laughs, holding up two hands. "You gotta admit, half the party needed it. My god, you would think no one ever used a vibrator before, the way they were asking 'now, how exactly do you use the tickler, Jon?' I couldn't take it sober, so I decided to spike the punch."

"That's right!" Allison recalls, giggling. "Jon was the only guy in the room. You're such a trooper. And we *all* know Kate's guest list was a sly trick to find out which neighbors liked to use these toys, and a way to horrify the rest."

"If you remember, we *did* end up with some new recruits after that party thanks to me, as usual." Kate swirls her wine and smirks.

"You're right, that was how you landed Chad and Heather," Jon says. "Are you inviting them? I'm not sure I like him pawing on you, Kate." Jon looks concerned.

"Chad I can handle. It's Roy that annoys me, but you love Lisa and they're a package deal." Kate rolls her eyes.

"It's too bad you have to invite the spouse. Actually, I like Roy, he's adorable and so tall, like six-six, right?" Allison asks.

"You only like Roy because you've never swapped with him. He bites, and not in a good way." Kate shivers.

"Good to know, because Marc likes Lisa too, something about exotic brunettes turns him on." Allison thinks of Carla and her smooth, tanned skin.

"No wonder your neighbors are so high on your list." Jon smiles, then seems to realize he may have stepped out of neutral territory. He glances from Kate to Allison.

Kate doesn't shy away from the topic. "Lawrence is undeniably hot," she says. "But sometimes men that good looking can't always deliver the goods…if you catch my meaning. I wouldn't get my hopes up, Allie. Even if you pull off a threesome with them, it's probably going to be a one-shot wonder. The fact you live next door is catastrophic." Kate throws her arms up dramatically.

"Don't worry, my hopes are in check," Allison assures her. She isn't entirely sure why Kate would generalize that good-looking men aren't great in bed. "I don't know yet if they'll go there, but we spent last night around the fire pit, and there was definitely sexual tension. His eyes are mesmerizing, and he doesn't turn away when I stare. It's so intense."

Allison gulps down her wine and extends her empty glass to Jon, who's ready with a newly corked bottle, but then remembers she's driving and pulls it away.

"Ah." Jon gets it. "You're driving home." He pours more into Kate's glass instead.

"You, my friend, have it bad. So? What about Marc and Carla?" Kate tries to be casual, but Allison knows this is a touchy question. Allison plays along.

"Carla is gorgeous. If Lawrence jumps, I think she will too. Marc is hesitant because of their proximity, but you know Marc. Sex is sex to men," Allison says with more bravado than she feels.

"So, it all hinges on Lawrence then. What will we do to loosen him up?" Kate twirls her finger through her blonde hair as she schemes.

"Wait a sec, before we go any further," Allison says brightly but firmly. "To get it straight once and for all, you're OK with Carla and Lawrence coming? And then we'll see what transpires?"

Kate takes a breath. "Yes," she says. "Their invitation stands."

Oh, thank you, Queen Bee, Allison thinks, her internal voice dripping with sarcasm.

"I know just the thing to get Lawrence into it," Jon breaks in, lightening the mood again. "He loves to drink the hard stuff. He had us doing Patron shots on the golf course. I'll stock my scotch and cigar bar with plenty of Patron and limes for Lawrence."

"I was planning on seaweed martinis as our specialty drink, but we'll offer a full bar, of course," Kate says. "The bar and food will be to the left and the dance floor will be right there between the veranda and the pool, with the band set up on a small stage to the right." She points through the open French doors.

"We'll string lights on the trees around the pool area and have some large standing candle arbors. For the pool, we'll add floating candles along with some dry ice in the deep end. The sunset hour will be to die for." Kate takes the last sip of her wine and saunters toward Jon.

Allison, fidgety and about ready to get home to her family, fingers a stack of mostly cream-colored cardstock on the counter. "What'er these?"

"Invites," Kate yawns. "I'm sure you got a lot of the same ones. A lot of people are having bashes tonight."

"Oh, I know," Allison nods. "It's hard to decide which ones to make an appearance at."

Allison is lying. She and Marc were invited to *one* get-together by an old childhood friend, but she puts that down to the fact most of the people she knows understand she and Marc do small gatherings at home with the kids for Independence Day.

"Right? Believe it or not, Jon and I talked about staying in tonight," Kate says. "After the wild brunch and all the planning we have to do, it seems like a good night to stay out of the fray. You've seen one Fourth of July bash, you've seen them all."

Allison's flipping through the invites and stumbles onto one from a young, hot, famous actor. "But this one's from—"

"Ah, yes," Kate grins, reading the card Allison's holding up.

"Jon's favorite movie star. His parties attract a…well, a less savory crew. We're a bit too old for the TikTok crowd, I think. Plus, I have to finish the guest list. I am having the invitations printed and delivered next week."

"When you put it that way," Jon nods, "I'm happy to stay in tonight and watch the Pops show. The Boston fireworks are better."

It's unusual for these two to stay in on such a big night. Allison bets they will swing by the Tik Tok party.

– 63 –

No Regrets

Kate

"It sounds like everything is under control," Allison says, sliding off her stool. "Well, except Kevin and Brooke. Are they coming, drama and all?"

Kate hears the question but is now imagining Marc in the pool with Carla and is regretting her decision to allow them to come. *Why is Marc getting to her like this?* Has she really fallen for Marc, or is she jealous that Allie, Jon, and Marc have plans that don't include her?

Kate thought she would be into Kevin. He's handsome and cocky, but she adores Brooke so much that she's pissed at Kevin instead. Not to mention his drunken behavior at brunch was a turn-off. It's too bad he's such a fuck-up. What's his deal? Maybe if she could figure him out, she could talk to him, reason with him. Help him pull his shit together. Jon told her he was a horny, narcissistic, overgrown frat boy with too much money for his own good. Then again, she thinks, *Maybe I'll find out for myself.*

"Oh Allie, you better sit for this one." Jon pats the stool Allie just stood up from with his hand. "I think Kate may have bragging rights here."

Kate has Allison's full attention as she parades out onto her veranda knowing Allie will follow her rather than sit like Jon wants her to. Kate takes a deep breath and stares out at the endless ocean.

She finally turns to Allison and says flatly, "We had a threesome with Brooke yesterday." She turns her attention back to the sea.

"What? No way! Where was Kevin?" Allison throws her arms up and turns back toward the kitchen to Jon, who steps outside and hands her a fresh glass. Allison takes a tiny sip, figuring she can afford another half of a glass and still be OK to drive.

Kate tells her everything that happened and Allison listens, her eyes wide. Kate takes a risk and shares the decision she's come to. "I'd love for Brooke to be our unicorn," she says, "but I don't want to get ahead of myself."

"Your *unicorn*? I thought you were too jealous for something like that," Allison says, her harsh bluntness annoying Kate.

Jon saves the day again. "All I know is the Doyles need a break from each other, at the very least," he chimes in. "If Kate is open to it, we might tell her she can move in with us for the summer. We have more than enough room for Brooke. I think she'd love spending her summer with us in the guest house."

"What about Kevin?" Allison looks confused.

"He might not be around. There's a chance he'll be in treatment," Kate answers.

"But I thought you said he started taking prescription drugs recently? How can he be addicted already?" Allison asks.

"The treatment is for *sex* addiction," Jon says.

Kate begins to laugh, a high-pitched cackling sound, at the

irony of it all. "Oh! There is something fundamentally wrong with that man, I am telling you. I see it in his eyes."

Kate watches Allison's face as they speak about Kevin and is convinced, once and for all, that her friend has a secret. At the first chance she gets, Kate plans to ask her about it.

"You know," Jon says as an aside to Kate, "it was so bad at brunch I think we should stop by and check on them. See how Brooke's doing, show some support, that kind of thing."

Kate nods. "Let's do it before happy hour."

Allison sets her near-full glass down on the table next to the pool. "I'd better get going," she says. "Lots to do for tonight. Let me know if you need any help besides the playlist for after the band, I've got that."

"Just bring your beautiful self," Kate purrs. "And please reassure Marc and your neighbors that there will be plenty of non-believers here, and the event will remain tame until the clock strikes midnight. Also, there will be a car service from the house, so no one needs to worry about driving home."

"I can't wait," Allison grins, and Kate thinks maybe, once and for all, they're going to get back to the place they were before things got weird. "Your party is going to be amazing. You are undoubtedly the best host on Nantucket. Thanks for the wine and the gossip. Bye, Jon!"

And with that, Allison turns and heads for her car.

– 64 –
Lobstah

Allison

Allison feels her husband's eyes on her as she walks in the door. He greets her with a quick peck and asks, "How did it go?"

"It went great," she says. "It was just like old times. But get this: remember that guy Kevin that you played golf with last weekend?" Marc nods. "Leave it to Kate, but she somehow lured his wife, Brooke, into the pool for a three-way with her and Jon."

"*No way*," Marc says as he throws lobsters into the pot.

"Yes way," Allison says. "I'm not kidding. Kate *is* irresistible, after all. You know better than anyone."

Marc's face darkens as he continues to prep the food. Allison takes note of this. Somehow, even though they made up, even though she enjoys being with her friend, Kate still manages to get between her and Marc.

"Babe, will you set up the strainer?" Marc casually engages his wife.

"Wait, you're done already? They're not even here yet," Allison snaps.

"I'm ahead of the game," he says. "I wanted to cook everything up ahead of time so I can throw it on the grill and have it ready in minutes. This way we can all relax and have a few brews before we eat. Why don't you open a couple?"

– 65 –

Young and Carefree

Carla

Carla catches herself whistling along to a tune while she puts together some food and drinks to bring next door. As she thinks back to the gorgeous welcome basket Allison brought her when they first arrived, she knows she is out of her league.

Allison seems to do everything perfectly, from running to throwing parties to helping her new neighbors feel welcome. She makes it all look so easy.

Wanting to match Allison's flawless execution, Carla works diligently to prepare and present the appetizers she plans to bring for the Fourth of July lobster bake.

Then come the cocktails. Carla found a refreshing blood orange mimosa recipe over the holidays last year, and this is the perfect occasion to mix some up. When they stopped at Bartlett Farms on their way home, she picked up a locally made, hand-blown glass pitcher that will showcase her signature drink beautifully. Carla carefully packs a cooler full of the drink's ingredients to create another batch in the event her cocktail is a success.

As she finishes the final touches, Carla notices her mimosa samplings have started to add up. Between the early morning road race and the sugar high from the candy store, the alcohol is going straight to her head.

She glances at her reflection in the mirror and decides her slightly ruddy cheeks, caused by a mixture of sun and alcohol, suit her. Island life has been good to her. Her sun-kissed skin has browned, and her muscles have grown lean and toned. Her hair has grown still longer and thicker, and she has a youthful glow.

Lawrence rounds the corner and catches her admiring herself in the mirror. She's embarrassed, but he's not laughing.

"You are gorgeous," he says. "You better watch it tonight, don't want to do anything to give Marc the wrong impression!"

He steals a brief but sensual kiss on his way out.

A light bulb goes off in Carla's mind as to why she is so giddy. It's as if the clock was set back years, back to her early law school days. She vividly remembers falling in love with Lawrence, with that affectionate side of him that got lost in the stresses of parenthood and work and owning a home. All the responsibilities of being an adult bring changes, and it's easy to forget what got them here in the first place. The love, the lust, the connection.

Back in those days, though, they were still kids. Carla's biggest worries were answering the professor's question correctly when called on and making new friends. This new home in Nantucket, their promise to each other to reconnect, and the kids being older have allowed them to turn back time.

If Carla were back in law school, she would ask Allison to be her roommate and her study partner. They would do happy hour together and go for runs.

She resolves to ask Allison tonight more about her swinging ways. Maybe it's more common with couples than she realizes, especially when their kids get older. Hell, Allison talks about it like it's no big deal. If it were years ago, Carla is pretty sure she would experiment, so why not now? Especially on an island twenty-seven miles out to sea. It's as if it doesn't count.

As she's thinking this, her husband breezes back into the kitchen.

"What a spread! Should I start carrying stuff over?"

"Just one more thing…" She fiddles with a garnish on the cheese platter.

"Carla, stop fussing over everything, honey," Lawrence pleads. "It all looks phenomenal. I'm sure they don't care if the chips are in a red bowl or a blue one."

"Leave me be," she says. "Take these platters over now, and I'll be right behind you with the drinks."

"With pleasure." He manages to grab several bowls and a platter using his hands and forearms and walks gingerly out the door.

Carla watches him go and realizes with a jolt that maybe, just maybe, she could see herself sharing him with someone she trusts. She follows behind him and thinks she *might* do something risky tonight, like agree to something she never would have before.

It depends on how things go.

– 66 –
Inquisition

Allison

Allison watches from the kitchen window as Lawrence approaches the front yard where Marc is playing Wiffle ball with the girls. Behind their perfectly manicured hedge, distant daisies wave in the gentle ocean breeze while the surf pounds the shore, and Allison thinks for the millionth time this is her favorite place on earth, this exact spot right here.

"Hey, Marc," Lawrence calls out as he holds up his contributions. Carla is right behind him carrying a giant pitcher of cocktails across the lawn.

"Excellent! Are you ready for some lobster? Follow me up to the house and we can unload those platters," Marc replies as he reaches out and takes one off Lawrence's full hands.

"Aw, you're ruining the game," Savannah whines.

"We'll be right back. Get ready for dads against girls!" Marc grins.

The three adults head up to the deck. Allison walks out to greet the Rossis, and she and Carla get the drinks set up for a toast.

She hears the girls start up their own ball game, minus the dads, so Allison pours four mimosas from Carla's pitcher and raises her glass. "Let's have a toast, shall we?"

"Cheers to celebrating our first of many Independence Days together." Marc raises his glass, too.

"Here's to our runners," Lawrence adds.

"To all our beautiful, loud, wonderfully exhausting children," Carla smiles as shrieks float up from the lawn.

"And to all of the people that fight for our freedom." Lawrence holds his drink high.

The four of them clink glasses. They are about to sip on their cocktails when Allison adds, "One more: To our family and friends, both old and new."

She winks at Lawrence, and to her great amusement, he nearly chokes on his drink. If Allison had any doubts before that their attraction is mutual, they're gone now.

Marc and Lawrence head down to grill the food and take turns hitting home runs with the girls while Carla and Allison sip on their mimosas on the upper deck.

Their families are a perfect match, Allison thinks, and she's already picturing them vacationing together in the winters, maybe in Aspen or Anguilla. She watches Carla sip her blood orange drink and is entranced by the shimmer on her lips. Carla twirls her hair and Allison realizes she's staring.

"These drinks are amazing," Allison says, snapping herself out of it. "You outdid yourself."

"They're really refreshing, but be careful, they sneak up on you," Carla warns.

"I don't even taste the alcohol," Allison laughs, taking a long sip.

"Trust me, it's in there," Carla laughs. "And it's already hitting me after our big run this morning. Thanks for getting me out to run an actual race. It was quite an accomplishment for me. You've really helped me get back into working out. I'm invigorated."

"Oh, my goodness honey, it's all you," Allison waves her thanks away. "You deserve a lot of credit. We've only been running for a few weeks and you just raced three miles without any hesitation."

"I feel like it's been so much longer," Carla observes. "I think you know more about me than friends I've had for ten years. I don't know why, but I feel like we've known each other forever."

"It's a Nantucket thing," Allison agrees.

Allison feels a change in the air. She rises and pours more drinks, and as she does, she watches Carla gaze out at the waves curling and crashing in the distance. She senses Carla is about to make some waves of her own.

Allison gets comfortable in her chair, adjusts her sunglasses, and waits. In a few seconds, it comes.

"So, um…" Carla begins, swiveling her neck to face her. "I wanted to talk to you about that chat we had the other day. I know I said the, um…*lifestyle* probably wasn't for us, but I kind of want to know how it works. I guess what I'm trying to say is, I have questions."

Allison doesn't intend to miss this chance but doesn't want to scare Carla off. She responds as lightly as she can, "I don't blame you. It was a lot to take in at once, I know. Does this mean you're thinking of dabbling? Or even…swapping?"

Carla's face remains impassive. "I'm not sure, but I know I'm not imagining the tension between the four of us. Once you brought it up, it was in my head. I can't speak for Lawrence, but I'm starting to think we could try it and decide if we like it or not. Otherwise it's going to hang out there, always lingering."

Carla sounds like she's thought about this.

"I would love nothing more, but I'm hesitant it will ruin our friendship," Allison feigns apprehension. "Our girls are so close, and we've bonded so deeply, so quickly."

"True," Carla says. "So, give it to me, how does it work exactly?"

"It's up to you and Lawrence really," Allison launches into it. "You should both decide together how far you want to take it beforehand. No surprises. If you're not into it, I suggest you leave the party by midnight or you may do something you'll regret."

"You make it sound so mysterious. What could possibly change so drastically at midnight? You all turn into vampires?" Carla laughs.

Allison raises an eyebrow and crosses her long legs.

"Vamps yes, vampires no," she laughs. "The temptation builds pretty fast, and after midnight the chances of you and Lawrence escaping are slim. Marc and I began with a ménage a trois with Kate while Jon watched. Then a few days later, I went with Jon and Kate while Marc watched. It wasn't full swapping to start, just foreplay."

Allison takes a deep breath, forcing herself to remain casual as her insides start burning with desire at the memory. She is now more obsessed than ever with getting the Rossis to join their group.

"Wait," Carla furrows her brow and giggles nervously. "Isn't that sort of a letdown? You get all worked up, and then nothing?"

Allison shakes her head slowly and raises one eyebrow, an old trick she figured out she could do in fifth grade. "Not when your husband is there watching and waiting to whisk you away for the most heart-stopping sex you've ever had," she says. "It's not all about the sex with other people. For many of us, that foreplay enhances and recharges our sex lives in our *own* marriages. Trust me, it works."

She can see Carla's mind spinning. Allison knows, because she was the same way—incredulous, her head filled with images of writhing orgies. But Kate took her hand, eased her in, and showed her the way, and now Allison is doing the same for Carla.

"I can see that working in the right scenario," Carla says carefully. "How long was it before Marc and Kate had sex?"

"It didn't happen right away, but it happened on its own time, naturally. The chemistry was already fierce, and we'd become friends. It came easy evolving to the next step over time."

She doesn't have to spell out that it's exactly the same with their new foursome.

Allison feels that old familiar jealousy rising. This time, though, she's not sure what's sparking the feelings: is it Kate, or could it be Carla? She seems interested in straight up sex with Marc, which shocks her; Allison thought Carla would be more interested in a little foreplay at first. Certainly not full swapping.

"So, if Lawrence and I decide to join, who would go first?"

"It's not always planned out ahead of time," Allison explains. "But I'm thinking maybe you and I could put on a show for our men and then disappear. Or we could—"

"Who would disappear?" Carla is officially intrigued.

Allison is shaken by Carla bombarding her with questions; she must be feeling those cocktails.

She's saved by the chaos before she can get too anxious about this sudden turn of events. The guys tromp up the stairs to join them, followed by the kids, and she and Carla hop off their sun loungers to help get dinner served.

Allison is grateful for the reprieve. Maybe she's not so sure she wants this. The back and forth is starting to get to her.

But then Lawrence, who is perspiring ever so slightly from the Wiffle ball game, comes into her view.

Oh, yes, she wants this. Allison has only fully swapped with Jon, who is a gentle, giving lover.

But lately, Allison is in the mood for someone to be primal with her and looking in Lawrence's eyes now, she *feels* it.

"I hope everyone is *stahvin*!" Marc calls out.

Allison is at the stove and pulling the side dishes out of her double ovens, and she and Marc lay out corn on the cob, steamers with drawn butter, lobsters, and roasted potatoes. And chicken nuggets, hot dogs with fries for the kids.

Carla jumps in to help and pulls the coleslaw, cucumber salad, and watermelon out of the refrigerator.

"Look at all this food! When did you guys have time to prepare all of this?" Lawrence asks.

"It's our yearly tradition, so we have it down cold." Marc smiles. "This is easily the best holiday of the year. When else do you get to drink beer all day, man the grill, light a bonfire, and watch fireworks?

The two families sit together at the festive round table decorated in red, white, and blue ceramic, matching cloth napkins, and a vase full of wildflowers. A mixed-fruit pie decorated like an American flag and sits high up on display on a side table.

They enjoy their food and some good laughs. Marc opens a nice Pinot Gris to go with the ladies' dinner and grabs another round of beers for himself and Lawrence.

"Lawrence, what time did Will say he would be home?" Carla asks as she looks towards her husband.

"He didn't say, but I would guess soon after the fireworks." Lawrence sounds confident enough.

"I wouldn't be too sure of that," Marc argues. "Those beach parties can go all night. Ask Allison. She's been to many of those parties when she was his age. You know she grew up summering here. I've heard she's seen many July fifth sunrises."

Marc glugs some beer and smiles mischievously at his wife.

When dinner is done and everyone is well fed and had more than their fill of sun, the sky darkens to night and everyone settles in to watch the distant fireworks ignite the sky.

– 67 –
Wake Up

Brooke

The call comes at precisely 1:11 a.m. It's an easy number to remember: 1:11. At first the ringing is part of her dream, a distant sound of someone else's phone. But it won't stop. Eventually the noise pulls her from a deep sleep into a semi-wakened state.

Brooke reaches over to his bedside table to make it stop, to shut it up. *Why is it so loud?*

"Is this Mrs. Doyle?" The deep voice on the other end continues without waiting for an answer. "This is Detective Wiley of the Nantucket police department."

The instant pit in Brooke's stomach was enough to make her gag. "Yes. Yes, this is Brooke Doyle. What's going on?"

She turns to Kevin's side of the bed. "Kev! Wake up. Something's happened."

Is it Charlie? Her mother? Who could it be?

She reaches out to rouse him, but she only hits pillows. Kevin's gone.

"What's happened? Oh my god, what's wrong?" It's a feral shriek into the phone.

– 68 –

Phone Tree

Kate

Kate jolts awake with her phone's shrill alert. She usually leaves Do Not Disturb on for all but close friends and family, so she knows this can't be good.

Her heart races immediately: *Caroline!* It's an emergency; has to be. Who would be calling in the middle of the night unless something horrific had occurred?

She sees who the caller is. *Not Caroline. Thank you, God.*

As soon as she hits the answer button, a woman's voice screams down the phone.

"Kate! I'm sorry to call so late. I need help. Kevin needs help!"

"Brooke?!" Kate lurches up in bed and whips around to wake up Jon. He's not there.

"Brooke, slow down, please. Tell me what happened. Take a breath."

Jon enters the room, yawning and groggy.

"Where were you?" Kate says in a stage whisper, hand over the mouthpiece. "It's Brooke. Kevin's in big trouble."

"Needed a glass of water." Jon, empty handed, perches by Kate at the edge of the bed.

Brooke is bawling. Kate puts the phone on speaker. "It's Kevin," Brooke says through sobs. "He's been in a terrible car accident, *and* he's been arrested, but they won't tell me why! I need a lawyer. And I need a ride! I don't have a car—he took the Jeep, Kate. I don't know what to do! Please, can you come over? I'm so sorry, I didn't know who else to call…"

Jon takes the phone from Kate and says calmly into the receiver, "You did the right thing, Brooke. We'll be there as fast as we can."

– 69 –
Attorney Evans

Allison

Allison rolls over when she hears ringing. She reaches over across Marc, eyes still closed, slaps her hand around and finds Marc's phone.

"Hello." It barely comes out as a word. She clears her sleepy voice.

"Hello? Oh, hi! Of course, it's fine. Yes. He's right here."

"It's for you, babe," Allison, groggy, her voice husky, says as she holds out the phone. Marc is already awake and rubbing his eyes. "It's Jon."

Marc yawns and takes the phone. They're both accustomed to late-night calls because of Marc's attorney practice. It's never fun to be woken out of a sound sleep, but they're usually comfortable assuming it's an emergency that doesn't involve them or anyone they love, especially when they know the girls are tucked safely in their beds.

"Hey, Jon," Marc says. "What's going on?"

Allison, fully awake now, gestures to Marc to put it on speaker; he nods and obliges.

"I need your help. It's Kevin Doyle. He's gotten himself into a spot of trouble."

Marc kicks into lawyer mode. He sits up straight and changes his tone from buddy-buddy to attorney-client. "What's happened? Is he OK? Is Brooke OK?"

Marc grabs the yellow legal-size notepad he keeps by his bedside. He has an identical pad of paper in his nightstand at home, too.

"They're both in good shape, from what we're told," Jon says. "Brooke got a call from a Nantucket detective a little while ago. Apparently, Kevin was out driving and plowed into some guy's fancy fence, and the homeowner heard the whole thing and called the cops."

"Was he drunk?"

"They said he was on something, but they didn't say what. The detective said Kevin was totally out of it and shouldn't have been behind the wheel. He submitted to blood tests already."

"First things first," Marc says crisply. "Get Brooke to tell him not to say a word to anyone. Not a single word."

"Got it," Jon replies. "I think they took him to the hospital, so hopefully he didn't blurt anything before that."

"He'll likely be arraigned in the morning if the doctors give him the all-clear," Marc says. "We need to get him bail. I'll make some calls first thing and find out when and where."

– 70 –
Waking Nightmare

Brooke

Brooke, a box of tissues within reach, sits at the kitchen table. She glances at the colorful, blown-glass clock on the wall. It's almost two-thirty.

Jon and Kate raced over when she called, and even took separate cars so Brooke would have a car to drive to the courthouse in a few hours.

"Please, I'll be fine now. You two have done enough." Brooke tries to smile. Her eyes are red and stinging. "I'll be OK on my own. Marc's going to text me when he knows about the arraignment and everything. I wish I could be at the hospital."

"You heard what the detective said," Jon reminds her. "They didn't think he was hurt. It's only a precaution. He'll be taken to jail as soon as the doctors see him. He's probably already gone by now."

Brooke grabs her tissue box and pulls another one out. "I know," she says. "I don't understand how this happened. Where was he going? We had nothing more to drink after brunch, and then we went to sleep together and the next thing I know, the police are calling. None of it makes sense."

"There, there," Kate says, wrapping her arms around Brooke's shoulders. "You need to get some sleep. All will become clear tomorrow. I'm sure of it."

They both kiss her on the cheek, and Brooke staggers upstairs with a glass of water, hoping to get a few hours' sleep before the arraignment.

Brooke is showered, dressed and ready well before the 10:00 a.m. court appearance Marc texted her about. She finds court terrifying, even when it's for work. Everything is so formal, so much is at stake, and there is often no mercy.

She, Jon, and Marc converge outside the courthouse.

"I can't thank you enough," Brooke says, handing Marc the suit he advised her to bring for Kevin. "We owe you such a debt of gratitude. Jon can tell you where to send the bill for your fees."

"No need to worry about that now," Marc replies. "What I'm interested in, Brooke, is what was going on with Kevin yesterday? We got his tox results back already. The guy was on enough benzodiazepines to kill an elephant."

Brooke shakes her head. "That makes no sense," she says. "Why would he be driving? where was he *going*? His last dose was at noon. We didn't drink anything at all last night, and he never took any more pills. They were half a milligram each, so the max he had yesterday was two milligrams. He had twelve hours for that therapeutic dose to leave his system. These results are wrong."

"How can you possibly know he didn't have any more when you weren't looking?" Jon asks. "He said himself that he was popping pills like Skittles."

"I know," Brooke says levelly, "because after a double vodka at the restaurant, he didn't notice me hugging him and grabbing the bottle out of his pocket. I've had possession of it since his last dose at noon yesterday."

Jon looks shocked by this information and falls silent.

"What if he has other pills that you don't know about?" Marc asks.

"I suppose it's possible," Brooke says, unconvinced. "But not here in Nantucket. I'm trained in this, remember? He didn't need to hide his pills. He was taking them in plain sight, prescribed legally by his doctor. This…this situation makes no sense."

"What are you saying, Brooke?" Marc asks, his brow furrowed.

"I don't know," she says quietly. "It's just not possible…"

"I'm afraid blood tests don't lie," Marc says somberly. "Kevin's benzodiazepine levels were through the roof. He should never have been behind the wheel of a car. He's lucky he didn't kill anyone, including himself."

Brooke has no other argument for it.

A half an hour later, she's sitting behind Marc as he makes his case before the judge for Kevin's release, and she hears as he agrees on what sounds like a very manageable sum, and a sheepish Kevin falls into her arms as he is dismissed by the judge and told to come back at a later date in September.

Brooke drives Kate's loaner car, an Audi usually reserved for Caroline when she's on Nantucket and confronts Kevin as they make their way back to their rental home.

"What the hell happened?" She asks. "Are you hiding pills from me, Kevin? And where the hell were you going at that hour?"

"I'm so confused," he cries, rubbing the sides of his head with both hands. "I remember Jon and Kate stopping by to check on us. Well, *you*, they wanted to see how *you* were, and next thing I know, I'm waking up behind the wheel of our Jeep. I swear I don't remember anything else, Brooke."

"You'll forgive me if I don't take your word for it," she says. "I'll be searching everything you own for more pills to explain those blood test results."

"Go to town," he says, his voice thin, pleading in such a way that Brooke almost believes him. "You won't find any. I promise. I didn't take anything or drink anything after brunch. On my mother's life."

– 71 –
Dress Stress

Allison

Allison and Carla are walking beach roads to Miacomet past the spectacular dunes and watching beachgoers arrive with their boards, coolers, and sand chairs. They park like tourists, too damn close to the dunes.

Allison shakes her head. "I remember when you could drive on all these beaches and it was like being on the end of the earth with no one in sight. Now the secret of our island is out."

Carla sighs. "That does sound perfect. But this…even like this, it's heavenly."

Allison feels a pang of sadness and tries to put her finger on where it's coming from. Maybe it's all the changes on the island and in her life. There's something making her very uneasy, and she can't shake thoughts of her sister when she was young and carefree walking this very path.

Breathe, Allison. She's heard that advice often over the years, and sometimes it works. As the seagrass sways, the sun warms her and the sound of the waves crashing is like a symphony, she lets it start to calm her.

Her attempt at a moment of peace is interrupted by an excited Carla. "Allison, you need to prep me for Kate's big party," she pleads. "I have three different dress options. You have to come over this week and help me decide."

Carla tilts her head and seems to sense Allison's mood. She reaches out and grabs Allison's hand. "Allie."

They both stop and face each other, and Allison sees her reflection in Carla's sunglasses. "Are you OK?" Carla asks, squeezing her hand.

Allison can do nothing but reach out and embrace Carla, holding her tightly as she realizes she hasn't had a friendship so real in a long time. "Promise me we'll be honest with each other no matter what," Allison says, pulling away.

Carla wipes a tear off Allison's cheek with one finger. "Of course! What's going on with you, Allie?"

Allison is walking again, and Carla falls in step with her. "I'm just tired," Allison says. "This island was my safe haven and now it's always some drama. Like the call Marc received at like three in the morning the other day. Jon's friend Kevin apparently is OK, but he crashed his car and got arrested. Marc is with him now discussing what comes after yesterday's arraignment."

Carla's eyes go wide. "When were you going to tell me this?"

"Sorry," Allison forces a smile. "I was dead asleep when the call came in, and I'm so foggy and melancholic today, I flat-out forgot. Now. Let's grab some iced coffees and sit for a bit at Bartlett's Farm before we head back. You can tell me about these dresses!"

Allison half listens to Carla go on about the green one with the straps. *What's going on with me?* She wonders as Carla carries on about platform shoes, gold jewelry and jewel tone dresses.

Carla notices Allison's not fully locking in and says brightly, "Let's head back."

On the way home Carla challenges Allison. "Let's pick up the pace and race home!"

Carla darts ahead before Allison knows what's happening. They've become pretty competitive these last few weeks, though Allison can still run circles around Carla. A part of her loves watching Carla as her confidence grows and she starts to shine. Marc has clearly noticed, too; Allison sees the way he looks at Carla and notes a burning intensity when the two of them lock eyes.

Alison takes off after her. In the final stretch, she sees Marc's car pulling into their driveway and both women kick it into high gear. Allison pulls in front of Carla as Marc steps out of the car.

Carla doubles over, still unable to catch her breath, as Marc watches intently.

"I see you weren't expecting Allie's fifth gear in the last fifty yards…she makes you think you're going to beat her and then she turns on the rockets," Marc laughs.

"You seem upbeat," Allison observes her breathing slows. "Did it go well?"

"About as well as it can when your client doesn't even remember leaving the house, let alone getting in the car." Marc rolls his eyes.

"Looks like it is going to be an interesting lead up to Kate and Jon's party," Allison says. "I wonder if Kevin and Brooke are still going." Allison feels her chest tighten. "I better call Kate and see if I can get a peek at the final guest list."

Carla offers, "Do you think she needs any help preparing?"

"I wouldn't worry too much about that," Marc points out. "You know she has a small army at her fingertips."

"Believe me," Allison shakes her head. "You have no idea what it takes to orchestrate the social event of the year. Clothes, jewelry, timing, the specialty drink, when the band goes on, when the candles are lit in the pool as the sun sets and the twinkling lights strung along the hedge turn on, the strawberries and champagne buckets in the cabana, the timing of slow songs…"

Allison grabs Carla, who's still breathless, and twirls her around. "This party is going to epic. I hope you're ready for it."

I hope I'm ready for it, Allison thinks nervously, but keeps smiling.

– 72 –

The Games Begin

Carla

Carla's nerves are on fire. She can't believe tonight is here.

Marc opens the door for Carla to climb into the back of the black Escalade, where she sits next to Allison. "Well, well, well," he grins. "Look at you two."

"What's up, my man," Lawrence slaps Marc on the back and hops into the captain's chair.

Marc holds out two ice-cold drinks. "I brought some roadies for the drive out to the Gibsons' place," he grins.

Lawrence takes one and Carla coos from the back, "Ooh, a Nantucket Red! My favorite."

"Carla, you're blowing my mind in that dress!" Allison places her hand on Carla's thigh and lets it linger. Carla is both excited and slightly unnerved by it because she knows it's a hint of what's to come tonight.

"I'm kind of freaking out," Carla whispers to Allison as the guys talk about surfing. "Like…who's going to be there that we know, did you find out if Kevin and Brooke are coming after all?"

313

Marc turns and reaches out to rub her forearm. "It'll be fun, I promise," he says. "The guests will be people you met at our party a few weeks back, plus a couple dozen socialites and billionaires that you might or might not recognize from the news. Kate and Jon only allow the crème de la crème of Nantucket society for this bash."

As they roll into 'Sconset and through the gates of the Gibsons' home, Carla sees partygoers walking up a granite path lined with lanterns and white rose petals. The front door to the home is massive, and it's manned by an equally massive bald bouncer dressed in a black suit checking off the guest list.

"Wow, they have security?" Lawrence asks.

"That's Jean-Pierre, their security chief," Allison informs them. "He's their most trusted advisor and with Jon's family money, they need someone who will have their backs. Not to mention this is invite-only and Kate doesn't mess around with her guest list."

"Oh, look, there's Logan Williams and Alexa Barlow from our party. You remember them, Lawrence," Marc says, cocking one eyebrow.

"Sure do," Lawrence replies, pretending not to understand the subtext.

The SUV rolls to a stop behind several other vehicles unloading well-dressed passengers, and the two men exit and help their wives do the same.

As soon as they enter the Nantucket estate, Carla is in awe. There's a wall of glass stretching along the oceanside with white linen drapes softly dancing through the open doors. Every detail and design has been meticulously thought out, and the décor is like nothing Carla's ever seen outside of Instagram and glossy magazines.

Oil paintings of landscapes and scenery grace the soft white walls. Beyond the main living room, Carla is drawn by a sweeping view of the custom-designed pool surrounded by hedges offering complete privacy from the rest of the world. Certainly, no detail has been missed from the covered daybeds wrapped in white sheers billowing with the soft breeze to the coordinating loungers.

"Hello, my loves." Kate appears from the stream of arriving guests and offers air kisses all around.

A server offers them all champagne from his tray, and when they all have a glass, Jon appears. "I have a toast," he says as he saunters towards the group.

"Thank you first to Allison for your help keeping us sane all day," Jon says, and Allison smiles back shyly. "We're so appreciative of our friendship with both you and Marc." He turns to Carla and Lawrence. "And it is an absolute pleasure to welcome the Rossis to our side of the island. I look forward to getting to know you both better."

"Cheers!" Their group says in unison while clinking glasses.

Marc shoots Carla a surreptitious look that gives her butterflies.

Let the games begin, Carla thinks as she takes a long swig of crisp champagne.

– 73 –

Seaweed

Brooke

Brooke and Kevin step out of the Uber and make their way to the grand entrance. Kate is there to greet them, and as their host gives her a quick hug, Brooke whispers, "I didn't want to leave him alone. He's feeling better and I promise he won't overdo it or take any meds. I hope you don't mind?"

"Of course not," Kate whispers back, and she sounds sincere to Brooke. "While I am surprised, I understand. It's absolutely fine."

"Hello, Kevin," Kate smiles politely. "Welcome to our Seas the Day party. We're happy you and Brooke could make it."

"It's an honor," Kevin smiles. "I'm a different person since you saw me last. Brooke didn't think I should come back to Nantucket so soon, but here we are."

Brooke thinks, *So, Mr. Charming is back. He better behave himself tonight. I don't want to have any more regrets.*

Kate beckons them inside. "Before I have to go back to my hosting duties, let me introduce you to my dear, dear friends Marc and Allison," she says. "Oh wait, I forgot you have met.

Consider this . . . proper introductions."

Brooke holds Kevin's hand as they follow Kate. "Allison, Marc!" Kate finds Allison at the bar, but Brooke doesn't see Marc anywhere. "Look who just arrived, Brooke and Kevin."

Allison immediately reaches out to envelop them each in an enthusiastic hug. "It's great to meet you both properly. That day at the club was utter chaos, wasn't it?"

If Allison had an odd expression on her face the first time she and Kevin met in the golf club parking lot, tonight she's happy, clear-eyed, and bubbly.

Brooke is relieved. She was imagining that Allison had taken a disliking to them both that day. And chances are she knows all about the arrest, unless Marc keeps his legal matters confidential.

Kate says, "Allie, can you see they get a drink and settle in? I must go outside and greet my guests. I'll see you all later." She waves and floats away.

"You'll see Marc at some point," Allison says to Brooke. "He's mixing and mingling. Now. What are you two having? Signature drink of the night is a seaweed martini, and it's to *die* for."

"Eh…I'll stick to club soda for now," Kevin says.

"Nonsense," Allison grins back. "You must try it." She proceeds to order three, and Brooke cringes as Kevin dives into his. Her first sip of this unique cocktail leaves a tingle on her tongue and instantly brings Brooke back to the first day she met Kate when she was feeling so hopeful and carefree.

As Kevin downs half of his in one gulp, Brooke notices him looking at Allison. *Always ogling women,* Brooke thinks. *He'll never change.* But wait, no, she has it wrong; he's *studying* her, and it's not lust she sees in his eyes.

She knows the two of them came into contact very briefly at the golf club, so maybe he's trying to recall that day. Whatever that odd look is, it makes Brooke uneasy.

A giant man in a tailored Armani suit—even in this hot weather—approaches them and leans in for a double air kiss with Allie.

"Ah, Jean-Pierre," Allison greets him.

"Kevin, this is—"

"No introduction needed," Kevin interrupts, offering a hand to the security chief. "We've had a few nights out in Boston with Jon." The men shake hands.

"This is my Brooke," Kevin says, and Jean-Pierre takes Brooke's extended hand and brings it to his lips for a soft kiss. "Ah, mademoiselle…. the pleasure is mine." Brooke blushes and starts to feel the stress melt away with the help of her martini.

Jean-Pierre heads back to work. Allison winks at Kevin. "Let's get another martini, shall we?"

This needles Brooke. *Why is she plying Kevin with strong drinks?*

Allison must know about Kevin, as her husband was called in the middle of the night about his dangerous crash caused by substance abuse. *Right? Or…is it possible Allison doesn't know?*

Either way, it's concerning. Brooke promised Kate her husband would behave himself tonight, and within fifteen minutes he's on his second martini.

As Kevin and Allison wait at the bar for their drinks, Brooke catches sight of a tall, curvy woman with silky black hair and enormous breasts who is staring openly at Kevin. Brooke shivers, and wonders if this is a normal part of the swinging lifestyle.

"Allison," Brooke whispers as her new friend hands her a seaweed martini. "Do you know who that woman is?" She points subtly.

"Come to think of it," Allison says, squinting to get a better look without being too obvious, "I've never seen her before. It's odd to see a woman alone at one of these things, I can tell you that much. Oh, well. I'm sure Kate will introduce us at some point. The night is young!"

– 74 –
Main Man

Allison

Allison played it off with Brooke, but she too wants to know who the single, curvy raven-haired woman is. Except for a few plus-ones of invited guests, Allison knows everyone here. She watches through the French doors as the woman zones in on Kevin from afar.

Jon approaches Brooke and Kevin, appears to say something utterly charming, and pulls Brooke away. Within seconds, the stranger slides up to Kevin and from what Allison can see, Kevin's eyes pop out of his head. The woman kisses him full on the mouth and Allison's jaw drops. *What would Brooke think?*

The woman pulls Kevin toward the pool area, out of Allison's view, and a shiver goes up her spine.

Carla's voice breaks through her focus. "Earth to Allison. Hello? You haven't had too many of these already, have you?"

Allison snaps out of it and giggles. When Allison brings her attention back to Carla, she senses her friend still needs to be eased into this kind of scene.

"Sorry, I can get lost in people watching at these things, can't you? Let me tell you who everyone is…"

"Oh, yes," Carla nods. "Please do."

Allison fills her in on all the players on the deck and indoors, discreetly pointing out the guests who will leave before midnight and those who are likely to stay and see how the night unfolds.

"Have you and Lawrence talked boundaries?" Allison whispers as she flips her hair playfully. Carla sighs and nods.

"We did. We came to an agreement of sorts, but I think we're both a little hesitant to put rules in stone since we don't have a great grasp on what it's really like, you know?"

"Oh, I know," Allison nods. "It's one of those decisions that can change everything. Thankfully, it's changed Marc and me only for the better," she lies.

Carla takes a last sip of her martini. "These are delish, but I need to switch."

As if on cue, a waiter appears. "Champagne?"

The women laugh and both grab a flute.

"I hope you're not too nervous," Allison says.

Carla shakes her head. "No, not at all. Lawrence and I agreed he would retrieve me before midnight."

"Oh," Allison raises her eyebrows. The Rossis are all over the place, and Allison doesn't believe for a second that they'll leave before midnight. "Well, then. Let's make the most of it before we all turn into pumpkins!"

They throw back their bubbly as the stars start to pop and the purple lights glow around the pool. While the band takes a break the DJ plays the song of the summer, and Allison drags Carla toward the dance floor. They pass by Kevin dirty dancing with the sultry brunette and Allison decides she'll have to find out who she is.

– 75 –

Sticker Shock

Carla

Carla catches a glimpse of Kate and Jon in a seductive dance with Brooke by the pool. She never would've guessed the sweet, innocent southern girl she's heard so much about would be a part of the late-night crowd.

Technically the afterparty hasn't started yet, but there's no denying things are heating up even before the clock strikes midnight. Carla needs to find Lawrence and talk to him again. She doesn't feel comfortable with how they left things, and she's having a great time on the dance floor with Allison and Marc. She's decided she wants to see this through—but how far she'll go is up for discussion with her husband.

She finally spots him, and to her surprise, he's leaning on the bar watching Brooke. Carla makes her way through the provocative scene on the dance floor to her man, leans into him, and gazes straight into his dark, seductive eyes. She feels his taut chest as they take a deep breath together.

"Let's talk," she says, pulling him toward the dimly lit pool path. They stroll off the path and onto the lawn.

They find a bench far from the main house, by a white picket fence bordering the neighboring yard.

"So…" Carla smiles shyly. "What do you think? Are we leaving at midnight? It's fast approaching…"

Carla places her head on his strong shoulder as she has a million times before, but somehow she feels a change is in the air, like if they do this tonight, they'll hit a point of no return. The risk alone is invigorating, terrifying, and, Carla thinks, absolutely necessary.

"Well…I'm having a blast watching you dance and flirt… and, yes, flirting myself," Lawrence admits, smiling back at her, treading as lightly as Carla has. She now truly *gets* why Allison kept driving home the point that both members of the couple must be on board for this lifestyle to work.

Her husband pulls her in tight. "But I think we have to draw a line," he says. "This is not something we can take back. There are no do overs."

Carla pulls back to look him dead in the eye.

"I agree," she says. "I'm loving the flirting and forbidden touches here and there on the dance floor. I feel like I'm at a club back in Boston after my final exams! But I…I have to admit I don't want another man inside me."

"*Whoa*," Lawrence practically shouts it. "No way that's happening!" He springs up off the bench. "Why would you even say that?"

She rises to meet him face to face. "I *said* it because these people have their 'couple boundaries,' and Allison thought we should have ours," Carla says, using air quotes and getting a little heated herself watching Lawrence amped up with jealousy.

"Definitely no." Her husband shakes his head. "Do Allison and Marc cross that line?" He seems flabbergasted, even though Carla thought he truly understood the lifestyle.

"To be honest, I'm not sure," Carla throws up her hands. "But I wanted to make sure *we* have our boundaries set."

She grabs his hand and pulls him close for a kiss. "Let's go back in, dance, see where the night takes us," she says. "But absolutely no sex with anyone else…right?"

"Agreed," her husband nods. "And if either one of us wants it to stop, we leave immediately, no questions asked. If one of us says 'Let's go,' we go."

Carla nods. "And no jealousy, no making a scene, and we stay within each other's line of sight at all times. No alone time with any of these bitches. I see how they are all looking at you," she winks.

He bursts out laughing. "That's my feisty wife," he says. "I can't wait to have you alone later tonight."

He lifts her up and spins her around, and then they make their way back to the scene.

76

Divisively Devoted

Kate

Kate, with Brooke standing by her, says goodbye to the last of the early guests then throws a look to their security chief, Jean-Pierre. He gives a slight nod, and she knows the clock has struck midnight and it's safe to shift gears.

Kate smiles at Brooke and takes her hand wordlessly. They head to the dance floor and immediately lose themselves in the music thumping through the mansion.

Out of the corner of her eye, Kate sees Jon standing at the edges, watching his domain.

Jon knows better than to leave his post, because if he did, both the men and women in the room would converge on Kate and Brooke in seconds. None of the partygoers would dare approach in Jon's presence. Kate watches him sip his cognac and pull out a Cuban cigar as he observes another scene unfolding out by the pool: Kevin and Michelle are heating up with a very public dance of desire.

Ah, Michelle. It hasn't been lost on Kate how the young dark-haired, eye-catching woman, a high-class escort Kevin has been seeing for months if not a couple of years, has attracted attention and questioning glances—particularly from Allison. So far, Jon's kept Brooke on the other side of the party, so she hasn't seen the sex worker with her husband yet.

Kate notices that Kevin is also watching Jon. *Glaring*, actually. Kate should be mad at Jon too, because she would never have allowed Michelle to come. Jon obviously slipped her in without telling Kate, and without putting her on the guest list.

Kate has already figured out why he did this; Jon knows all too well Kevin can't resist Michelle, and how poisonous her presence will be to the Doyles' marriage. Kate feels a pang of annoyance, but she's also swept up in the moment. She'll wait to decide if this was a betrayal, or if it was actually a shrewd move on Jon's part.

Jon moves in on Brooke and seems to forget all about Kate for the moment. Kate moves away and begins flirting and groping with other partygoers out by the pool while keeping a hawk eye as Brooke unbuttons Jon's white linen shirt. Brooke pulls the last button, popping it off his shirt, and runs her hands up and down his sculpted chest and his firm, masculine waist, then onto his shoulders.

Jon runs his fingers through her golden locks and kisses her gently but deeply, pressing his full body into hers. Kate has never seen Jon this besotted. His complete focus on Brooke, to the exclusion of everything else happening around him, gives her pause. Something's different this time. Something Kate doesn't like.

She watches Jon pull abruptly out of Brooke's grasp. He takes her hands and pulls them to his lips; then says something Kate can't hear.

Kate decides to focus on herself and her own pleasure, which is the point of these parties in the first place. *Fuck it.* Kate brazenly heads out to the pool area and joins Kevin and Michelle in their sexy romp.

Kevin smiles languidly and embraces Kate when she approaches, planting a sensual kiss on her lips as Michelle massages his firm ass. But Kate knows a distracted man when she kisses one. She opens her eyes to see him staring at Brooke, who is so obviously under the spell of a man who was once Kevin's close confidante.

So deep of a spell, Kate thinks, that Brooke hasn't even appeared to notice another woman all over her husband just outside.

Kevin looks down as Kate slides down his leg while Michelle mirrors her on the other side. Kate sees in Kevin's eyes that he wants nothing more than to hate fuck Kate as he watches Jon gently caress his wife.

Why does he have to sexually dominate his lovers? Kate knows now with a cold certainty that Jean-Pierre's detective work was spot on; Kevin cannot control his impulses.

As Kevin grabs Kate and Michelle from behind, Michelle nips at his lip while Kate undoes his striped Vineyard Vines bowtie.

"Why don't we head inside?" Kate suggests deciding to play with fire.

Kevin glances toward Brooke and Jon embracing, and he looks crushed when he sees Brook rush into the house, seemingly upset.

Kate watches Jon take off after Brooke. Kevin tears himself away from Kate and Michelle and pushes through the hot, steamy crowd. Kate leaves Michelle looking dumfounded as Kate follows Kevin and Jon.

Tearing into the house, Kevin gains on Jon who is using quick, phony smiles and hellos to pacify guests vying for his attention. Kate can see Kevin is operating on pure adrenaline and rage. As he flies past Jon he checks him with his shoulder, clearly determined to find Brooke. In a matter of seconds, Kevin spots Brooke distraught in the kitchen and approaches.

Kate intently watches Kevin and Brooke. Neither of them notices the various people who are watching their marriage implode in real time.

Kevin slides his hand over Brooke's as she grips the counter. He straightens himself and runs his hand through his sweaty hair. Brooke turns and fixes a cool gaze on her husband.

Kate, who can't hear anything they're saying, then sets her attention back to Jon, who remains laser-focused on Brooke and Kevin.

Kate is behind Jon now, hidden in the low lighting. Jon is too focused on his new conquest to notice. To Kate's surprise, Brooke's body language changes, and she's now listening intently to whatever Kevin is saying to her.

Jon's shoulders tense up at watching this, and Kate thinks, *What is happening here? Is he too far gone for this woman already? Did I miss the signs? Am I too late?*

Kate doesn't plan on losing sight of her husband again tonight. He's up to something, and she's going to stay on him until she finds out what it is.

77

Blessing and a Curse

Brooke

"**B**rookie, please don't leave me," Kevin is begging. "I love you…*only* you. I don't know why I can't control myself. I feel like a failure." He hangs his head. "Do you even know how much my life depends on you; how much I've relied on you from the very beginning to save me?"

Brooke has never seen this kind of humility from him. *Ever.* He leans in for a quick, gentle kiss, and she goes with it.

"I don't deserve you, Brooke," he says when they pull apart. His voice is strong and sure, though she knows he's had a bunch of cocktails.

"I know," she replies, consumed with emotion.

He wipes her tears with the back of his hand as he searches for the expression on her face.

"I love you, Brooke," he says. Something in his voice alarms her. It's different from any other time since she's known him. "I always will. But you deserve more. More than I will ever be able to give you, and I want you to be loved in the same way that *you* love."

Brooke feels sick hearing his words. She wasn't ready for them, or to see genuine relief on his face. He turns his back to her and calmly makes his way towards Jon. He places a hand on his old friend's back, a gesture of approval and defeat. He nods to Jon and walks away.

Brooke is flabbergasted that Kevin had the capacity to turn and walk away. Not only did he bow out, but he made it seem gallant, the bastard! This has been her problem with him from day one: he's the one in the wrong but *she* feels bad for him. His hired girlfriend is here in Nantucket and he is groping her, but Brooke feels bad for him? *Really?*

She's kept her cool all night with Jon's help, but of *course* Brooke saw the brunette crawling all over Kevin. After a few probing questions, Jon explained exactly who Michelle is but no one seems to know why she mysteriously showed up. She suspects Jon is covering for Kevin, who must have brought the sex worker here in some twisted bid to make Brooke jealous.

Brooke watches Kevin stagger away toward the bar, and decides her habit of trying to please him, to chase him, to placate him, ends now. Brooke lets the sweet night air fill her lungs and turns her eyes on Jon.

Brooke, hardly an aggressive soul, takes several long strides, steps to Jon, and firmly grabs hold of his arm, wrapping it around her waist. She looks into his eyes and is overcome with emotion. Jon's expression makes Brooke feel like there is no other woman on the planet but her.

Brooke suddenly notices all eyes on her and looks to Jon in a panic.

Jon grabs her hand and leads the way. "Follow me Brooke, I

have a surprise for you. I hope it's everything you ever dreamed of."

Brooke feels her heart unclench for a moment. This isn't wild lust he's showing for her; it's something entirely different. She follows Jon away from the curious eyes. Finally they arrive at a much quieter place. Jon opens a door and Brooke sees only darkness inside before she realizes there are stairs going down.

Jon guides her through the door, shuts it behind them, and holds her arm as they descend the steps. At the bottom are lavish, purple, velvet curtains hanging in the ornately arched doorway, which must be at least twelve feet high.

On the other side of the curtain is a long hallway that reminds Brooke of a medieval castle she and Kevin once visited in Ireland. The hall is lit by candles and the walls are lined with beautiful, smoky-colored marble. She notices that they pass several rooms with similar purple velvet drapes; some are closed but she peers into a slightly open one. Brooke spots an ornate chandelier dimly flickering against several leather couches. On the couches she's surprised to see several couples engaging in more intimate counters. It's a lot to take in.

She hears laughter in the distance behind her but resists turning around and continues to follow Jon who leads her up a set of stairs and back outside onto a covered blue stone patio.

"Welcome to our guest house," Jon says. "Let me give you a tour of your new oasis."

Jon opens the set of French doors and Brooke takes in the peaceful sitting room with a magnificent view of the Atlantic. She is mesmerized by the distant dark ocean lit only by the moonlight dancing off the water. Brooke lets out a deep sigh and feels the stress dissipate from her body as she steps out onto a balcony that faces north.

Brooke sees flickering lights and hears the faint sound of music from the main party. Two Adirondack chairs with footrests and white, down-filled cushions await them with a bottle of champagne.

"Sit and enjoy the view," Jon says. Brooke obliges and Jon pops the champagne and fills two flutes with the bubbly. He passes her a fresh glass, then holds his glass to hers and toasts.

"To new beginnings." Brooke hastily raises her glass and clinks his, then downs her champagne.

"Brooke, look at me." Jon gets down on one knee and starts to remove her strappy sandals.

She's buzzed, so she allows it, and tries to read his intense expression.

"I know what you've been through, and we both know you need time to recharge," he says, now caressing her sore feet. "With all that has happened, you're one of the strongest women I know. I feel bad for Kevin, but he has the ability to make you want to help him, to fix him. You and I know the only person who can help Kevin is Kevin."

Brooke knows what Jon is saying is true, but the unbearable need to save him from himself remains overwhelming. Brooke so badly wants to embrace this gentle and kind soul in front of her and pretend Kevin does not exist, but something feels wrong, and she resists.

She says, "You and I both know he is not going to get help. He is going to self-destruct. I feel responsible."

"Oh, Brooke, you can't put this on yourself," Jon argues,

rising to sit next to her. "You love him, you have given more than most would give, and if it were not for you, he would have self-destructed long ago. He'll drag you down with him, and you know it. Hell, he knows it. Do you think he walked away because he doesn't love you? No, he walked away because he does. In fact, I think it was the most courageous thing he's ever done."

Jon pulls Brooke to her feet and holds her tight. She knows he's speaking the truth. She can't put Kevin's demons on herself; she needs to live for herself, for Charlie. She needs to listen to this man in front of her who has saved her and held her and made her realize that it is alright to put herself first.

Brooke leans back and says two words, "Thank you."

Jon leans over and kisses her on the forehead.

"Brooke, you can stay in these guest quarters for as long as you like," he says. "I hope you will feel comfortable here for the rest of the summer."

Brooke starts to feel dizzy and whispers, "Jon, I think I need go to lay down." She begins to stand but loses her balance. Jon is there to catch her and he carries her to the bedroom. Jon flips on a light, and a crystal chandelier glows over the crisp white duvet accented with soft purple and orange flowered pillows.

Brook begins, "I…I…don't…" Jon lays one index finger over her lips.

"Shhh…. get some rest. You've had a long evening. I'll bring you breakfast on the balcony in the morning."

Brooke puts on a small smile and lays her head on the plush pillow.

78

Midnight Madness

Carla

Carla can hardly believe she's still at the party—and that she's finally feeling Marc's hands on her. He pulls her close as they dance, their palms touching as they raise their arms in the air. They are one with the music. He locks his warm hands over hers and turns her around, her arms now crossed in front of her body. She begins to move her voluptuous body against his, feeling him rise under her coaxing.

They bump into another couple as they dance. Carla observes a dark-haired beauty, her bright-orange sundress dropped from her shoulders, being ravaged by a blond-haired man. The man looks up and locks eyes with Carla. Carla gasps, her heart in her throat as she recognizes this man is Brooke's husband.

Carla's body is screaming *yes* even more loudly now.

"Carla," Marc whispers her name into her ear as he spins her back around to face him.

She feels like she has no breath, no air left in her lungs. She gazes into Marc's eyes and melts into him, unsure if she's weak from desire or hesitation.

"Are you doing okay?" Marc takes a quick nibble on her lobe as he asks.

"Yes," she mouths as she licks her lips, needing more.

Her brain does not seem to be attached to her body. Her own mind is shaming her: *This is your friend's husband, your neighbor, your children's friend's father, what in creation are you doing? Where is your husband? You know, the father of your three children?*

Suddenly Marc jumps back as if he is listening to her thoughts. His chest is rising and falling quickly, and she admires his built body through his tight black V-neck.

"Let's join our partners." Marc says as they make their way through the crowd that has formed around the steaming pool.

As they slide in between half-dressed, hot bodies, she feels them grooving against hers. They are all moving in rhythm with the pounding dance music.

They pass through the rose-covered arbor, leaving the soiree at the pool barely visible. Catching her breath, Carla is clinging to Marc and can feel his tense bicep under her hands. He begins to caress her with his strong, skilled hand.

As he steps toward her, they're suddenly in the shadows, separate from the purple light shining on the dance floor up the pathway. His mouth is recklessly on hers with such intensity their lips thirst for more. Indulging in the moment she tastes his desire and feels every twist and turn, his teeth grazing her lip she playfully pulls back enticing him to come in for more. She lunges back into him kissing deeper and with even more passion. She hasn't felt this much passion since...

"Let's go." Marc snaps her out of her fog and pulls her back into the purple light, towards the dance floor. The pulse of the music is still beating.

Carla can feel every nerve in her body; she is on the verge of imploding. A faint attempt at composure leaves her breathless on the dance floor.

There, amid the sultriness, she sees something she thought she'd been prepared for, something she agreed to. It is her soul mate dancing close with Marc's. Marc circles behind Allison, and Carla releases her grip, stalking behind Lawrence. She wraps her arms around her husband, squeezing his toned chest as he is rubbing his hands slowly down Allison's thighs.

Carla cannot believe they are doing this. *Are they really going to do this?* There is a rush of adrenaline surging through her she has never felt. She feels so invigorated and so sexy, like she is the most desirable woman in the world.

79

Embracing Desire

Allison

As Lawrence slides his hands down Allison's hips and onto her firm outer thigh, she watches Carla come up behind him. The lavender scent of Carla's perfume wafts over them.

Allison watches Marc dirty dancing with another woman and it turns her on more. Carla slides to the side of both Lawrence and Allison and he leans into her, as Allison and Carla writhe on his hips. Lawrence passionately kisses Carla, making his way to her ear to ask, "Do you want this?"

Allison is right there as Carla replies, "Yes, do you?"

As Allison slowly reaches down and holds on, Lawrence turns and unleashes a deep, forbidden kiss on Allison. She gasps and bites his lip hard. She then leans into Carla and moves from Lawrence's lips to Carla's. Lawrence looks like he's about to explode.

Allison leans back into Lawrence's firm body, and they lose themselves in the excitement. Marc approaches Carla and fondles her breasts as he consumes her arching neck.

"Why don't the four of us head inside," Allison whispers as

she presses Lawrence's hand against her tensed lower abs. "Come with me, let's grab a bottle of champagne."

When they reach the mahogany bar, Allison removes a chilled bottle of champagne from a silver ice bucket. They circle back to Carla and Marc who they lost back on the dance floor. On the way, Lawrence pops the cork on the bottle and takes a swig and hands the bottle to Allison. They fall into the rhythm of the slow song next to their partners. As Allison reaches one hand around Lawrence's chest, she places the bottle in his hand. She runs her hands under his shirt and then up his muscular, sweaty back, feeling him tense under her touch. Allison watches intently while he drinks from the bottle then turns to passionately kiss his wife.

"You are both so hot," Allison whispers in his ear as she lightly nips his earlobe.

Marc is massaging Carla's neck while locking eyes with his wife. He gives Allison a look she knows all too well and lifts his perfectly shaped brow. Allison maneuvers her way around Lawrence's body, touching and dancing her way to Carla.

"We need a room," announces Allison. "It's time." Allison knows just where to go.

Allison links her arms with Carla. They pass several rooms with closed velvet curtains until they reach one still open. Their husbands follow them through the mahogany archways. Once inside, Allison wraps her hand around the champagne pulling Lawrence's hand towards her aching chest. She takes a small sip from the sweating bottle before passing it onto Marc, and she stares into Lawrence's dark eyes.

Allison is startled to feel someone unzipping her dress. She turns and meets Carla and they come together in a long kiss.

Lawrence's strong hands move down to her ass with a determined force. Allison feels an intense tingling shoot into her.

Allison looks up into Marc's eyes for her next cue. He motions to the left, and Allison moves to face Lawrence. With his rigid, clenched jaw, he nearly suffocates her as he kisses her. She feels his rough hands pulling her dress down to the ground as she embraces him with both hands and gasps in awe. She feels him pause and sees his eyes float to Carla and Marc.

Allison abruptly steps back, and as she does, Lawrence moans. Carla, hearing her husband's familiar sounds of desire, leaves Marc and joins her husband. Allison looks to Marc and senses his heart must be pounding. He is lying on the soft leather couch, aroused and ready for his wife.

– 80 –
Enough

Carla

Carla has never felt this desirable and sexy, except maybe the first time she and Lawrence met.

Allison and Marc stuck to their boundaries and set off on their own, leaving Carla ready for Lawrence more than ever because of her encounter with Marc. When she was removing Marc's white linen shirt, she had felt the power of his manhood beneath her and was overcome with lust as she felt his chiseled arms, the arms she had been longing to touch.

She had tasted the sweat on his lips and saw the look of desire in his eyes, and she realized how much he had been lusting for her too.

Now, as Lawrence puts his mouth frantically on hers, Carla feels like someone is watching her.

She jumps to her feet and sees Jon smirking in the shadows of the purple velvet curtains. Their eyes meet momentarily, and then he disappears.

Lawrence appears to have seen Jon too. Carla holds Lawrence's face in her hands and kisses his distracted lips in a frenzy. She notices Lawrence watching Allison and Marc out of the corner of his eye.

Carla pushes Lawrence down on the matching leather couch while she climbs on top of him; she sees Marc's laser-like eyes locked in on her. They watch while one another makes love to their spouses.

Carla feels her blood pumping as the stare turns to an occasional glance, and her imagination has Marc under her. She can feel Lawrence as he clutches her hips with a tight grip. She can hold on no longer.

81

Nightcap

Allison

Allison is breathless and draped over Marc. Her head is on his chest, and his heart feels as if it will explode against her ear.

She catches a satiated Lawrence glancing over at them.

Allison feels triumphant knowing she not only got these two into the lifestyle, but that they found it satisfying and exciting. Allison is thrilled she and Marc have an alternative to Kate and Jon.

Her job should be done. She should be spent.

But Allison Evans has one last, difficult move to make before she can truly enjoy the rest of the summer.

She glances over as Lawrence, still looking like he's in awe, and she lets out a little laugh. He joins in and after a moment, it seems he can't stop.

Now the four of them are giggling releasing tension and lightening things up. Carla and Allison are trying to fix their hair, pulling back ruffled strands. Carla pulls down her sundress.

"Now I know why everyone runs around in sundresses," Lawrence says. "Oh, and did anyone see Jon being a peeping

Tom? What the hell was that all about?" He throws his hands up as his eyes grow wide.

"He loves to see who is in his playrooms," Marc says with a shrug.

"We're lucky he didn't come in and ask to join." Allison laughs as she rolls her eyes. "Technically, that's not entirely the way it's done. But his house, his rules, I guess."

"Join?" Lawrence says. "That would've been a buzz kill." They all nod in agreement.

Allison does one last check of her hair and dress then heads to the door. "I'm going to get some water. I'll be right back."

"Water? Is that how you want to celebrate our group romp?" Marc turns to Lawrence. "Why don't we head out to the pool for a late nightcap and cigar?"

Allison agrees. "Good idea. It's time to celebrate! I'll meet the three of you by the pool in a few."

She needs to make sure Carla doesn't follow her. Marc winks and Allison slips out the door before Carla is ready.

82

Fairy Tales

Kate

Jon moves alone through the last stragglers in the main party room. Most of the guests have retreated to private rooms, so he cruises through easily. He slips down the stairs again, through the basement hallway, and works his way towards the guest house.

He tiptoes into the room he designed for her and watches Brooke lying on the bed. He sighs and whispers, "I love you."

He gasps and whirls at a sharp noise behind him.

"Surprise, asshole," Kate says, glaring at him and blocking his way out. "What's the matter? You don't seem happy to see me, *darling*."

Brooke is pretending to be asleep, and Kate is fine pretending she's not there.

"Kate! What's wrong, my love?" Jon blinks innocently. Kate's not fooled. Not anymore. "I've been looking all over for you."

"Bullshit," Kate replies, her voice like ice. "How could you do this to me?"

Jon wasn't alone racing around catering to his pretty little princess like he thought he was. Kate was on his heels the whole time; she made a promise to herself not to let him out of her sight tonight, and she kept it.

"What's *wrong*? What's *not* wrong? Are you in love with Brooke?" Kate's seeing red but trying not to lose her cool.

"Oh, don't be ridiculous." Jon gaslights her.

"You leave me out there with Kevin and that whore so you can play knight in shining armor, and now his poor wife is…what? Our *roommate*, Jon? Did you ever intend on asking what *I* thought about all this?"

Kate flails her arms towards Brooke, who by now is most definitely faking her slumber because no one would be able to sleep through this argument.

"Oh, *please*, Kate, like you weren't enjoying every minute of it," Jon snarls. "I was watching you." He moves towards her.

"Don't you dare touch me! You think I don't know you set this whole thing up?" She says this more as an accusation, less as a question.

"I love your temper. Are you feeling jealous?" He smiles and gives her a sly look.

When she doesn't respond, Jon continues, "Kate, you know you are the sexiest woman on the island! What has you so frazzled, my dear? Is it what you saw in the playroom?"

"Don't try to make this about Allison and Marc," she snaps. "This is about *you* and your creepy behavior."

Suddenly, Brooke pops up and swings her legs off the bed. She stands up and rubs her eyes.

"Hello, Kate," she says coolly. "You think you know what's

going on, but you don't know the half of it. Check this out."

Brooke uncurls her hand and reveals something that starts to make a whole lot of things make sense. In an instant, all of Kate's suspicions are confirmed by what she sees.

Kate immediately recognizes pills inside the small clear plastic bag Brooke is holding; she went through a brief stint of pill popping herself a few years back. Thankfully those days are over. She knows that Kevin has had issues with these recently. And most importantly, Kate knows that Jon knows.

"Did you find those in this room, Brooke?" Kate asks, trying to keep her voice from wobbling.

Did Kate ever really know the man she's married to? Could the man she loves and promised to spend her life with really be this much of a psycho?

Jon interrupts, "What are you looking at? What's in her hand?"

Brooke, who had turned away to show Kate her palm, can't keep quiet and her tone turns accusatory. "You should know, Jon. I found them under the Adirondack chair where you were sitting."

Jon quicky checks his now empty pocket.

"Why would you do this?"

Jon, now understanding that he's been caught, lunges at Brooke to retrieve the pills.

Kate realizes with a chilling certainty that Jon has been plotting to remove Kevin from the picture by whatever means necessary. She reacts with pure rage, grabbing the leaded crystal vase from the side table and slams the side of Jon's head with the force of a mad woman.

The pills go flying, Brooke screams, and Jon drops to the floor with a thud, clearly unprepared for the force of the blow. He lays motionless on the ground.

"Jesus, Kate!" Brooke cries. "What is *wrong* with you?"

"Brooke, he deserves it. He drugged your husband and then put him behind the wheel of a car!"

"You people are seriously deranged," Brooke argues. I need to go find Kevin and get the hell out of here."

Jon remains still and blood has begun to spread on the white carpet around his head.

Kate starts to grasp the seriousness of the situation. She nudges her fallen husband with her foot. "Jon? Jon… are you ok?"

Brooke hesitates at the door, turning back to look at Jon on the floor.

The vase is still in Kate's hand dripping blood all over the carpet. "Jon, wake up," Kate tries again as her voice starts to quiver.

Brooke turns and dashes out the door. Kate is torn. Does she stay with Jon to make sure he's OK? Or does she follow Brooke and make sure the woman doesn't talk?"

Fear grips her as she comprehends the trouble that will follow if Brooke doesn't back her up. She kicks the bag of pills out of sight under the bed and sprints to follow Brooke, bloody vase in hand.

– 83 –

Seeing Things

Allison

Crap. Where is Kevin? Allison's plan to confront him and make him regret ever meeting her and her sister can't work unless he's still on the premises. Allison wants to antagonize him, let him know he'll never be allowed inside Nantucket society, that he and Brooke—his kind wife is collateral damage, unfortunately—will never be welcome at any of their parties again.

Kevin's ego is fragile despite his frequent bravado, and Allison knows this, and she plans to hit him where it hurts.

Allison knows damn well who this man is now, she is sure of it. It had been bothering her since the golf club parking lot, when her gut confirmed what her eyes couldn't be sure of: This was the guy from her past.

To make absolutely certain of who he was, Allison had made a point of driving Marc to the arraignment that morning, insisting she wanted to support their friends. She sat in the car and watched as Kevin left the court a free man, with no hat or sunglasses, no cocky stride. Kevin was a hungover, beaten man and Allison recognized his face and the way he moved like sixteen years hadn't passed since he changed her family forever.

He is the reason her sister isn't on the island body surfing the waves, taking beach walks, and playing with her nieces Abigail and Savannah, who adore their aunt.

Allison knows the statute of limitations has likely passed for pressing charges, so this confrontation she's planning tonight will have to be catharsis enough. She's determined to confront him now and to finally move on.

It happened the year she lived in Philadelphia with Billy. The couple had settled nicely into their two-bedroom condo and the perfect life. The job market was hot for MBA graduates willing to work sixty-plus hour weeks, so it didn't take long for Allison to land a highly paid position.

Billy's new job was also demanding and kept him out late several nights a week, which was fine for Allison since she was half asleep on the couch by ten after her long workdays. Allison and Billy traveled together almost every weekend. Work hard, play hard; they were living the dream.

On a Friday night before a long weekend, Allison was waiting for her younger sister Laura to arrive. Laura was what Allison missed most about Boston. Although they talked several times a week, it wasn't the same as when they both lived in Beantown. Back in those days they could go for a walk, a coffee, or a drink whenever they wished.

Billy's childhood friend was also visiting for the long weekend. Although Allison had only seen pictures of this good-looking man Billy was so close to, she secretly hoped that he and Laura would hit it off. Laura, two years younger than Allison, was still getting over a tough breakup with a guy she thought was the *one*.

Laura arrived to a tearful reunion with her sister, and then the four of them went out on the town. As the night progressed, it appeared Allison's wishes might come true. They enjoyed dinner and drinks, then ended up at a night club for music and dancing.

What happened after that remains a hazy memory for Allison; she can't seem to remember how they got back to the condo. If only the night could have ended here, if only they'd all cabbed it home and gone to sleep.

For a while after, Allison would spend hours upon hours wishing she could turn back time and rewrite the script. She would imagine what the weekend could have been, dreaming about how it should have unfolded rather than remembering what actually happened. Maybe the next day they would have enjoyed a leisurely late brunch at her favorite cafe with some background jazz while they laughed at their disco dance moves the night before. Maybe she would have heard more stories of Billy when he was a kid.

It starts to dawn on her why, years later, Laura is still single and pours everything into her job and her volunteer work. Why she has crippling anxiety to the point where she can't travel, thus why she's never on the island for any holiday.

Once back at the condo, Billy and Allison had gone to bed. Allison now remembers her sister in deep negotiations on why she deserved to sleep in the second bedroom. Any gentlemen would not have required negotiations and would have offered to take the couch. Allison can almost hear her sister now, insistent that she deserved it since she was there first and all of her bags were unloaded already. That argument seemed to play out in the end, Allison thought, as things got silent after that.

She *must* find Kevin. She has some time. Marc, Lawrence and Carla seem to be determined to see in the wee hours of the morning and are still sipping Jon's high-end booze and smoking Cubans by the pool.

She wonders if he left or, fingers crossed, maybe he decided to take a solitary stroll outside. It's worth a shot.

Allison strides out back where the party has really wound down. She spots the shadow of a figure moving along the clifftop in front of her. The gait, the shape of the man, the gut feeling— it all says *Kevin*.

Allison heads down off the deck to investigate. She's about thirty yards away, but the night is like deep space with endless stars that aren't quite bright enough to reveal who the man is. She cannot quite make out if the mysterious figure is Kevin or someone else. As she grows closer and opens her mouth to say his name, she realizes it *is* him.

He appears wasted, and she smiles to herself for this first victory; it's what she wanted all along. The minute he'd walked in the door tonight she'd begun plying him with hard liquor.

First, a few martinis and then, during the pre-midnight she'd kept handing him vodkas with lime and soda, hold the soda. Just past midnight, she spotted Kevin sipping on whiskey with Jon, so chances are he is now well primed, just as Allison wanted. She wants him to be defenseless. She wants him to suffer like her sister is still suffering.

Allison easily catches up to the stumbling drunk and walks behind him as he heads to the cliff's edge. She can't calculate how far the drop is, but it's well over a hundred feet through thin air, brush and then finally rocks and the eroding beach below.

Then he hears her, and whirls around.

"Oh…hello," he slurs. He's barely conscious. "Aren't you a preeey gurrrl."

Allison's horrific memories are brought to the surface by Kevin's voice. She is listening, but from afar, like someone eavesdropping on another person's conversation.

"I know you," he slurs, pointing at her. Allison is close to warning him away from the edge.

"You do," she agrees. "Or should I say you know my sister. Remember your friend Billy? I lived with him in Philadelphia when you met my sister."

"That's right, you're Billy's girl."

"*Was* Billy's girl," Allison corrects him.

"Howz your sister these days?" Kevin continues in a slurred voice. "Whas her name?"

"Her name is Laura," Allison bellows into the night, her voice loud and sure. "And you attacked her."

"Ohhhhh…"

He stumbles back and falls on his hand in some brambles. They're now five feet from the cliff edge. Allison thinks maybe he is not suicidal after all, nor is he in danger of going over since he's flopped on the ground.

"Is she angry?"

"What do you think? You are so pathetic."

"Oh," he says again, closing his eyes and crawling towards Allison. "Well." He's drooling now.

"Do you remember?" She hisses. "Do you remember what you did to my sister that night?"

It was silent at their Philadelphia condo until it wasn't, until

Laura's screams could be heard blocks away. Allison rushed into the room to find this asshole pinning Laura's hands down, completely naked and on top of her. Laura's body was twisting and turning trying to get out from under him and she was screaming over and over, *No, no, no. Get off of me!*

Allison tried to pull him off, but he swung a punch which landed on her left eye causing her to lose her balance and fall back.

Billy, help! Allison had screamed.

It was a shit show. All that Allison could hear were her own screams for Billy and her sister's screams for her. It was an eternity before Billy left his bed and strolled into the room.

What's the problem? he'd asked with no urgency.

Dude, I am trying to get with Laura, give us some space. Kevin was acting like Allison wasn't even there.

Get him off of her! shouted Allison.

Nah, let them be, was Billy's response. The four words that ended it all.

Allison ran back to her bed and somehow wrangled her sister out from under the 200-pound man. The two sisters ran out of the condo and sat on the sidewalk shaking and sobbing by each other's side. They waited for the day to break, snuck back in the condo packed up their clothes and personal items and left Philadelphia for good.

"Actually, I take it back," Allison says to Kevin now. "She *is* angry."

Not too loud, she tells herself. She doesn't want to call attention to them from the remaining stragglers at the party or from Marc, Lawrence, and Carla out by the pool.

"And so am I. And so are my parents, who are home with her this week on the mainland because she can't be around crowds or fireworks."

Allison looks up at the stars and thinks, *How am I having this conversation right now? How is this Kevin the same guy who violated her sister at a time she needed to find someone stable?* Allison's guilt starts to tear at her core, because it never would have happened if Laura didn't come to visit her. The feeling of wanting to turn back time is all too familiar.

If she can't turn back time, she now wants to forget, forever. She wants to go back to the party, back to the music, back to Marc. She doesn't want to think about that dreadful night. But this is her chance to speak up for her sister who couldn't.

"You destroyed her faith in men, her faith in herself. She deserved better. And you deserve to rot in hell," Allison says.

"Ehhhh," Kevin moans from his place on the ground. "Slut was prolly askin for it. They always want it."

As Allison fights the urge to kick him in the teeth, she notices Kevin start to get up and stumble toward the cliff; she's pretty sure he's so out of it he doesn't know where he is. He begins to sway, clearly with no clue how close to the edge he is getting.

Allison has a split second to decide if she should warn him of the deep drop at the back of his heels. Or if she should remain silent and let things take their course and hope that maybe justice will prevail after all.

She remains frozen, fighting her basic instincts. And then he collapses again, falling slightly forward, only inches from the edge.

"Help me," he slurs.

"Help you? Go kill yourself," she mutters under her breath.

"I needa get 'ome. Or to a hopsital. That whore rooned my marriage." He speaks nonsensically. "And Jon . . ."

He flails off the path, inching closer in a dangerous direction, toward a drop-off that would surely injure if not kill him.

Allison makes her decision then and there, finally.

Kevin Doyle is not her responsibility. His safety is not her job.

Allison leaves him mumbling and gurgling, and she quietly walks backward toward the house, wiping her footprints in the patches of sand behind her with one bare foot as she goes, making sure to leave no trace.

What happens now is out of her hands.

– 84 –
The Fall

Allison

This is how Allison finds herself on the back deck, leaning against the railing in full view of the couple lounging inside, a large glass of water in hand. She's wracked with disappointment and feels an odd lack of relief for how she confronted Kevin after all these years.

Yelling at her sister's attacker didn't bring her the joy she hoped for, nor did it spark the desired high of revenge served cold. She hated having to relive that scene, but maybe now she can finally let it all go.

And then, Kevin falls. Allison watches the blur of his body disappear into the abyss. She loses her breath, then screams as she drops her drink.

She needs to call 911; she left her phone behind the bar before going off to find Kevin. Harder to track her movements that way.

She races inside and bumps into the couple, Bobby and Siobhan, who casually saw her filing her water mere moments ago. They are now on their feet and moving toward the French doors.

"Did you see that?" Allison screams.

"What the *hell?*" Bobby confirms, his voice cracking. "Did someone just jump off the cliff? Let's go check it out!" He's clearly freaked out.

"Be careful, its dark and full of brush. You need to take the beach steps down to try to find him."

"Him? You know who it was?"

Allison realizes her slip as she runs past them. "I'm going to call for help."

Allison bursts into the smaller staff kitchen off the living room at the front of the house, and there she runs smack into Brooke and Kate standing close, talking in tense, hushed tones.

In Kate's hand is a bloody crystal vase.

– 85 –

Just an Accident

Kate

Kate's face goes white when she sees Allison.

"We need to call 911," Allison says calmly.

"Why? What happened?" Kate is asking this question while still holding the bloody vase.

Kate is still confused at Allison's emergency. "Did you see Jon, is he okay?"

"Jon? Wait, what happened *here?*" Allison asks, reaching out to grab the vase from her friend's hands. "What's all over your vase."

"Allison, that's blood."

As her eyes grow wide. Allison, on auto pilot, sets it in the deep sink and scrubs, scrubs, scrubs, then adds Clorox spray from underneath the sink, and scrubs some more. There are too many nooks and crannies.

"Fuck it," she says, leaving it in the sink.

Kate grabs it back. "We need to destroy this vase or at least put it where they'll never find it."

"You don't even know what happened," Brooke says looking at Allison.

"Well, it can't be good. Are you going to tell me or not?" Allison says.

"You won't believe it," Kate replies, shaking.

Allison notes that Brooke is the strong one for once. "Brooke?"

"Long story," Brooke tells Allison, meeting her eyes unwaveringly, "Jon put me to bed in their guest house that he'd been secretly decorating for me. At this point I realized he had something more in mind for me than sex. When I was looking around, I noticed a bag of pills on the ground under the chairs where we were sitting. It must have slipped out of Jon's pocket when we were sitting and talking."

"I don't understand, who's pills are they?"

"Jon's. It turns out he drugged Kevin that day he got arrested. He slipped them in his drink when they came over to check on us that afternoon. And then later that night he snuck back to our house to talk a wasted Kevin into the driver's seat of the Jeep. Kevin didn't know if it was New Years or New York when he got behind the wheel of that car." Brooke takes a breath.

"But *why*?" Allison is floored. She can't believe she didn't see it, that she had *sex* with someone like this. She feels sicker and sicker by the moment.

"Because." Kate replies, regaining some composure. "He's obsessed with Brooke. I didn't realize until it was too late. He wanted to frame Kevin or get him out of the picture however he could."

"So, then what happened?" Allison prods.

"I followed Jon most of the night, and confronted him when he went back to check on Brooke. He probably wanted to jump in bed with her and I called him on it. Brooke was asleep but our argument woke her up.

"That's when I pulled out the bag of pills and showed them to Kate. Jon all but admitted what he had done to Kevin," explains Brooke.

"I was so furious and confronted Jon." Kate takes a pause, then twists the truth a bit by adding, "Then he came at me, so I hit him over the head with this."

She points to the vase.

"Oh my god. is Jon *dead?*" Allison asks.

"Fuck, I hope not." The gravity pours over her. Kate presses a button on the wall and calls, "Jean-Pierre!"

Allison slips back into practical mode. First things first: protect the three of them.

"OK. I'm calling 911 about what just happened out at the cliff—"

Allison stops short. This is Kevin's wife, a woman who clearly loved him through his bad acts and terrible treatment of her, and his slip off the cliff and possible death is going to traumatize her. They don't have time for Brooke to fall apart right now.

Allison decides she has to keep the act up—for *everyone*. She was never on that cliff, doesn't know who fell, assumed the person fell because wouldn't that be the normal assumption if you were watching from the Gibsons' deck? Allison has Bobby and Siobhan as her alibi through the whole thing. No way she had anything to do with the unfortunate fall of Kevin Doyle.

"Brooke, you two need a believable story about where you've been for the last half hour. Now, go figure out a way to smuggle that thing out of here and get rid of it, even if you have to throw it over the cliff. And one of you needs to go and see if Jon still has a pulse! Hurry. You have about five to ten minutes, max."

"What are you going to do?" Brooke asks.

"I'm going to call 911. There's been an accident. I think someone went over the cliff. I'll fill you in after I call for help."

"What do you mean someone *went over the cliff?*" Understandably, Kate can barely comprehend the new development. "Who?"

Allison is already dialing.

Brooke's eyes change, and Allison believes a part of her knows it could be her husband who's in trouble. Kevin is self-destructive, wasted, missing—it would certainly add up.

"I need to go find Kevin and get out of here," Brooke cries. "I don't know how I got so swept up in your scene, it seemed like a great escape from my problems, but you all are *much* worse off than Kev and me."

Brooke turns away and races out in search of her husband.

The dispatcher tells Allison that others from the party called as well, and that an ambulance, police, Coast Guard and a Life Star helicopter are all on the way.

Allison hangs up and Kate grabs her hand, leading her to the empty parlor around the corner. Kate closes the door and says in a panicked voice, "We need to shut Brooke up. She could take me down, and Jon too, and though I don't give a crap about him right now, unfortunately our fates are intertwined in this particular situation."

"How are we going to do that?" Allison throws her hands up. "And more importantly, what are we going to do with the vase? It's still in the kitchen sink!"

"I don't know…" Kate thinks aloud. "If we bring it through the party someone will see us. If we smash it in the kitchen, someone will hear it. We don't want to call attention to ourselves—"

"Or *do* we?" Allison interrupts. "If we smash the vase in there right now, and people hear it, there will be witnesses who can say the vase broke when Jon was nowhere near you—"

It's Kate's turn to interrupt. "Yes! And the cleaning crew is here until dawn, and they can pack up the shards with a ton of other garbage that will be long gone before anyone puts two and two together. Let's go!"

They run back into the kitchen and Kate raises the vase out of the sink. "Protect your eyes," she says, and Allison complies and backs away. Kate turns her head and smashes the vase against the corner of the marble countertop, into smithereens. She grabs a shard and slices the palm of her hand. Her blood splatters onto the floor.

Like clockwork, two kitchen staff race in at the ruckus. "Oh, Mrs. Gibson! Are you OK? Let me get that cleaned up for you. Oh no, you are bleeding."

"Thank you so much, Margie," Kate smiles ruefully. "I was washing it out and I think I had a few too many drinks and *oops*, it slipped out of my hands."

Kate wraps a dishtowel around her hand and pulls Allison away again, back into the parlor. "Your turn. What the hell happened out on the cliff?"

As if coming out of a trance, Allison tells Kate a version of the story. She tells her she saw Kevin sipping whiskey with Jon one minute, then saw him again as he passed her at the martini bar, and then she hadn't seen him after that. She explains she can't be sure it was him, but she saw a body slip off the cliff and she thought whoever it was had Kevin's build.

"Jesus, Allie. Is there a chance you're wrong? Maybe the

vodka has impaired your vision and you were seeing things. Was anyone else there on the path?"

Sirens float through the house now, distant but drawing closer.

"Absolutely not," Allison replies, though Kate is staring through her friend like she knows. Like she can sense Allison is acting strangely. "We need to focus on you and Brooke right now. Are you ready for this?"

"As I'll ever be," Kate replies grimly, taking a deep breath and composing herself.

After-Sex Smoke

Carla

Marc and Lawrence have their feet up on the outdoor loungers and are puffing away at their cigars with an after-sex glow. Carla has drifted to sleep with her head on her husband's lap after trying to stay awake waiting for Allison's return. Lawrence starts to laugh and his shaking jolts her out of her slumber.

"What time is it?" she asks, eyes half open. She has a vague memory of someone screaming in her dreams.

"No clue," Marc responds after finishing his sip of whiskey.

"Did you fall asleep, babe?"

"I think I did…where's Allison?"

Marc looks around like he hadn't noticed she wasn't there. "Good question. Your man Lawrence and I have been swapping old college stories and the time slipped away."

The two men dive back into to their reminiscing and Carla sits up and looks around. There aren't many people left outside. A few standing over by the martini bar, but the lights are still twinkling, the fires blazing, and the music is still playing.

Carla begins to grow impatient, looking over her shoulder every few minutes for Allison. The husbands seem to be having the time of their lives but Carla's buzz is turning into a headache and her mouth is parched. She rises and tells the guys, "I need some water. And why is Allison not back yet? It must be close to three a.m. I need to get home soon for some beauty sleep."

Carla heads inside and collides with Brooke in the doorway.

"Brooke, have you seen Allison?" Carla asks after she recovers her balance.

Brooke answers Carla's question with her own: "Have you seen Kevin anywhere?"

"Last I saw Kevin he was either dancing or stumbling and mumbling to himself spilling his drink and heading away from the house."

"When was this?" Brooke is visibly upset.

"It was before I fell asleep, so not sure how long ago. Poor guy is going to be hurting tomorrow, or I should say today. The sun will be coming up soon."

"I need to find him and get out of here. I'm done with this place."

"I want to leave too, I am exhausted. I don't know how they can stay up all night at our age." Carla asks again, "Have you seen Allison?"

Brooke takes a deep breath, "She's inside near the kitchen, where the caterers were set up. I'll show you if you help me find Kevin after."

"Thanks. But are you OK, Brooke? You look like you've seen a ghost."

"Uh, no, not really. This night has taken a turn."

It sure has, Carla thinks to herself as she remembers their foursome not long ago.

"What do you mean?" Carla wonders if Brooke joined some group sex too and is also feeling a pang of regret.

"I um, I really don't want to get into it. Allison can fill you in."

"*Allison*? How would she know? She was in our group room."

"What? What are you talking about? Just ask her when you see her."

Carla's head is swirling. Whatever happened has Brooke upset, but how could it involve Allison if Carla was with her most of the night? Would Allison have joined another room while they were all out by the pool?

No way, Carla thinks, by now completely discombobulated. *How long was I asleep?*

Brooke locks arms with Carla and leads the way towards Allison.

– 87 –

Come Clean

Brooke

Carla and Brooke did not find Allison and Kate in the server's kitchen. Brooke's panic begins to take over and she thinks she is going to throw up. She runs to the sink and notices the vase is gone. She desperately needs to get out of this mansion and breath in some fresh air so she can think straight. As she nears the front door Carla stops her in her tracks.

"Wait, what's in here?" Carla's curiosity kicks in and she pushes open a closed door to a mystery room near the foyer. Inside, they discover Kate and Allison. The parlor is a lady's version of man-town; decorated like a Tiffany's Fifth Avenue Manhattan Cafe with a stunning platinum and diamond chandelier casting a dim glow over the famous Tiffany blue colored décor and plush inviting French seating. The lit candles and white roses would have all been enjoyed much more if the circumstances were different.

Kate and Allison appeared deep in conversation in hushed tones which Carla quickly interrupted, "There you are, you left me with the boys, and I fell asleep waiting for you. Where can I get some water, and can we leave soon? I am starting to feel hung over."

Kate and Allison whip their heads around as if surprised by the interruption.

"Brooke! There you are, can we talk?" Kate asks with a sympathetic smile and in her sweetest tone.

"No, we can't talk. I need to find Kevin and Carla just saw him so she is going to show me where he is."

"You just saw Kevin?" Alison asks, surprised.

"Well, it was before I drifted off and I have no idea how long I was sleeping so I'm actually not really sure how long ago I saw him."

"Why are you so surprised, and where have you been?" Carla adds sounding suspicious.

Brooke interrupts, "Hold up everyone. I need to find Kevin, now. Carla, you said you would help me. Let's go!"

Kate, the host, and ringleader steps in front of the door. She closes it and demands, "No one is going anywhere. We all need to talk and get our stories straight. Everyone, take a seat."

Carla spots a large crystal pitcher of water and matching goblets. Allision suggests, "Carla, why don't you pour yourself a glass and listen."

Brooke rolls her eyes but takes a seat. "You have exactly five minutes, Kate. After that I suggest you check on your husband's head wound, the one that you inflicted, and I am going to grab Kevin and we are leaving."

Carla spits out her water, "head wound? What happened? Oh my God are those sirens?'

"We don't have time to explain now, Carla. I will fill you in later," Allison tries to keep the focus on getting out of here without any trouble.

"Brooke, you're in the process of adopting that sweet little troubled boy, right?" Kate interjects.

Brookes shoulders relax at the thought and a small smile emerges. "I am, and little does Kevin know how close we are to finalizing the process with Charlie. He could be moving in with us as soon as we get back from Nantucket. Why are you asking me this?"

"Because it is very important for you to listen to what I am about to tell you if you want to make sure the adoption does not get derailed."

Flashing Lights

Kate

Kate somehow convinced Brooke to take their car service home with Carla and Lawrence. Brooke didn't want to leave without Kevin, or without knowing if it was Kevin that Allison saw stumble over the edge of the cliff. But she trusted it was the best option to avoid the police and any possible blemishes that could end up on her adoption application as a result of this regretful night. Brooke had enough of Kevin, and it was clear her love for Charlie outweighed her love for Kevin, and Kate used this to her advantage.

All the police, ambulance and fire department vehicles parked in her front driveway light up the night sky. Kate watches as one of their security guards rushes the EMT's toward the guest house. She observes the fifteen or so guests left at the party as they gather around, gossiping, and desperate to leave. She can't wait for this to be over. But of course, the cops said in no uncertain terms that no one can go yet.

Jon is whisked away on a stretcher from the guest house towards the ambulance. Jean-Pierre is by his side, and he has a towel wrapped around his head and blood dripping down his face and staining his clothes.

"Sir, sir," a young cop is calling as a paramedic loads Jon into the ambulance.

"Not now," Jean-Pierre, a strapping Frenchman, barks. "Mr. Gibson needs to get to the hospital *immediately*."

"We understand that sir," a rookie cop who looks like he's twelve says. "But sir, can you tell us who did this to him? Was he assaulted, sir? We need to know who—"

"It's a party. He had a bit to drink and fell on a glass table," Jean-Pierre snaps back. "There's no need for police. Unless falling is against the law?"

The kid's right-hand quivers as he takes notes. "N-no, sir. It's not illegal. Thank you very much."

Meanwhile, another set of officers and paramedics were directed to the cliff area around the back of the house. They were told someone slipped off the cliff, but no one knew for certain who it was or if they were ok. After much effort weeding through the brush and cutting away to release Kevin's body, they were able to confirm a pulse and call for back up to assist him to an ambulance. As they load Kevin into the back of the second ambulance, they are able to ID him as Kevin Doyle. The officer radios this information to the Detective.

Detective Wiley approaches Kate, who's standing by the first ambulance trying to look upset about her husband's injuries.

"What a coincidence, it is the Ambien driver from a couple of weeks ago. He has been the talk of the NPD," he says.

"What are you saying?" Kate asks.

"We found the man in the brush below the cliff. Lucky for you, and your homeowner's insurance company, he still has a pulse. It's the same guy who was in Court," the detective says. "Before you go, Mrs. Gibson, I see you have some cameras on the property. A lot of them. We'll need to check the footage."

Kate says nothing as the gurney is lifted into the ambulance.

"I'm their security chief," Jean-Paul steps in. "I can tell you *all* the cameras were off. The Gibson's friends are well-known, successful people who count on our discretion, and we make it a point to leave all surveillance off for events such as these. Any further questions, you can direct them to Mr. Gibson's lawyer."

With that, Jon is loaded into the ambulance, and Kate makes a show of sniffling and crying with worry as she approaches him and says in his ear, "This isn't over."

The paramedics shut the door and Allison appears by her side as Kate watches it pull out. Moments later the two see a second ambulance, the one carrying Kevin, follow not far behind.

Another cop is interviewing a couple with a blanket over their shoulders as if they have any reason to be in shock.

"Where were you when Mr. Doyle fell from the cliff?" He asks.

"We were in the living room," the woman replies.

"Yes," her boyfriend nods along, "Allison chatted with us just before the guy fell. She was getting some water and then went out to the deck."

"Who was this?"

"Allison. Allison Evans," the woman says. "She is a very close friend of Kate, our hostess this evening."

"Where was Ms. Evans when Mr. Doyle fell, to your knowledge?"

"She was standing on the deck when we saw the body go off the cliff," the man says shaking his head vehemently. "Then she immediately ran back in, screaming for help."

"Absolutely no chance she had anything to do with this," the woman agrees. "It would have been impossible. I could literally see her from here when he fell."

The detective nods. "That's good enough. For now. You two are free to go."

Kate stands alone. Detective Wiley speaks to Kate again, his notebook out and pen in hand.

"You still use notebooks?" Kate remarks. "Wouldn't iPads be more efficient?"

"Ma'am," he says, "I'm going to need to know where every single person on this property was at the time of Mr. Doyle's fall, and that includes your husband when he returns. Now. Let's start with you, Mrs. Gibson. Where exactly were you for the last hour?"

Jean-Pierre steps in, "With all due respect, Detective, Mrs. Gibson needs to go be by her husband's side at the hospital. She won't be answering any questions at this time."

What would Kate do without Jean-Pirre. He stayed back while the questions for the remaining guests lasted well into the new daylight.

Kate takes a car service with Allison and Marc to check on Jon. On the way, reality starts to settle in. The adrenaline that helped her keep her cool with the cops wears off the minute she buckles into the car. Her thoughts shift to Jon and Kevin and she wonders about the possibility that either could be seriously hurt. She's grateful to have Allison and Marc with her as she enters the emergency room waiting area.

They approach the registration desk and hear a nurse say, "DOA."

Marc's head picks up as he clocks the acronym. "You had a dead on arrival?" His voice is weary.

Kate's face turns pale and she wobbles, falling backward. Marc catches her and calls for a nurse.

Allison and Marc carry Kate to a seat and a nurse comes running over with smelling salts.

"Is she going to be okay?" Allison asks the nurse.

Before the nurse can respond, Kate's eyes flutter open.

Marc turns to the nurse. "Please. We need to know who the DOA is. We know both men who were recently taken here by ambulance. Was it one of them?"

The nurse replies, "I'm so sorry, but I can't share that information. Why don't you finish checking in at registration and I'll make sure your friend here is OK."

Marc snaps, "This is Jon Gibson's wife. She needs to know if her husband is still alive."

– 89 –
The Truth, or Something Like it

Allison

As Allison exits the Nantucket Police Department with Marc a few weeks later, she sighs with relief. She didn't expect it to be this easy. The investigation into the events of that night were half-hearted at best, but Marc cautioned her there's always a chance a rising star in the department will find a loose thread and tug at it.

Kevin Doyle never made it to surgery that fateful night. He died in the ambulance, and a doctor at the hospital pronounced him. When Allison found out this news, the guilt of goading him and leaving him by the cliff, no matter how much she wanted him to pay for what he did to her sister, left her in bed for days. She lied and said she had the flu as she didn't have the strength to tell anyone exactly what happened out by the cliff.

"Are you sure it's over?" She asks Marc, who takes her hand as they walk back to the car. Allison doesn't look back; she never wants to see the inside of the Nantucket police station again.

"It's over," he assures her. "Which it should be. These were accidents, pure and simple, and the department knows that. I don't know why you're so worried. Is there something I'm missing?"

He searches her eyes and watches for her tells, which usually include fluttering her eyelashes nervously and clearing her throat too much.

"I just . . ." Allison stutters. "I just really love you, and our life, and it feels so fragile recently. I feel fragile." Her eyes well up. "I need to tell you something, something that has rocked me to my core since before I met you."

She feels Marc's arms envelop her as she sobs. Right there in the parking lot, Allison shares her and her sister's encounter with Kevin. She wants this to be the last time she has to remember that night. But she knows she still needs to talk to her sister, to provide her with some kind of closure.

As of now Marc believes Allison went looking for Kevin to confront him, but never found him. The late-night couple who saw her get water told police Allison was on the deck when Kevin went over the edge. She wasn't anywhere near him. Kevin was wasted on benzos and booze, and he fell. Or jumped. The coroner ruled it an accident. It wasn't suicide, it wasn't murder. But the people on the island all had their own theories. It seemed there was more talk of suicide than murder throughout the ensuing weeks. Part of Allison understands that still could be the case. Kevin very well might have jumped.

That gray area should be good enough for Allison's conscience. But it isn't.

Marc pulls away and Allison takes a tissue out of her handbag. As she wipes her eyes, she considers revealing the truth about what happened on the cliff in the minutes before Kevin's fall, but something stops her. She can't risk Marc thinking less of her. She can't give him another reason, in addition to gorgeous Kate and his new plaything Carla, to not want to be with Allison. She also wonders if, as a steward of the law, she'd be putting her husband in a dangerous position by confessing.

"Oh Allison, baby, I'm so sorry," Marc is saying. "I feel awful for being friends with him this summer. If I'd known, I'd have told everyone to stay away, and I certainly would never have represented him."

"I know," she sniffles.

"Please, no more crying. It's over," he assures her gently. "They told me flat-out they're not filing charges, partly because dead men can't speak, and because Jon isn't going to invite any sort of police presence into his complicated life. The case is closed. There was no evidence to tie any of the partygoers to any wrongdoing."

Marc holds her as she calms down. *He really is my rock*, she thinks.

Allison knows Marc has his suspicions, but he could never make all the pieces fit together and she feels better now that he knows at least one of her big secrets. Allison hasn't told Laura yet, but now that the legal mess is over, she's going to figure out a way to tell her sister how much Kevin suffered for what he did. She will tell Laura that he got what he deserved, and they can take solace in knowing that he will never ever do this again to another woman. Hopefully this will allow Laura to finally move on. But if she tells her everything, will her sister think she is a horrible person too? Her sister may not need to know the details maybe just how much of a screw up Kevin Doyle turned out to be which ultimately led to his death.

It does seem like they're all in the clear. The cops seemed to care more about digging into the world of swingers and ménage a trios than they did about what led to the bloody end to that party.

However, it's not lost on Allison that there is irreparable emotional damage and countless rumors washing over her and her friends like a red tide. The pineapple parties had to be put on hold. But that didn't slow Allison down. She had been so proud of her conquest of her neighbors, and she didn't want to lose what she worked so hard to achieve. Allison made sure they had a few more nights of encounters with the Rossis before the summer was over. It was such a great escape. This is what kept her mind off things the most. But now it seems the case is finally closed.

They pull apart and Marc gets his keys out of his pocket, ready to drive to 'Sconset.

Allison decides to risk asking him one more probing question. She can't shake an uneasy feeling and is increasingly desperate for reassurance. "Do you think it could have been suicide, Marc? I mean, Kevin was so wasted, who knows what really happened…?"

Marc thinks for a moment, and Allison realizes he very well might suspect something, but is letting it lie. *Smart.* She vows never to tell him about her role in Kevin's demise—for both their sakes.

"I don't think we'll ever know," Marc says, sending her a meaningful glance. "And I think that's OK. We can leave it where it is. The fact someone told the detective they saw a woman up on that cliff with Kevin that night has pretty much been discredited, and that's the only question remaining as far as

I can tell. One witness isn't enough to make any kind of case and police treated the drunk person's claim with contempt, from what I read in the report."

"*What?*" Allison swallows hard. "Who…who said they saw what? And who did they think was with him?"

"Ah, that's right. I forgot I'm the only one who's seen the full police report," Marc says. "It doesn't name the witness but says a party guest thought it might have been Michelle. That maybe it was a lovers' spat gone wrong."

"How can they be sure it *wasn't* Michelle?" Allison chokes the words out.

"Jean-Pierre vouched for her whereabouts," Marc said. "He told the cops Michelle was in a back room waiting for an Uber."

Marc clicks the key fob to unlock the car. Allison moves to the passenger door and Marc starts the engine.

"What I don't buy is Kate's story," Marc says, pulling out of the lot. "Did you see her in the hospital cafeteria that night?"

"Yes, and you grilled her like a witness in a case." Allison rolls her eyes. "But she stuck to her story. She insisted that Jon had a panic attack and passed out."

"C'mon, Jon is the coolest guy I know under pressure," Marc shakes his head and pulls out of the lot. "A panic attack? Really?" That gash on the side of his head took 22 stitches and the poor guy is still getting migraines."

Allison shrugs. This isn't her truth to tell. Marc gave Kate every opportunity to tell him what happened. She even had the protection of his attorney-client privilege. But she never said a word. And the only other person who knew the real story was Brooke, well and Jon of course.

Kate had called Brooke to tell her the tragic news even before the cops could do an official notification. Brooke raced to the hospital, coolly took in what happened from police and hospital staff, refused to speak to any of the rest of the group, and within two days boarded a ferry off Nantucket.

When Marc tried to call her a few days later, her number was no longer in service. Marc has warned Jon and Kate not to rest easy as he has a feeling she may be back with a team of lawyers.

Marc guides the car on the winding roads out to 'Sconset where everyone is waiting to hear the outcome of their meeting at the station. She stares out the window as tears stream quietly down her cheeks and onto her neck. If only she had not stared into his soul and uttered those three words. As they pull into the palatial property on the cliffs, Allison's anxiety is through the roof, she feels as though she may vomit.

While initially there was the relief that none of their friends were formally charged with assault, or worse, attempted murder, Allison always has anxiety bubbling beneath the surface. A lot has changed in the past few weeks. It's mid-August and the colder nights confirm that summer is winding down. Their little club has been exposed through hours of questioning. The dirt dug up on everyone on that guest list will keep the cops downtown talking for years.

If they only knew the half of it. Everything that went on was bound to lead to a dramatic ending with the amount of suspicion, anxiety, desire, and jealousy that spread amongst them all. Allison wonders what will happen to their friendships now that the case is closed. Sustaining this lifestyle is exhausting. And worse, she fears Marc might be falling in love with someone besides her.

Allison follows her husband as he walks around to the back of the house. They turn the corner, and she takes in the expansive lawn and the breathtaking view that she will surely miss once they leave the island at the end of summer.

When their friends catch a glimpse of Marc approaching the house, he raises both his hands and pumps his fists. Allison watches Marc lock eyes with Carla. Carla blushes and all of Allison's feelings of relief are gone.

She feels a fresh, smoldering burn in her gut that feels something like anger toward the woman who'd been her best friend this summer. Carla breaks eye contact with Marc and rushes over to hug Allison.

"Everything's going to be OK," Carla says in her ear. "Isn't it amazing?"

"Everything's just perfect," Allison says through gritted teeth, squeezing Carla a bit too tight.

THE END

ACKNOWLEDGMENTS

We would like to thank all of our family and friends for their love and support. A special thanks to the early readers who provided your feedback throughout this process. And finally, to Sara Hammel for getting *The Cliff* over the finish line with her endless guidance and knowledge.

—*Adrienne Leigh Summers*